Praise for *The Greatest Lie of All*

"Pages fly by as the storylines tangle, as love is revealed, and we discover that it's not just endings and beginnings that matter, but also the middle parts of our lives where choices are made. Cantor has penned a witty and mesmerizing novel with suspense and intrigue, and then the most important thing of all—heart."

—Patti Callahan Henry, *New York Times* **bestselling author of** *The Secret Book of Flora Lea*

"A heady whirlwind of secrets, fame, family, and love, *The Greatest Lie of All* is Jillian Cantor at her absolute best. I devoured this late into the night and loved every single thing about it."

—Allison Winn Scotch, bestselling author of *The Rewind*

"Prepare to be pulled into an addictively twisty maze of secrets and lies, heartbreak and love. Once you open the covers, you'll need to forget everything else in your life because you won't be able to put down this compulsive story until you reach its startling end."

—Natasha Lester, *New York Times* **bestselling author of** *The Paris Orphan*

"*The Greatest Lie of All* is irresistibly juicy, twisty, and layered. It explores the stories we tell about ourselves to conceal our truths and the lengths we'll go to protect our hearts. Fans of Taylor Jenkins Reid will love this one."

—Annabel Monaghan, bestselling author of *Same Time Next Summer*

"Truth ultimately trumps fiction, and Cantor does not miss a beat in this unputdownable, richly textured propulsive tale, in which heartbreak ultimately blossoms into unexpected love. Readers will devour this one."

—Lisa Barr, *New York Times* **bestselling author of** *Woman on Fire*

"A twisty, turny, delight of a story. Nothing is quite what it seems when young actress Amelia Grant visits the home of a legendary romance novelist in preparation for a role. Jillian Cantor's *The Greatest Lie of All* is perfect for fans of *The Seven Husbands of Evelyn Hugo*. An addictive read!"

—Jamie Brenner, bestselling author of *A Novel Summer*

Also by Jillian Cantor

JILLIAN CANTOR

THE
GREATEST
LIE
OF ALL

PARK
ROW
BOOKS

PARK
ROW
BOOKS™

ISBN-13: 978-0-7783-1091-4

The Greatest Lie of All

Copyright © 2024 by Jillian Cantor

Park Row Books
22 Adelaide St. West, 41st Floor
Toronto, Ontario M5H 4E3, Canada
ParkRowBooks.com

Printed in U.S.A.

For G, B and O, the ones I love, always.

"The human being who acts is the human being who lives."

—Lee Strasberg

PROLOGUE

Amelia

SOMETIMES THE END of everything sneaks up on you when you least expect it.

I read that once, in a Gloria Diamond novel. Only she was referring to an asteroid. For me, the end came as a 32 DD red lace bra.

It happened on a rare rainy day in LA, two months after my thirty-third birthday. Two days after my mother had died.

She had collapsed quite suddenly in her garden, my mother. And forty-eight hours later, I found myself numb and standing in the open doorway of my walk-in closet in my underwear. I knew I needed something to wear to the funeral home to discuss arrangements, but I couldn't figure out how to step inside the closet and choose what that should be. *Young woman with newly dead mother.* It was a role I didn't yet understand and didn't want. I stared at all my clothes blindly, as if I'd never seen any of them before.

"How about this?" Jase stepped around me, walked into the

closet and pulled out a hanger with a simple black shift dress. Was it mine? I had no memory of buying it. The tags were still on.

"She hated black," I reminded him. My mother had been in love with color, from the pink azaleas in her garden to the color-splattered abstract art she made in her studio to the bright orange plates she'd serve us brunch on each Sunday.

Jase raised his eyebrows, and I took the dress from him, ripped off the tags and quickly slipped into it. I glanced at myself in the floor-length mirror. The dress was shapeless, and I looked pale and powerless.

Jase walked up behind me and hugged me, whispering one more apology over not being able to accompany me this morning. His shooting schedule was intense. The director would get mad if he called out last minute.

"It's fine," I told him, again. Work was work. And he had fought so hard to get this far. It wasn't like I could be mad he hadn't planned ahead. No one could've expected my healthy fifty-eight-year-old mother to collapse in her azaleas when shooting schedules had been made. I'd just wrapped shooting on a supporting role in an indie film, so luckily my schedule this week was clear. My mother always had impeccable timing.

"Are you sure?" Jase released the words slowly, tickling my ear with his breath. When I nodded, he spun me around, planted a gentle kiss on my forehead. He took a step back, nodded approvingly as he glanced over the blah black dress, then flashed what I knew by then was his TV-doctor sexy grin. The smile was an apology, or a promise, or maybe by then it was more like a tic. Since he'd taken on the role of heart surgeon/heartthrob on the überpopular *Seattle Med* last year, my boyfriend's face had become familiar to every woman in America. But it had come to feel strangely unfamiliar to me.

"I'll be okay," I heard myself saying. And in spite of everything, I was still a good actress. I sold it.

"I know," he said easily. Then he shouted after me as I walked out: "Call me if you need anything, though."

"I won't," I yelled back.

But it turned out, I did need something.

Halfway to Pasadena on the 10, I realized I hadn't grabbed my wallet, and I called Jase to see if he had time before the shoot to drop it off, or if he could at least text me a picture of my credit card so I had the number to pay. But Jase didn't pick up, and if he'd already left for his shoot, he'd be no help.

I sighed and got off the next exit on the freeway to circle back. I knew I would be late for the appointment now; my mother had abhorred lateness and, more, she had never understood what she termed my *spaciness*—a lifetime of forgotten wallets and missing socks. But then it hit me, she would never know about this. A dead woman couldn't get angry. And suddenly I had to pull off to the side of the on-ramp because I couldn't see the road through my tears.

By the time I made it back to our apartment again, my face was puffy from crying, and I clutched a crumpled tissue in my hand as I unlocked the door. I was blowing my nose as I walked inside, so I almost didn't notice that random red bra strewn across the floor until my foot caught on it in my path to the bedroom.

And even then, I disentangled it from my foot, picked it up and tossed it aside. I couldn't process what it was, why it was there. I kept on walking like an idiot to my bedroom; all I knew in that moment was that my wallet was still sitting on my dresser. I opened my bedroom door and suddenly everything—and nothing—made sense. Jase was lying on our bed completely naked, a blonde woman with too-bronze skin, also completely naked, straddling on top of him.

"Jase?" I ran toward the bed and said his name like I was in some stupid movie of the week, and I was too naive to understand what was happening. What had been happening, right in front of me.

The naked woman turned at the sound of my voice and then I recognized her: Celeste Templeton, Jase's gorgeous twenty-two-year-old *Seattle Med* costar.

I had this weird moment after she turned where I was nearly eye level with her breasts, and I found myself wondering if they were real. They couldn't be. No one had authentic breasts that large and that perfectly symmetrical. Did they?

"Shit, Melly. It's not what you think," Jase said. But he didn't move right away, and neither did she. Until she finally shifted off him to grab a blanket and I noticed her breasts barely moved. Definitely fake. I was trapped inside some awful cliché, and all I wanted to do was run. I had to get out.

"I forgot my wallet," I finally heard myself saying, my voice coming from somewhere far away, above me, apart from me, the way it did when I auditioned for a role. I grabbed my wallet from the dresser and tore out of the room, then out of our apartment.

Just as I stepped outside, it started to rain. It had been raining on and off all week, and rain had been forecasted for today too. But I stood there, letting the water wash over me because, of course, I'd forgotten my umbrella too. And there was no way I was going back inside for it now.

Water flattened my curls and ran down my face, pelted my arms and soaked my ugly dress. My skin felt both numb and raw at once. But I stood there, in the rain, as the understanding hit me, that everything I was and everything I thought I knew, suddenly it was gone, just like that.

THREE MONTHS LATER

Amelia

THE FIRST THING I noticed as the car reached the end of the long tree-lined driveway was that Gloria Diamond's house seemed smaller than it should've. After the buildup and negotiating to get here, the secrecy surrounding my arrival, the limo sent to pick me up at the airport and that long twisty driveway—when the car finally emerged through the morning mist and Pacific Northwest pines, I'd expected *The Gloria Diamond*'s house to be a mansion. But instead, it was just a two-story redbrick Colonial, with a surprisingly dilapidated black shingle roof. It was large enough for, say, a family of four, but not enormous or spectacular by any means.

It was the first indication that maybe I didn't fully understand what I'd gotten myself into. But I brushed that thought aside as we pulled into the circle up front. I let myself out of the back seat, and I accepted my roller bag as the driver retrieved it from the trunk and wheeled it to me. He stared at me, and I wondered briefly if I was supposed to tip him, but I had no cash on me, so instead I offered him my most charming smile, a thank-you or an apology. And then I wheeled my bag up to the bright red front door and rang the bell.

I heard it chiming on the other side, and then the high-pitched bark of what sounded like a small dog. I waited for a moment, the dog continued to bark, but no one came to answer the door. Gloria's assistant had gone over every meticulous detail of my arrival on the phone yesterday—they were definitely expecting me.

As I waited there on her doorstep, I felt the briefest flash of doubt. I was the one who'd insisted that if I was going to play Gloria Diamond in the biopic of her life, I needed to spend a few days getting to know her first. But I hadn't exactly been functioning at my best these last few months either. Coming here felt like ripping the Band-Aid off my rippling grief, back to the world, back to work.

I had only been back to my apartment once since the morning I'd found Jase and Celeste Templeton in my bed—to pack this roller bag with essentials. I'd escaped to my mother's empty house in Pasadena with its bright (but too-quiet) colorful rooms, which had been both a balm and haunting in the wake of her sudden death. I'd considered staying inside her house forever with her needy, elderly orange tabby and the remnants of her unfinished life and artwork. But as I'd settled her estate, it became clear I would have to sell her house to pay off her credit card debt. And when the Realtor not so kindly suggested I should move out so the house would show better, and when Liza, my agent, called to pitch me this role the next day, it all felt like fate. The original lead had dropped out; shooting would begin ASAP, and a lead role in a big-budget biopic would be an amazing opportunity for me. Things were finally coming back together. At least, I hoped they were.

If nothing else, taking this role forced me to leave LA. The Pasadena house was being scrubbed and decluttered probably at this very moment, and hopefully a sale would come quickly too. Eventually, I'd have to deal with finding another place to live. But for now, I would spend the next six days with the world's biggest bestselling author, The Queen of Romance, Gloria Diamond, interviewing her, studying her, before shooting on her biopic was set to begin an hour north in Belles Woods next week. This was the first thing I'd felt truly excited about since my mother died and, maybe, that was partly because my mother had been Gloria Diamond's biggest fan.

The red door suddenly swung open in front of me, and a brown Chihuahua dressed in a diamond-studded black sweater ran out and circled my legs, still yipping.

A woman stepped out behind it. She looked young, younger than me, with thick tortoiseshell glasses framing her bright blue eyes, black hair pulled back into a tight ponytail at the nape of her neck. Tate Finley, Gloria's assistant, I assumed. We'd emailed several times and had spoken on the phone once, and for some reason I had expected her to be much older. "Sorry," she said, nearly shouting so I could hear her above the barking. She knelt to address the dog. "Jasper, sit," she commanded.

Jasper ignored her and continued circling my ankles and yipping.

Finally, she scooped him up in her arms, he gave me a sad little final growl baring a few crooked teeth and then started to pant. "I'm so sorry. I was trying to get him in his crate, but he escaped. Amelia, gosh, welcome. You're even more gorgeous in person than on TV." Then she added, "I hope you're a dog person."

I warmed from her compliment and smiled. But I was definitely not a dog person. I was probably not a cat person either as I'd left my mother's elderly tabby in the care of the (likely incapable) Realtor who had pretty much been ready to promise me anything as long as I agreed to leave the house before she listed it. "He's cute," I lied.

"He's a pain in the ass. But he's the love of Gloria's life." She laughed, but I was pretty sure she was only half kidding.

There was no dog in the script, which I'd finished reading on the flight. But it was based on Gloria's real-life love story with her husband, who'd died tragically young. Her first novel, which she published only a year and a half after his death, drew from this real-life romance, and it was that story that had sky-rocketed her to global fame. Nearly thirty years and thirty books later, she'd never remarried, but apparently The Queen of Romance was obsessed with her yippy dog, *Jasper*, who I realized now weirdly had a name only two letters off from *Jase*.

"Sorry," Tate said again, and the word rolled out of her so easily, like she was used to constantly apologizing. "Come on in. I didn't mean to leave you out here. It's so damp and chilly. You'd hardly even believe it's almost summer."

"I like it." I breathed deeply, letting the cool heavy air and the mist permeate my lungs. Never mind that we were a mere hour from Seattle, which I'd come to despise only in the theoretical sense for its fictional presence in Jase's (and Celeste Templeton's) show. *Seattle Med* was, of course, actually filmed in Burbank. And I really had to stop thinking about how everything reminded me of Jase.

Tate stepped aside and gestured for me to follow her into the house. "I'm just going to put Jasper in the laundry room in his crate," she said. "Take a seat in the library." She slung the dog under one arm and gestured with her other toward the seating area in the room off to the right of us.

I walked inside the library but didn't immediately take a seat. Instead, I was drawn to the bookshelves that lined every inch of space on the walls of the large open room. They were filled from floor to ceiling with Gloria Diamond books, towering rows and rows and rows of pink and purple spines, in every language imaginable.

When Liza called me last week with the offer to play Gloria in the upcoming biopic, *Diamond in the Rough*, she threw around words like "breakout role" and "amazing opportunity" and glossed over the catch—that I would only have a short time to prepare before shooting began.

I'd stared at the bookshelves in my mother's home office as Liza had continued talking too fast on the phone, like she thought she really needed to convince me. I'd counted—my mother had exactly twenty-seven Gloria Diamond titles, taking up two full shelves of space. I'd probably read at least ten of them myself. "I'll do it," I'd told Liza, before she'd even finished explaining about the short timeline to me.

"Great," Liza had said, sighing on the other end with relief. Like she was shocked I hadn't turned her down. "I knew you would," she lied. It was a good role, but short notice was short notice, and let's just say I hadn't exactly been receptive to most of what Liza had been sending my way since my mother's death. But this had felt different. Gloria Diamond had been my mother's favorite author. And here, standing amongst all Gloria's books, *inside her house*, I suddenly felt swept with certainty. I'd made the right decision.

I ran my fingers across a row of Gloria's books now, spines in so many languages, it felt like her own personal literary UN. I recognized my favorite, *Love at the End of the World*, in Spanish, recalling words from my few years of Spanish class in high school. *Amor al Final del Mundo.* I picked it up and ran my fingers across the embossed pink and gold letters, wishing I could call my mother and tell her that I was here, in *The Gloria Diamond*'s personal library.

"I see you've made yourself at home with my books." An icy voice rang out from behind me, startling me, and I quickly put the book back on the shelf where I'd found it. The voice didn't belong to Tate; I knew it was Gloria before I even turned around. I took a breath and composed my character first. *Young, eager actress. Go.* I spun on my heels and offered her my best doe-eyed smile.

Gloria stood in the doorway, and like her house, at first glance she appeared much different than I had imagined she would. Smaller. Older. Frailer. In the author photo on the back of her latest novel, she was bold, glamorous, sparkling, with smooth cheeks, bright cherry lips and big blond hair. But standing before me in black leggings, a baggy hot-pink sweatshirt, no makeup and her hair in a thin ponytail at the nape of her neck, she appeared plain, a little wrinkled and certainly every one of her nearly sixty years. The author photo must've been old, heavily retouched or both.

"I'm going to have to ask that you refrain from touching my things while you're here," she said, her words crisp, like she was cutting the air with a knife. Liza had said Gloria had been a bit reluctant to agree to my request of spending time with her before shooting began. But that didn't quite hit home until right now.

I forced a smile. "I was admiring some of the foreign editions of your books," I said. "It's impressive to see them all in here, like this. You've had quite an amazing career."

"Admire with your eyes next time," she snapped.

I bit my lip and nodded, not wanting to say what I really thought, that of course I would have to touch things in her house while I was staying here, trying to get to know her. But we could get to that later. First, if I were going to become Gloria in only one week's time, I needed to get on her good side. I walked toward her now and held out my hand. "Amelia Grant," I said. "It's so wonderful to meet you in person."

She cleared her throat and didn't take my hand, so I dropped it back to my side. "I know who you are," she said.

Of course she did. I was just hoping she'd reply with what she wanted me to call her. *Gloria? Ms. Diamond?* Or her real name, *Mary?* Or more formally, *Mrs. Forrester?*

"Have a seat." She pointed to the couch, and I complied, and I moved to the far end, leaving room for Gloria to join me. I smiled at her warmly, hoping that might get her to soften, open up to me.

But she remained solidly in the doorway, her arms crossed in front of her small chest, her eyes locked steadily on my face. Was she trying to imagine if I could pull it off, the younger version of her? Any version of her? I wanted to assure her that I would, and I could. I'd played more taxing roles, but perhaps I'd never played one I was so personally interested in. Excitement fluttered in my chest, and I remembered again, *this* was why I was an actor. The challenge and the thrill and the hunger to become someone else, and to do it flawlessly.

Gloria was still in the doorway, and the silence between us began to feel heavy. "I love your books," I finally said. "I'm thrilled to have been cast in this role. My mother was your biggest fan. She recently passed away, quite suddenly, and…" I stopped talking when I realized I had nothing else to add to that. She passed away quite suddenly, and what more could I say except that now she was dead? And soon her house and all her things would be gone too.

"I'm very sorry to hear about your mother," Gloria said. It was the first kind thing she said to me and yet her tone was reserved. She was the opposite of what you might expect from the woman who'd written all the best love stories of the past thirty years. I would need to practice that later, if I truly wanted to get her character right, making even the warmest of words come off the tongue like ice.

"Thank you," I said. "I appreciate that." But all the *sorry*s in the world couldn't bring my mother back, not even the great Gloria Diamond's.

Gloria stared at me for another moment, opened her mouth to say something else. But then pressed her lips together tightly, as if she'd quickly changed her mind. "Tate will be back shortly, and she'll get you settled in the guest room," she finally said. "Take the afternoon to yourself, and we can talk at dinner tonight—six p.m. sharp in the dining room. Don't be late."

She spun on her heels and turned, and that was the first time I noticed that she was using a cane, dragging her left foot behind her ever so slightly as she walked out.

Amelia

I FIRST MET Jase ten years ago in a method-acting workshop in West Hollywood.

I was twenty-three, with a shiny (and useless) theater and dance degree from UC Davis, and I'd promised my mother that if I didn't book at least *one* real and paying acting job within my first year out of college, I'd apply to law school. I was pretty sure we both knew I was never cut out to be a lawyer, but I agreed to it because she also agreed to let me move back into her Pasadena house rent-free for the year. My mother was perpetually tough on the exterior, soft on the interior. Whatever hard line she'd pretended to draw in the sand that year, we both knew she would renegotiate our terms in twelve months' time if I asked.

Still, I wasn't sure she was wrong back then about acting. I was approaching the end of that first year, still completely jobless, verging a little bit on hopeless. I had yet to find an agent, and open casting calls had led me nowhere. Then, at one more failed audition, I picked up a flyer for a method-acting workshop. The cost was only twenty dollars, and so I decided to go, because why not?

It turned out I hadn't read the flyer all that carefully. It wasn't a class on the Method, an extension of the Lee Strasberg Institute (also in West Hollywood) as I'd assumed, but a class on *a method*, taught in the dark basement of a Unitarian church by some random aging "actor" who I was pretty sure was trying to scam a handful of us out of twenty dollars.

"Want to get out of here?" The inarguably gorgeous guy sitting in the folding chair to my left leaned over and whispered to me, as the instructor told us he was beginning with a guided meditation.

"Me?" I whispered back, though there was no one else sitting even remotely around us. The only other people in attendance—three septuagenarian women huddled together in the front row—should have been our first clue that this class wasn't legit.

He didn't wait for me to answer before he stood. He turned to me again, shot me a beautiful, full-faced smile, revealing dimples in both cheeks, perfect white straight teeth and sea-blue eyes that dare I say twinkled even in the dim fluorescent lighting of the church basement. What else could I do but stand up and follow him?

We ran up the stairs, then out onto the street, laughing. We ducked into a dive bar a few doors down and each got a beer.

"I guess what they say is true," Jase told me, his smile crinkling all the way up to the corners of his eyes. Even in the dark and smoky bar, I was sitting close enough to see the stubble on his chin. But it looked intentional, calculated, not sloppy. If he were going for a type, it would definitely be *scruffy, sexy guy in his twenties*. Probably a carpenter.

"What do they say?" I took a sip of my beer and tried to look and act as cool as him, like I hung out here, drinking with

sexy actors all the time. But then I betrayed myself by bump-
ing my beer bottle against the edge of the bar, spilling a little.

Jase chuckled, grabbed a bar napkin and wiped up my mess.
"If it looks too good to be true, it probably is," he said.

"You say this in reference to...yourself?" I asked.

He laughed, a genuine, hearty laugh, that shook in his (extremely well-muscled) chest. "Twenty dollars... No audition
necessary..."

"Ahh." I took another sip of my beer and felt myself relaxing a little. "The method class."

Jase nodded and explained that he'd been living in New York
up until a few months ago, studying Method for real, at the Lee
Strasberg Institute there. But he left when he got cast in a pilot
out here. That lasted a whole two months, though, before the
pilot got scrapped. He'd recently gotten a job working at Tar-
get while simultaneously going to auditions. He was trying to
save up enough again to take more classes, and he'd been lured
in by the affordable price on the flyer today.

"Twenty dollars," I said, taking another sip of my beer. Not
spilling this time. "We should've known."

In a Gloria Diamond novel, that moment in the dive bar
would've led in a straight line to our happy ending. But in real
life, our relationship was winding, messy. Complicated. Tiny
studio apartments and arguments over loading the dishwasher.
Failed audition after audition. Then a few minor successes,
which led to a few bigger ones. A few small movie roles for
me, and then *Saving Addy*, a show that lasted two seasons before it was canceled. Ever since, I'd been getting a fairly steady
stream of offers and roles. So maybe I wasn't a household name
or winning an Oscar, but I was making enough to support myself and live pretty comfortably in LA, which was no small feat
for an actor. Then last year Jase got his big break, a lead role on
Seattle Med, and within weeks his popularity exploded. Which

led us to that rainy morning, ten years after we first met, when Jase was naked in our bed with someone else.

That morning, he ran after me.

He stood there in front of me outside of our apartment building, still shirtless, in the pouring rain, and he swore what I had just witnessed in our bedroom was only part of *the Method*. Celeste's character, an intern named Molly, and Jase's character, cardiologist Dr. Ryan Matthews, were about to have a steamy scene in the on-call room at their next shoot.

"It doesn't mean what you think," Jase told me. His face blurred through the rain, or maybe through my tears, and he sounded so sincere, it was almost like he believed it himself, like he didn't even realize where the line between real life and method acting was anymore.

"You know what?" I finally said to him. "Fuck the Method."

Then I dramatically spun on my heels and attempted to run to my car, but through the haze of teardrops I didn't notice the giant puddle in my path until I stepped right in it, soaking my favorite black flats and splattering mud on that awful black dress.

I found myself thinking of that moment, sitting in Gloria Diamond's dining room a few hours later. It had begun to rain, and water pelted the large picture window behind the long rectangular dining table where Tate had told me to sit. I'd told Jase to *fuck the Method* a few months ago. But also, wasn't that exactly why I was here? Ten years dating Jase, ten years as a working actress, had made me into a believer. To play Gloria, I would have to become Gloria, understand what she was truly like beneath her dazzling, but always guarded, public persona.

The sound of her cane thumping against the hardwood interrupted my thoughts, and I looked up. She entered the dining room, made-up and dressed up and sparkly now, Jasper's tiny nails clicking at her heels as he trailed right behind her, a black diamond-studded bow tie around his neck. Gloria wore a sleek white pantsuit; her platinum blonde hair was elegantly piled on top of her head, and there seemed to be so much more of it than earlier that I was certain she was wearing a wig. A long string of diamonds hung from each ear, just heavy enough to tug her earlobes down like teardrops. And her lips were the color of a bowl of summer cherries. I'd changed into jeans and a black tee and had washed my face after Tate had shown me to my room upstairs. Now I felt desperately underdressed.

I stood to greet her, and Jasper let out a low growl. "Sit," Gloria commanded, and I wasn't clear if she was talking to me or the dog, but we both listened.

Then Gloria took her seat at the head of the table, stared at me and frowned. I made a mental note to at least do my makeup before I saw her next time. "Everything to your liking here, Amelia?" Maybe she intended for her question to be kind, but it came out sounding annoyed.

"Yes, the guest room is huge. And lovely." And that was true. It was large, maybe larger than the apartment Jase and I had been living in up until a few years ago in Studio City. And nicer too. Liza had originally booked me a hotel in Seattle, but Gloria had argued that it was an hour away and too inconvenient for us to meet, and the truth was, I'd liked the idea of settling in her space for a few days, anyway. Her guest room was nicer than a hotel room, with huge floor-to-ceiling windows that looked out at an expanse of pines and steel-gray sky. It had a plush king bed, a large sitting area with a TV and a desk, and even its own en suite bathroom.

Tate carried in plates from the kitchen, and I wondered if she was cook in addition to personal assistant and perhaps housekeeper too. She served Gloria first, then put a plate down in front of me: a giant hamburger served on top of romaine lettuce leaves. I stared at it and bit my lip.

"You're not a bleeding-heart vegetarian, are you?" Gloria asked me, eyeing my reaction.

I technically was both *a bleeding heart* and a *vegetarian*. But I used to eat meat, back before I moved in with Jase, who didn't. I made an effort to smile warmly. "Of course not," I lied. If Gloria ate meat, I should eat meat too. *If I were going to play her, I needed to be her.*

I hesitated for a few more seconds, but then wrapped the burger in lettuce and took a large bite. It was exceptionally… meaty. I chewed it slowly, remembering that the truth was I gave up meat not for Jase and not for the sake of the environment (which I did care about!) but because I didn't even like it. "It's great," I lied again, chewing slowly.

Gloria cut her burger with a knife, eating it in dainty delicate bites after dipping it in the pile of ketchup she'd poured in a giant circle on her plate. I watched her for a moment, then grabbed the ketchup and made an equal circle on my own plate.

"All right," Gloria said, in between bites. "Let's go over some ground rules, shall we?"

Rules? I dipped the meat in the ketchup like she was and forced myself to swallow another bite.

"While you're here this week, we'll meet between the hours of one and two each day to go over the script. I write in the mornings from six a.m. to noon and need complete quiet, so I am not to be disturbed during that time, no matter what. Tate can prepare lunch for you whenever you'd like. Dinner is promptly at six." I nodded and she continued. "You should find everything you need in your room, but if not, give Tate a list. She goes into town in the mornings while I'm writing to shop for the day. And last but not least, as I mentioned earlier, you are not to touch anything, except what's in your room. I value my privacy above everything else." She paused, took another bite of ketchup-soaked meat. I did the same and felt my stomach turn. "I've been told you require these few days of face-to-face time with me to perfect your craft, and I can respect that, as long as you respect my rules."

Her words were heavy but precise, and I felt as if a bus had driven right over me and left me in a flat little outline of myself in the middle of the road. I suppressed the urge to tell her that wasn't how this worked, that everything I'd need to truly know her could not be restricted to one hour of conversation per day. I didn't want to simply sit down and hear her rehash what I'd already read myself in the script. I wanted to carefully examine the small minutiae of her real life and her real self, the way it felt and tasted and smelled and looked and sounded.

"Could I watch you write tomorrow morning?" I asked her. "I won't say a word—I only want to observe what you look like when you're working."

"Absolutely not," she said quickly. "I'll be available between one and two to talk, like I said. Ask Tate for anything you need between now and then."

And then, just like that, she blotted her mouth with her napkin, pushed back her chair and walked out of the dining room, Jasper running off behind her.

I finished off the lettuce leaves on my plate after she got up, leaving the rest of the burger. I felt unsatisfied by their limp crunch and bland taste. Or maybe it was that I was upset, or… sad? A nagging heaviness settled in my chest, the same feeling that had been overwhelming me these last three months, sorrow or dread or despair. And now, I'd left LA, but my mother was still very much dead. Jase had still cheated on me. The tabloids had still made it out to be all my fault.

No one had even reported on Celeste. Everyone blamed *me* for the breakup. I wasn't pretty enough, young enough, famous enough. The gorgeous *Dr. Ryan Matthews* deserved better. As much as I'd wanted to argue and fight back, Liza had talked me down, convinced me it was better to ignore the press than start a battle with Jase. A battle I would certainly lose in the court of public opinion. And besides, I'd been in no shape to fight locked up in my grief in my mother's house in Pasadena. I was hoping to finally change the narrative with the recent announcement in *Variety* about me being cast last minute as Gloria Diamond.

I'd also thought I would come here and completely lose myself in Gloria, in this role, forget all about the tabloids, and Jase. About losing my mother. As an actress, you can do that. Slip into another life, and for a little while, all your own problems disappear. Unfortunately, so far, Gloria wasn't making that very easy.

"You all finished?" I looked up, and Tate was hovering, her eyebrows raised, staring at the half of burger still on my plate.

"Yes." I pushed the plate toward her. "It was delicious," I lied. "Thank you."

She hesitated for a second before picking up the plate. "There are snacks in the pantry in the kitchen, and fresh fruit in the fridge. If you get hungry later or anytime, help yourself."

Tate's offer seemed to directly contradict what Gloria had just told me, though maybe food didn't count as *things I was not allowed to touch*. I bit back a sarcastic comment and thanked her instead. "I'm full now," I told her, which strangely wasn't a lie, even though I'd barely eaten dinner and had skipped lunch all together unless you counted a small bag of pretzels on the plane. It was that feeling, that nagging heaviness. It filled me up. Swallowed me whole. Grief was both amorphous and all-consuming.

"Well, if you change your mind…" Tate said. "Oh, and there's coffee in your room if you want some in the morning. Gloria doesn't eat breakfast but we have eggs and oatmeal—"

"I don't eat breakfast either." I supposed Gloria and I had one whole thing in common. "And I saw the Nespresso in my room. That will be amazing."

Tate hesitated before she spoke again. "I loved you in *Saving Addy*." The words fell out of her in a rush, and her cheeks reddened slightly at her fangirl moment. I smiled, and I felt myself relaxing for the first time since I'd walked into this house. *Saving Addy* had been fairly popular. And my character, Addison Hemlock, had been an endearingly lovable hot mess, who was always getting herself into (and out of) trouble. The hook of the show was that Addy almost always eventually learned how to *save* herself. It had been a challenging role for me, balancing comedy with the darker moments of Addy's life, including her struggles with anxiety and depression.

"Thank you," I finally said to Tate. "That's very kind. I'm glad to know you watched."

Tate smiled. "And don't mind Gloria. She's just…" Her voice trailed off and I thought of several words to finish her sentence, *difficult* being the kindest one. But then Tate surprised me by adding, "Nervous."

"Nervous?" I asked. "Because of me being here?"

Tate nodded. "Yeah, and about the movie in general. She's a very private person. You see how she lives, all the way out here. Isolated." She gestured to the woods behind us. "This is all very much out of her comfort zone."

I glanced out the window now and the rain had stopped. It was nearly dusk, and the sky glowed a pale orange. The evergreens shimmered with leftover raindrops in the half-light, a beautiful and pearlescent green. I stared at them, considering what it must be like to live in such isolation, amongst all these trees. It was beautiful, but so achingly quiet.

"Anyway, I'm off for the night as soon as I finish cleaning up from dinner." I realized Tate was still talking. "But if you need anything else, text me at the number I gave you, okay?"

Tate had handed me her card earlier and I'd already put her number in my phone. I nodded now. "Is it safe to take a walk out here?" I gestured to the woods on the other side of the glass window.

"Safe?" she repeated, like she didn't understand the question.

"I mean, will I get murdered if I go take a walk through the woods now?"

She laughed. I couldn't tell if she was laughing with me, if she wanted us to be on good terms and in on the same joke, or if she thought I was absolutely absurd for asking her in the first place.

"Eaten by wild animals," I clarified. "Kidnapped by creeps lurking out there."

"I've never personally encountered either," Tate said. "There are deer and maybe some foxes, but chances are you'll come back alive." She chuckled again. "Town is about a mile down the main road that way." She pointed toward the front of the house. "I wouldn't walk that now, though. It'll be dark soon and there aren't any sidewalks, but tomorrow morning you definitely could. Or I could drive you to get anything you need."

I shook my head. "I don't need anything in town. I just wanted some fresh air before bed." And if I couldn't explore the inside of Gloria's house, at the very least I could explore the outdoors, feel and smell and observe the woods where she'd lived for the last thirty years.

"Twenty minutes walking in the woods now shouldn't kill you," Tate said. Then she added with a perfectly straight face: "At least I would hope not."

Outside it was damp from the rain, a little chilly. It felt like winter in LA, and I really needed something warmer than the thin cardigan I'd dug out from my suitcase.

I shivered as I stepped out the door, wrapped the cardigan tighter around my chest, and I considered going right back inside. But then I stood out on the stoop for a moment, took a deep cool breath. The dampness settled and expanded in my chest and that heaviness subsided a little. A walk in this air would soothe me, and it would also help me think about how to approach Gloria. Both the woman inside that house, and the role in *Diamond in the Rough*. I thought about what Tate said, that she was *nervous*. And I wondered what I could do to put her at ease, get her to open up.

I was considering that as I walked down the porch steps, and then almost immediately walked right into someone running up the path. His hands caught on my shoulders, and I wasn't sure if he was steadying me so I wouldn't trip over him or grabbing me. "What the hell?" he said.

Tate had laughed when I'd asked if I might run into any creeps, and yet, I hadn't even made it past the porch.

He took a step back, examined me as if trying to place me. And I did the same for him. He was only a little taller than me, with thick brown curly hair and glasses. Cute, in an academic kind of way. He didn't look like a murderer.

"Are you the new Tate?" he finally asked me.

I shook my head. "Nope. Are you?" He didn't look amused; his frown creased deeper. I took a step to move around him and he shadowed me, so I stopped and looked up again.

"Who the hell are you, then?" he demanded, brusquely. It wasn't like I was recognized everywhere I went or anything, but strangers still occasionally called out for Addy when they saw me in public. His question felt mildly offensive after Tate's warm recognition.

I frowned. "Who the hell are you?" I said it calmly and icily, channeling my inner Gloria Diamond. I met his eyes and refused to flinch, though I felt my heart thumping in my chest.

"This is private property," he said, pulling his phone from his jacket pocket. "You're trespassing." *Trespassing?* I saw him tap 9-1 on the phone screen.

"Wait," I said. "I don't know who you are but I'm not—"

Suddenly, the front door swung open behind us, and he lowered his phone and looked up. "Will, is that you?" Tate's voice called out.

Will?

Diamond in the Rough ended when Gloria and her son moved to the Pacific Northwest after her husband George's unfortunate death. She wrote her first novel there—here—while her son, and I could remember the exact line, *ran feral through the woods*. Her son, I remembered his name now too: *Will*.

"Oh, have you two met?" I realized Tate was still talking now. "Will, this is Amelia Grant, the actress portraying your mother in the biopic. Amelia this is Will—"

"Gloria's son," I said softly, cutting her off. That was the jerk in front of me, blocking me, accusing me of trespassing: Gloria Diamond's adult son.

Amelia

THIS WAS THE way Gloria's story began: *I found George Forrester, the love of my life, on a Saturday in the fall of 1981. I would lose him less than ten years later.*

I held my copy of her memoir in my lap the next afternoon, my finger nervously tracing the dust jacket on the book, my eyes falling on that line, as I waited for her on the couch in the library.

After my walk last night, I'd gone up unnoticed to my room. And I'd spent this morning sitting in there, trying to prep for the role and my meeting with Gloria today by watching old interviews I found with her online. She was a totally different person in those interviews: warm, magnanimous, sparkly. In a one-on-one with Oprah from the mid '90s, Gloria was svelte, tan and practically drenched in diamonds from head to toe: shoulder-length earrings, a large diamond choker and a diamond-encrusted gold sweater. Oprah asked her about her own love life and Gloria laughed warmly and touched Oprah's arm before saying that the love of her life was gone, but that he lived on in her books. Oprah shook her head, called Gloria *magical*, and Gloria practically beamed.

The thump of Gloria's cane jolted me now, and I glanced at my watch. Precisely one o'clock. Of course, it was. I opened the notebook on my lap and jotted down: *Exactly on time.*

I looked up and she was in leggings and a baggy sweatshirt, similar to how she was dressed when I'd arrived yesterday. *Casual writing clothes?* I jotted in my notebook, thinking about how they were very different from her dinner clothes and of course, her Oprah clothes. She sat down across from me, and I smiled hoping to ease her nerves. "Thank you again for taking this time to talk with me. How was your writing this morning?" I asked her.

She frowned, and I imitated her, trying to match her expression. Was this the real, unvarnished Gloria Diamond? Oprah-Gloria had had a totally different, happier look. A bright full-faced smile that I'd been trying to practice in my bathroom mirror before I'd walked down here. If I was going to play her, I needed to understand this dynamic—her private versus her public self.

"We'll start at the beginning," Icy-Gloria said now, ignoring my question about her writing. She was still frowning as she eyed the book in my lap. I wondered what her face looked like when she was at her desk, creating a story, wrapped up in another world, a love story. I imagined that relaxed, softened her. At least I would hope it did.

"The beginning," I repeated, my eyes glancing over the first line of her book again. "When you met George?"

"Amelia, do you define your own beginning with a man?" She arched her thin, penciled eyebrows, and I almost thought she looked amused.

I opened my mouth, then closed it again, not exactly sure what to say. Her memoir literally began with a line about her meeting George. Finally I said, "Okay. So what's the beginning, then?"

"I was born in Ohio as Mary. Mary Franklin. But everyone

called me Mare." I nodded. Wikipedia had told me that much before I'd even stepped on the plane at LAX. She was Mare Franklin, then Mare Forrester after she married George. Gloria Diamond was a pen name—but after several years of using it, she supposedly made it her legal name too. Twenty-eight years later, everyone seemed to call her Gloria, on and off the page.

"Do you ever go by Mare anymore?" I asked her.

She shook her head. "Mare disappeared that night George died."

That seemed to contradict what she'd just said about not *defining herself with a man*, but I nodded anyway.

It was Jase who had first suggested I should have a stage name, an acting name: Amelia Grant sounded beautiful and sophisticated and perfect. She didn't spill beer on the sticky counters of dark West Hollywood bars, and she certainly didn't trip into puddles when her entire life was falling apart.

But I'd come up with the name myself. Become *Amelia* myself. I wasn't about to take it back because we broke up. My mother had been the last person left to still call me Annie. Now it felt almost foreign whenever I'd see my real, given name on my credit statement each month: *Annie Gaitlin*. I was no longer that woman without even my mother to claim her existence out loud every Sunday at brunch in the garden. And it occurred to me that maybe that was what Gloria was saying about George too. That after he died, there was no one left who remembered who she was before, who she used to be.

Her memoir mentioned George's death only briefly, as if even all these years later it was too painful for her to write about it. He'd died at the age of thirty-two of carbon monoxide poisoning. Gloria and Will fled to a rural estate in the Pacific Northwest immediately after it happened. She wrote her first novel. Will grew up a *feral child*. And her love story with George lived on in her work.

"You must've loved him a lot," I finally said, figuring that was safe territory. It was, after all, the claim of the entire biopic, that her brief period loving George had become the inspiration for every single one of her thirty bestselling romance novels.

Gloria didn't say anything for a moment, and she turned and looked out the window. It had started raining again, hard drops rattling the glass, obscuring the woods beyond into a blur of brown and green. "I didn't let go of Mare because of George," Gloria finally said. "I just became a different version of myself after him. A better version." She paused for another moment. "Mare never knew how to get exactly what she wanted."

"And Gloria did?" I asked.

"Gloria *does*," she corrected me.

Gloria ended our session abruptly at two, as she'd promised the night before. And I'd gotten only a page of scribbled notes that didn't tell me much beyond what I'd already read in the script, her memoir and Wikipedia.

"You look confused. An hour with my mother will do that." I looked up and Will stood in the doorway now. I was surprised he was still here. I'd googled him last night and found he was a trial attorney in Seattle, and I'd decided that explained his immediate jump to me breaking the law. An occupational hazard—maybe I wouldn't hold it against him.

In the light of day now, he was not unattractive, creepy nor even slightly mean-looking. He leaned against the doorframe easily, smiling, exposing an endearing dimple in his left cheek.

"Maybe a little confused," I finally said. "Or, not exactly sure what to make of her yet."

He laughed. "That sounds about right." He had a gentle, kind laugh, and he struck me as the opposite of his mother in every way. If she was ice, he was warmth and light. "Sorry about last night," he continued. "My mother failed to mention that the lead actress would be staying with her a few days before filming began, and she's had some crazy fans in the past. I thought you were one of them."

I closed my notebook and stood, walking to the doorway and holding out my hand. "Apology accepted. Let's start over, shall we? It's nice to meet you, Will."

He took my hand, shook it. Held on to it a beat longer than was necessary while he stared at me, examining my face as if wondering how I could possibly become his mother.

"I'm supposed to take her up to Belles Woods for the beginning of the shoot next week," Will explained. "And she asked me to come stay here and help her get ready for a few days first. Of course, she neglected to mention she had other company until after I arrived. Then she promptly ordered me to stay away from you."

I could hear her saying it again, *Don't touch my things*. Did shaking Will's hand count? I took a small step back, gently extracting my hand from his. "Pretend I'm not even here." I paused. "This was all arranged last minute when I quickly stepped into the role after Therese Hadley quit, and I'm really just observing for a few days, anyway. Studying for the part. I'll try not to get in your way."

Our hands were no longer touching but Will's eyes hadn't moved from my face. "You're assuming I listen to her," he said. There was a hint of something in his voice, but I couldn't read him well enough to tell if he was annoyed with his mother or simply curious about me.

He finally averted his eyes from my face, and he was no longer smiling. So what he said next was completely serious, stoic even. "Just do me a favor. Play the *real* her. Not that bullshit romance queen version of her she presents to the world."

"And who exactly is the real her?" I asked. The words *icy bitch* sat on the tip of my tongue, but I wouldn't dare utter them out loud.

Will didn't say anything for a moment and then finally, he shrugged. "I sure as hell don't know."

Mare

1981

MARE FRANKLIN MET the love of her life on a Saturday, in the fall of 1981.

But the problem was that she introduced him to her roommate, Bess, on Sunday.

There would be other problems too, of course, bigger, weightier problems than Max Cooper. But at the time neither one of them understood that yet. Mare only understood that she had never felt anything as intensely as she felt standing close to Max. It was the way she imagined it would feel if she allowed herself to get too close to a fire. The heat, at first, would radiate, warm her skin, make her feel completely and utterly the most alive she had ever felt. Until she took one more tiny step and then it would burn her, cause her to cry out in pain, redden and blister. Destroy her.

Bess, though, didn't think about things like that. She just thought that Max was unbearably kind.

Max *was* unbearably kind. But that wasn't what drew Mare to him. It was something else. His eyes. They were a pale blue, the exact color of the June sky she'd stared up at while daydreaming once, lying in the grass in the field behind her father's house in Ohio as a little girl. That sky she daydreamed would take her away, take her anywhere else. It was ten years later when she accidentally walked straight into Max and caught on the blue of his eyes. But she still found comfort in that exact shade of blue.

Saturday afternoon in the fall of 1981, and she was in the library, on the third floor, looking for a very specific volume of Shakespeare sonnets for her Seventeenth-Century Lit paper. Her eyes trailed the spines on the shelf until she hit the right number. She stood up on her tippy-toes to reach for the book, and then suddenly, he was there, having come from the other side. They were both reaching for the same book on the same high shelf at the same exact time.

Their hands met, and she turned, startled, at the brush of his fingertips against her own, suddenly face-to-face, eye to eye, with this...man. *That blue.*

"Sorry." He laughed and let go of the book. "You can have it." *Unbearably kind.*

"You don't need it?" she asked. He must have, or else why would he have climbed all the way up to the third floor and meandered down the narrow rows to exactly this spot?

He shrugged sheepishly, smiled at her. His blue eyes were deep and thoughtful and held on to her face in a way that made it impossible for her to look away. "I could always write my paper on Marlowe instead," he said.

"God, don't do that." She laughed. Professor Treacher had nearly put her to sleep last week reading Marlowe aloud in class. Seventeenth-Century Lit was a required class for all English majors and, so far, the worst, most boring class she'd taken in college. She hadn't become an English major to analyze four-hundred-year-old love sonnets filled with impossible diction and written exclusively by men. She wanted to be a writer, a literary novelist, who wrote fearless women as they truly were.

"You're in Treacher's class too, huh?" He grinned, a small knowing grin. She had never noticed him there, but the class was in a large lecture hall, early in the morning, and it was all she could do to stay awake, much less be aware of her surroundings.

She nodded. "English major?" she asked him, wondering why she'd never seen him before in any of her smaller seminar classes.

"Minor," he said. "Double poli-sci and history major. I plan to go to law school."

"So are you taking Seventeenth-Century Lit by choice?"

He laughed, and it was a deep full laugh that shook his undeniably broad shoulders. "Bad choice, huh?" Then he added, "I transferred this year, and it was the only lit lecture still open when I registered."

That brought up so many things she wanted to know, where he'd transferred from. Why? But instead she said, "The fact that it was still open should've told you something."

"Apparently." He chuckled. "I'm Max, by the way."

"Mary," she said. "But all my friends call me Mare." She said it so quickly without even thinking about it, as if they were already friends.

"Nice to meet you, Mare."

She pulled the book from the shelf, held it out to him, an offering. "We could share it," she said. "I'm free this afternoon if you are."

And as soon as the words were out of her mouth, she regretted them. She immediately understood she had said something foolish, something that she might never be able to take back.

★ ★ ★

She had just turned twenty years old, a few weeks before that Saturday afternoon in the fall of 1981. An English major who studied so much she had a 4.0, she also wrote a feminist column for the college's newspaper in her spare time. (So far this fall she had covered both the new Princess Diana *and* Sandra Day O'Connor.) But she had vowed to make it through college with a degree, not a husband. Her older sister, Margery, five years earlier had made it through one year of college before dropping out *without* a degree, but with a husband *and* a baby. That was not going to be Mare's fate—she'd promised herself that. And she had thus far made it so by studying on the weekends instead of going out to parties with Bess. College was the blue sky too. It took her away from home, from her father, and she would never let herself go back there.

But then there she was, the beginning of her sophomore year. The shared Shakespeare sonnets in the library led to a shared coffee, led to catching a late afternoon showing of *Body Heat*, led to a beer on the worn couch in his small studio apartment, led to his lips finding hers. Fire coursed through her, making her suddenly stupid from the overwhelming warmth that traveled instantly from her lips, down her chest to her core, her legs, her toes. She couldn't even think, and she kissed him back.

Maybe it was the beer or the sizzling heat that lingered from the movie. But this was the kind of kiss she'd only read about in the Harlequin romances she'd snuck under her covers to inhale with a flashlight as a preteen. The kind that made you restless and reckless and hungry. She forgot everything, and she had to have more. She pulled him to her and kissed him harder.

If Max hadn't pulled back first, she wasn't sure she ever would've been able to stop kissing him.

"I'm sorry." He breathed the words more than spoke them, as if he couldn't get enough air. What was he sorry for—kissing her, or stopping? "I've never...felt this way...before," he finally stammered.

It was those words that jolted her back, that made her remember who she was, what she wanted. Not a man. She felt certain, after only this one afternoon, she could disappear into Max forever if she allowed herself to lose control. She couldn't ever lose control.

"I have to go," she said.

She stood so quickly, she knocked over her plastic cup of beer, but she didn't stop to clean it up. She ran out of his apartment, fleeing into the crisp fall night, where a cool breeze hit her face, calming the fire that still rose and swelled in her chest as she took the long way back to her dorm.

The next morning, the RA called their room—Mare had a guest in the lobby.

"A guest?" Bess inquired, her thin brown eyebrows raised. Mare didn't have guests. Not male guests, anyway. (Female guests were permitted to come up to the room on their own.)

"Must be a mistake." Mare shrugged. The Shakespeare volume was heavy in her lap, and in spite of herself, she thought of last night's kiss and hoped it was him. *It couldn't be.* She hadn't told him her last name or where she lived. It definitely wasn't him. But what if it was? She put the book down on her bed and stood.

"I'll go downstairs with you." Bess followed behind, grabbing a sweater off her desk chair on the way out. "Just in case it's someone trying to murder you," she added somewhat cheerfully. Tiny little five-foot-two Bess, who weighed all of ninety-five pounds, would not have been Mare's first choice for backup. Still, it was unlikely it was a murderer. More likely it was a mistake. Mare didn't protest and held the elevator door open for Bess to get in.

On the way down, Bess threw the sweater she'd grabbed

over Mare's shoulders, and that's when Mare realized she wasn't wearing a bra. Mare lost and forgot things. Bess remembered and found them. It was why they were the perfect roommates when they were paired together freshman year. And best friends ever since. "Thanks, B," Mare said, for probably the millionth time since they'd been living together.

"If he's a murderer, I hope he's cute," Bess said, as the elevator doors opened into the lobby.

But Max Cooper was not a murderer. (At least, Mare didn't think he was.)

He was sitting in a lobby armchair, facing them. He smiled at her, stood. Mare walked off the elevator and she wrapped Bess's sweater tighter around her chest. "How did you know where I live?" Her tone was accusatory, biting.

"You know him?" Bess whispered from behind her, sounding more shocked that Mare actually *knew* a guy than if there had been a real murderer waiting for her.

Max walked toward them, holding up his arm. "You forgot this," he said. That's when she noticed her wallet was in his hand. "Your student ID had your campus address. And I thought you'd be in a panic looking for your wallet. So I just came here to return it…" His voice trailed off.

"Thank you," she murmured, and she meant it. She softened a little, smiled sheepishly. Took the wallet from his hand, careful not to let their fingertips touch even the slightest bit as she inwardly chided herself for leaving her wallet behind and not even noticing.

Bess stepped forward and held out her hand. "Hi, I'm Bess, Mare's roommate. And you all know each other how?"

"We don't," Mare said quickly.

"I mean, we kind of do." Max stared at her, ignoring Bess's hand. Or maybe he didn't notice Bess at all, as his eyes, those intense blue eyes, were trained so heavily on Mare's face.

"Are you two…dating?" Bess exhaled the words in disbelief.

"No," Mare said quickly. Then she added, "We're in Seventeenth-Century Lit together. I guess I left this in the library yesterday. Thank you for picking it up."

Max opened his mouth to correct her. But then he suddenly did seem to notice Bess there, and he closed his mouth again, as if he understood the *Body Heat*, the beer, the kiss, could never be mentioned. Ever. "Yeah," Max finally said, his voice flat. "The library. We both needed the same Shakespeare book for our papers."

"Leave it to Mare to get so distracted by Shakespeare that she forgot her wallet." Bess rolled her eyes and chuckled. "I swear she would lose her head if it wasn't attached and she didn't have me to keep it in place, wouldn't you, Mare?"

"I would," Mare confirmed.

Max bit the corner of his lip a little, and Mare remembered with a sudden, overwhelming rush of warmth what those lips had felt like against her own. She wanted to take one step closer to him, to kiss him again. She wanted that so much that it terrified her.

And that's why she said what she said next: words that would haunt her through the rest of college, her twenties and even a good forty years after that. "You know what?" she said. "I have homework to do. But I think you two might actually have a lot in common and really like each other." She paused, as if already knowing she'd put something in motion that she'd never be able to take back, no matter how much she might want to later. "Bess, why don't you take Max out for coffee, to thank him for being so kind to your roommate?"

And then she turned and got onto the elevator, riding up the six flights to their dorm room, all alone.

Amelia

"AMELIA?" TATE CALLED my name, then knocked on the door. I opened my eyes and glanced at my phone on the nightstand. 6:48 p.m. Apparently, I was late for dinner.

After my session with Gloria and strange conversation with Will this afternoon, I'd come back up to my room, crawled underneath the covers in the giant and extremely comfortable king-size bed and had fallen asleep. I'd drifted into a hazy dream about my mother, where I'd been walking with her in her garden in Pasadena, trying to tell her that I had taken on a role she would finally, truly be excited about. But she couldn't hear me, and she kept disappearing in between the yellows and pinks of her roses and azaleas every time I reached out for her. Almost close enough to touch. But not quite. Tears pricked my eyes now, and I bit my lip to keep them at bay.

I took a deep breath, stood and walked to the door. "Sorry," I said to Tate as soon as I opened it. "I fell asleep and lost track of the time. Is Gloria upset?"

"Not at all," Tate said easily. "She just commanded me not to feed you since, I believe her exact words were, 'I shouldn't have to explain promptness to a girl of that age.'"

"Oh my gosh, I'm sorry. I'm sure I can DoorDash myself something. I don't want to cause any trouble."

Tate chuckled. "You most definitely cannot out in these parts. I made you a salad and put it in the fridge. Just to clarify, if I read your expression right yesterday, you are a vegetarian, yes?"

I nodded and fought the urge to grab Tate in a hug as I felt overwhelmed by her kindness, by the way she was oddly mothering me even though she was clearly younger than me. I saw a flash of my mother again in her roses, and another wave of grief crested in the hollow center of my chest. I was thirty-three years old, and I still desperately needed a mother. How pathetic was I?

"Gloria gets especially anxious about eating on time on Tuesdays because *Seattle Med* is on," Tate continued. "She's kind of obsessed. Tonight is the beginning of the two-part season finale."

A laugh rose in my throat and came out of me more like a strangled cry. *Seattle Med*. Gloria and Tate must know about me and Jase. It had been covered in all the tabloids and entertainment magazines. And Tate knew who I was—she'd watched *Saving Addy*!

"You're welcome to join us." Tate was saying now. She glanced at her Apple Watch. "If you can be down there in the next seven minutes. She doesn't do streaming. She watches it live, on cable TV. Promptly at seven." Tate paused and stared at me, and for a few seconds I couldn't figure out what to say. Did Gloria actually expect me to join her? Was she deliberately trying to torture me?

"I hate *Seattle Med*," I finally said. I wondered if it was possible that Gloria didn't know I'd spent years sleeping in the same bed as *Dr. Ryan Matthews*. Tate had to know. But if she wasn't going to bring up Jase, I certainly wasn't. "I can't stomach medical shows," I added coolly. "I don't do blood."

Tate smiled and nodded. "I hear you, but this show is more affairs and sex than surgeries or blood."

Affairs and sex. I remembered a brief flash of Celeste's perfectly round breasts, Jase insisting it was all really a professional interaction. *Method.* Tate was still smiling, but I wondered now if she was trying to get some inside information about the breakup out of me? Liza would've been proud—I pressed my lips into a tight smile and said nothing.

"Well, if you change your mind," Tate said. "The screening room is in the back of the house. Walk through the laundry room and open the door on the other side. It used to be the garage, but Gloria converted it a while back since she doesn't drive. Just don't come in after 6:58 or she'll get mad."

I nodded, letting all those small tidbits about Gloria settle so I could jot them in my notebook when Tate left. She wasn't all that old—I wondered when and why she had stopped driving. And did people really still watch shows live, on cable, at the exact time they actually aired? But it seemed clear that Gloria liked things the exact way she liked them, and she thrived on her very rigid routine. Was this part of what was making her nervous about the upcoming film shoot? Or was there something more to it?

"Salad's in the fridge," Tate reminded me, and then she added, seemingly out of the blue before shutting the door, "The screening room is very well insulated. Gloria can't hear a thing from the rest of the house when she's in there."

I sat down on the bed after Tate left, considering everything she'd just told me. I knew that the first part of the *Seattle Med* two-part finale was two hours long, Tate had said that Gloria had to watch it *live on cable*, and also that Gloria couldn't hear anything in the rest of the house while she was in the converted garage. Was Tate trying to help me learn more about

Gloria by hinting that if I were to snoop around, Gloria would never know?

I stood, swallowing back any guilt I felt at that thought. But it wasn't like I was going to damage her stuff or hurt anyone. I only wanted to learn more about her. I *had* to learn more about her if I was going to do a good job playing her.

Gloria's office, where she worked on her books each morning, was at the other side of the upstairs hallway. Tate had pointed it out when she'd given me a brief tour yesterday. I walked out of my room now and stepped carefully down the hallway toward it. I suddenly had this weird feeling of my mother's presence all around me, the way it had just been in my dream. Even though she'd stopped talking about law school after *Saving Addy*, I couldn't help but feel now that it would've been this role that would've finally made her genuinely proud of my chosen career.

This is for you, Mom, I thought, as I stopped in front of Gloria's office door. Though the truth was, she probably would've hated that I was blaming the trespassing I was about to do on her. And as much as thinking about her had pushed me to say yes to this role initially, now that I was here, it was beginning to hit me what a huge boost this could give my career. That if I succeeded as *The Gloria Diamond*, then maybe it would mean Jase hadn't left me behind in the dust of his mega success, but instead, that we had both finally moved upward in our careers, only in vastly different directions.

But then I felt annoyed even thinking again about Jase. And I pushed thoughts of him and *Seattle Med* away as I reached my hand up to the door. It was closed, and it occurred to me, likely also locked. But I tried the knob and felt a wash of surprise as it easily turned and the door opened into the dark room.

I blinked, trying to adjust my eyes to the darkness, worried if I turned the office light on Gloria would somehow know, or sense me up here. The light from the hallway flooded a small pathway to a large desk in the center of the room. I glanced behind me, back into the hallway one more time. Still empty—of course, it was. They were all in the screening room/former garage, even Will and Jasper, probably already watching Jase have sex with Celeste on-screen right at this very moment. *Been there. Done that.* Lucky me, I'd already witnessed it live.

Certain I was completely alone upstairs, I tiptoed into her office, following the slant of light to her desk.

Her desk glimmered in the yellow light from the hallway. It had a large glass top, with what appeared to be diamonds embedded all along the sides. Were they real? I ran my finger softly along the cool sharp edges and decided that they probably were. Now *this* was the kind of detail I was looking for. Gloria Diamond wrote each morning at her million-dollar desk, literally ensconced in diamonds. I suppressed a laugh as I moved to examine what was on the desk itself.

Half the desk was taken up by a huge monitor, with a closed laptop sitting in front of it. It felt strangely high-tech for a woman who was currently watching her favorite show on *live cable television*. But then I noticed a stack of yellow legal pads next to the laptop, covered with handwritten scribbles—that felt more like Gloria. Her handwriting was messy, and I couldn't exactly make out the words in the semidarkness. But I suspected they were book ideas, plot points, characters, scenes.

A little shiver ran up my spine and settled over me. No matter what feelings I'd had about Gloria, the woman, I remembered the way Gloria, *the writer*, had made me feel when I read one of her novels. There was that thrill of sneaking them off my mother's bookshelf as a teenager, reading them late at night in my room when my mother was already asleep. Back then, Gloria's words had made me believe that love was something real, something even I could feel intimately coursing through my veins, pulsing in my own young heart.

As an adult, in real life, I'm not sure I'd ever felt with Jase what I'd felt imagining myself as one of Gloria's heroines. My own parents had gotten divorced when I was almost too young to even remember them together. (My father had remarried and moved to New Jersey by the time I was twelve.) My mother never dated anyone after that. I understood by now that Gloria's fiction truly was *fiction*. But still, I'd read her latest novel after Liza had called me about this job last week. And for a few hours, I'd almost believed again.

But it wasn't like Gloria's own life was filled with the kind of love she wrote about either. Here she was, living in the middle of these desolate rain-soaked pines with her little dog, her existence isolated, rigid and ornery.

She had experienced it once, though. With her husband, George. *The love of her life*.

I noticed a framed picture sitting behind the stack of legal pads: a young woman and a young man with their arms around each other. Was that him? Was that them? Gloria and George. Or, no, *Mare* and George. Was this actual proof that the kind of love she wrote about truly existed?

I turned on the flashlight on my phone and shone it across the photograph. This woman was Gloria for sure. She was a little younger than she was in the photograph on the cover of *Diamond in the Rough*. But unmistakably the same person. The man she was holding on to, though, was...unfamiliar. I picked up the frame, held my flashlight over it and examined the photograph more closely. This man was definitely not George.

Gloria and George's 1983 wedding photo was also included in *Diamond in the Rough*. In that photo, George was much taller than Gloria, strikingly so, by at least a foot. His hair was curly and dark brown, and his face was round, much like Will's. But the man in this picture was only an inch or two taller than Gloria. His hair was straight, dirty blond, and his jawline was square.

Yet, their arms were wrapped around each other, their cheeks pressed together, their smiles wide enough to swallow the camera whole. Then my flashlight caught on a tiny orange date stamp in the bottom right corner of the photo—*October 1986.* Three years after Gloria married George?

"What are you doing?" A deep voice cut through the darkness. *Will.* I let out a little startled cry and jumped, dropping the frame. Luckily it landed on the stack of legal pads in front of me and didn't shatter. I quickly picked it up and put it back where it had been on the desk when I'd walked in here. "Jesus, Amelia." Will entered the room, and reached for my arms, encircling my wrists with his fingers like they were handcuffs. "I didn't peg you as a thief."

I uncurled my fists, revealing my empty palms. "I'm not stealing anything," I whispered, trying hard (and failing) to keep the edge of guilt from my voice.

He stared at me for a moment, but still didn't let go of me. The slant of light from the hallway hit the contours of his face and I tried to read his expression. His eyes were dark; he was angry or maybe he was confused.

"I'm sorry." I whispered an apology, not totally sure why I was still whispering. Gloria and Tate wouldn't hear us anyway. But it felt wrong to even speak in here, much less at full volume. "I shouldn't have come in here. I just wanted to see where she wrote. Understand more about who she is." I paused waiting for him to say something but instead I heard him breathing hard, air rattling his chest like he'd run too fast to get here. I thought about telling him that Tate had given me her tacit permission to snoop, but I didn't want to throw her under the bus, so instead I added, "I really wasn't going to take anything. Or even touch anything."

"And yet, you were touching something when I walked in," Will said, finally letting go of me and reaching across the yellow legal pads to pick up the frame and look at the photograph himself.

I ran my finger over my right wrist, tracing the outline of where he'd just touched me, and my skin still felt hot there. Will was ignoring me now and staring at the picture, frowning.

"Who is that man? Do you know him?" I asked. "It's not your dad, right?"

Will shook his head, and I wasn't sure if he was trying to say it wasn't his dad or he didn't know. Or both. He put the picture back down on the desk. "We shouldn't be in here," he finally said.

I nodded and then followed him back out to the hallway, quietly shutting the door behind me. Will stopped at the top of the stairs, like he was trying to decide if he should rat me out.

"You won't tell her, will you?" I pleaded with him. "I promise my intentions were all good."

He slowly turned back around to face me. His expression was so neutral, I couldn't read him at all. Was he sympathetic, or did he want to get his mother to throw me out?

"This movie means a lot to me," I said. "I just want to get to know her, so I can play *the real her*, like you said."

"The real her." He frowned and turned away from me, and then I felt certain he was going to go interrupt Gloria right this very minute to tell her what I'd done. I'd have to leave right now, tonight. Would I have to give up the role too?

But then Will turned back to me suddenly, his expression more neutral again. "Do you want to go get a drink?" he asked. "I could really use a drink."

Mare

1982

BESS WAS THE one to blame for George. Mare would tell her that years later, yell that at her, in fact, in a fit of rage and jealousy and pure frustration. *It was all Bess's fault.* Everything that would happen, everything they would lose, it all came down to the fact that Bess brought George and Mare together.

The whole truth was very different, of course. Deep down, Mare knew that. Bess knew that too. (Probably.) The truth was soaked in beer and the tenuousness of an icy sidewalk, a too-cold night that numbed them.

But the truth was also that Bess handpicked George from her psychology study group for Mare. He was *handsome, a gentleman, perfect*, she relayed as she'd practically forced Mare to go on the date that she had set up, without Mare's permission.

"Well, why don't you go date him, then?" Mare had snapped, as Bess told Mare about George while she fiddled with Mare's hair, running her delicate fingers through her wild brown waves, trying, failing, to tame them.

Bess laughed as she twisted Mare's hair back into a low bun. Because by then Bess had been dating Max Cooper for nine months, and she couldn't even think about looking at anyone else. Why would she?

"College is more than half over," Bess pleaded with her. "Just give him a chance. For me," she wheedled.

What wouldn't Mare do for Bess? Nothing. This included.

And so in spite of her own objections, she went on that date. She met George for coffee and sticky buns at the campus diner, where he held the door for her, pulled out her chair. Regaled her with a charming story about his recent soccer win. He was a gentleman. Handsome. Perfect. Just as Bess had promised. He bent down and hugged her out on the sidewalk in front of the diner afterward. He held on a second too long, a little too tight, like he didn't want to let her go. That might've been perfect too, except the problem was, Mare felt absolutely nothing. But maybe, she told herself, that wasn't the problem. That was the solution. What was safer than dating a man she felt nothing for, after all?

When Bess said it would be nice if Mare had a boyfriend so they could pair up, do everything as a foursome, the truth was Mare agreed. She didn't want to be Max and Bess's third wheel. She didn't want to spend her junior year in her dorm room alone either while Bess was out with Max.

And so, she went on another date with George (burgers and milkshakes and *An Officer and a Gentleman*). He kissed her in the theater when the credits rolled, and she let his lips stay on hers for three whole seconds (she was counting) before she pulled away. George laughed, and brushed a thumb softly across her cheek, told her she was *adorable*.

"I like you," George said then, nonchalantly. "We should date."

"I like you too," she lied. Well—it wasn't really a lie. She didn't *dislike* him. But she didn't like him, the way he liked her.

Still, in a matter of weeks, she was caught up in it. She was George's girlfriend, and together they were half of Max and Bess's foursome. There were more movies and football games, cheering on the sidelines for George at soccer, late nights at a dive bar sharing pitcher after pitcher after pitcher of beer.

And then there was the snowy night in December.

She had been George's *girlfriend* for four months by then. They'd all had too much to drink that night, and they were stumbling back toward George's apartment to drink more. Bess giggled from somewhere behind her, and she heard Max say, "Bessie, what are you doing?" his voice filled with laughter.

Bessie.

The tenderness in his voice hurt her, a physical ache in her chest, and Mare suddenly lost her footing, sliding on the icy sidewalk. George quickly caught her, held on to her and kept her from hitting the ground. And then his breath was warm against her freezing cheek as he said, "Let's ditch them."

"Let's not," she said, struggling to pull herself back upright, but she continued to slide and George held on tight so she wouldn't fall.

"Yes, let's." Bess giggled again from behind her.

Mare finally steadied herself and turned around to frown at Bess. Only Bess was too drunk to notice, and instead Mare accidentally caught Max's eyes, their blues glinting in the sheen of the streetlight overhead. She had not let herself look directly at him like this since that morning last year in the library, and now it felt blinding, like she'd just stared directly into the sun. She snapped her head back forward, clung tighter to George.

"Come on, Maxy. Let's ditch them." Bess's drunken voice rang out too loud. And maybe right then everyone knew what she meant, what was about to happen.

The inside of George's apartment was dark and it was too cold—the landlord controlled the heat—and it never rose above sixty-six degrees in the winter. Mare flopped on his second-hand couch, not even taking off her coat.

George pulled two more beers from the fridge and came and sat down next to her. He opened the bottles, handed her one, but she was too cold to drink something chilled now. Or maybe she was too tired. She was thinking about Bess and Max all alone. What were they doing at Max's apartment? Though Bess and Mare discussed almost everything else, they never talked about sex, at least not since Bess had been dating Max. But Bess was too drunk to do anything now, tonight. Max was much too respectful to try. Except maybe Bess had sobered up on the rest of their chilly walk. She felt a little nauseous thinking about the two of them having sex in Max's apartment, right at this very second, knowing there was nothing she could do to stop it.

"You're a million miles away," George said, touching her cheek, stroking it with his thumb. She extricated herself and took a sip of the beer, if only to keep her hands and her face occupied.

"I should probably go home," she said, her voice dull, her breath frosting the air as she spoke. "It's too cold in here."

"I'll warm you." George moved closer, wrapping both arms around her. He slid her coat down, and pulled her into his lap. Pressed up against him, she had a moment of clarity. And she suddenly understood what was happening, what he wanted.

"I don't think we should, George," she said. In four months, she had already said this to him a handful of times. But no other nights had been so cold, so hazy with beer.

He planted a soft kiss on her neck in response.

Then his kisses trailed up her neck, to her lips. And he started unbuttoning her shirt with one hand while still holding her close to him with the other.

"George." She said his name again. "Maybe we should wait."

He stopped kissing her for a moment. "But what are we waiting for?" he asked softly.

She was unable to form a reasonable answer, and she finally

shrugged. He grinned and tugged down her bra, his fingers trailing across her breast. She shivered, chilled from the cold of his touch, and he smiled, mistaking her reaction for pleasure.

He slid his fingers down her stomach, unbuttoned her jeans. All the alcohol made things muddled, and she felt oddly distant from her own self, as if she were watching this scene unfold, rather than participating in it. She could not think of one single answer to his last question. *What was she waiting for exactly?*

"I want you, Mare," George whispered.

But she didn't want him. She wanted Max. Except she didn't say that.

She didn't say anything at all, and she didn't push him away either. He kissed her again, and now she felt herself kissing him back. Because it suddenly felt easier to do what he wanted, to just give in, than to try and stop it.

Amelia

FIFTEEN MINUTES AFTER he'd caught me snooping around in his mother's office, Will and I pulled up in front of an extremely questionable (and run-down) shack nearly obscured by pines a few miles down the road from Gloria's house. A flashing neon sign out front said Ba; the *r* wasn't lit.

I followed him inside, thinking this place screamed more *most likely to get murdered* and less *grab a drink with a friend*. And the fact that it was mostly empty inside, save one table with two middle-aged men in leather jackets, didn't do much to change my perception. But I was in it this far, I doubted I could easily order a car all the way out here in the middle of nowhere and, anyway, I wanted to pick Will's brain. The fact that he'd invited me to get a drink made me think maybe he had things to share about his mother, and if that was the case, I was willing to ignore my surroundings.

"Not what you're used to out in Hollywood, I'm sure," Will

said, laughing a little as we took a seat at the bar. "But a drink is a drink, isn't it?"

"Sure," I murmured, unconvinced that was even remotely true.

But I ordered a glass of pinot noir after the bartender told me it was local and Will ordered a beer on tap. The drink was kind of beside the point.

"You don't watch *Seattle Med*?" I asked Will, half joking before taking a sip of my pinot noir. I let it sit on my tongue for a moment before deciding it actually wasn't half bad.

Will shook his head and looked confused, like he'd never heard of it before. I wondered if he was living under a rock. Because it seemed like everyone on earth watched *Seattle Med* and loved Jase's Dr. Ryan. "I don't watch much TV," he said, and I resisted the temptation to roll my eyes. Clearly Will was one of *those* people. He probably sat around at night reading. And not romance novels. Whatever it was lawyers read for fun, law briefs, or maybe if he really wanted to unwind, the *New Yorker* or classic literature. But I guessed that also explained why he hadn't recognized me yesterday when we first met.

"Well, Tate told me it's your mother's favorite show," I said. "They were watching the season finale tonight. I thought everyone was down there watching," I added sheepishly. "Including you."

"Ahh, so that's why you broke into her office." He took a sip of his beer and seemed to be swallowing back a smile, like catching me was now, in hindsight, more amusing than alarming.

"I didn't break in," I clarified. "The door was unlocked."

"My mother would definitely disagree on that fine point."

He was definitely right. I sighed. "If you think I was really breaking and entering then why did you bring me here? To get me drunk before you ratted me out to Gloria?" I gulped my wine. It burned the back of my throat. I'd have to take back my earlier assessment—it was not very good.

He chuckled and shook his head. "I just wanted to get out of there and you looked like you could use a drink too." He paused and took another sip of his beer. "This is why I never come stay at her house anymore," he added. "It's suffocating."

"So why are you staying at her house now?" I asked him. If he worked and lived in Seattle, he was only an hour away. And even if he wanted to attend the beginning of the shoot, that didn't start until next week.

He frowned. It was, of course, none of my business. But I was curious. "She's been nervous about going up to Belles Woods for the shoot. She pleaded with me to come stay with her for a few days first, to help her prepare. And she's still my mother." He sighed and I tried to absorb everything he was saying. Most of all, there it was again, what Tate had said too: she was *nervous*.

"Nervous about what?" I pressed, wondering if he'd answer the same way Tate had.

He shrugged, took a slow sip of his beer. "I guess it's one thing to write lies about your life and another altogether to *see* them play out."

"Lies?" I asked, turning to look more intently at him.

He took another sip of his beer. "You know she writes fiction for a living, right?"

"But *Diamond in the Rough* is based on her memoir. Nonfiction. Her real-life love story with your dad."

Will raised his eyebrows in response, and I stopped talking for a moment, pushed the wet cocktail napkin around the bar counter with my finger.

"I'm really sorry about what happened to him, by the way," I added. "It must've been hard for you." My own dad had left, gotten remarried and moved away before I turned twelve. I wasn't very close to him in my adult life, but we kept in touch with the occasional text every few weeks. At least I knew he was out there and okay, living across the country with his new family; he hadn't perished in a tragic accident.

"It was a long time ago," Will said, running his fingers through his hair. "I can barely remember any of it now."

"So then why do you think your mother's memoir is lies?"

He shrugged. "The *New York Times* review called *Diamond in the Rough*, a 'portrait of a happy marriage,' but the only thing I remember is them fighting. I have this vague memory of hiding out in the kitchen pantry while they threw things at each other."

I let that sink in. George in *Diamond in the Rough* is kind, generous, loving. A quiet bookworm who devotes his life to a young Gloria. Fighting? Their son hiding in the pantry while they threw things? But memory was a funny thing, and Will had said he could barely recall his father. Maybe he was mistaken or remembering some isolated incident that had stuck with him.

"You know what," he interrupted my thoughts. "Never mind. I shouldn't have even said that. It doesn't matter what I think, anyway. I'm sure you can pull off anything because you're a great actress or whatever." I wasn't sure if I should be offended by his "or whatever," if he was being serious or facetious, but I really was very good at acting. I *could* pull off anything if I worked hard enough to learn the part. "Seriously. Don't listen to me. I just…had a moment after seeing that picture again," Will continued.

"Seeing it again?" I asked. "So you do know who the man is in the photograph?"

He shook his head, then hesitated for another minute. "No, I don't know him. But I've seen that picture before. Once. The night my father died."

Will was my age or maybe a little bit older. The picture seemed like an oddly specific memory from that night, especially since he said he couldn't remember much from that time in his life. "You must've been what…five years old at the time?" I asked him.

"Seven," he said. "But that picture is one of the few things I remember from that night."

"I don't understand," I said.

"My mother went back inside our house right before it exploded. Not to save him. Not to save me. She went back inside for that damn picture."

It made no sense. How could a photograph be more precious than her husband or son? But Will's expression was drawn, his face pale. Seeing the picture again had shaken something in him, this much I fully believed. "Why do you think she would've done that?" I asked him. "And how come you never saw the picture again until now?"

He laughed a small bitter laugh. "Why? Well, I would guess that she loved him, whoever he was. More than me. More than my father." I shook my head, confused. How could that possibly be right? "As for why I didn't see it until tonight… Do you think I was ever allowed in her office? And unlike you, I am a rule follower."

"I'm a rule follower!" I insisted. But the truth was, maybe I wasn't anymore. I used to be. Now, after losing so much, I wasn't sure I still saw the point in playing it safe.

I looked up again and Will was staring at me, tracing my cheekbones slowly with his eyes.

"I really am a good person," I said, but my voice floundered a bit. Was I? Or could I only play one on TV?

"I'm not sure who you are yet, Amelia Grant," Will said softly.

"I am Gloria Diamond," I said, projecting with a stony coldness in my tone, forcing a confidence I did not at all feel.

He smiled a little and shook his head. "Jesus. You actually did sound like her just then. That's actually pretty fucking creepy."

"Amelia, how dare you get my son drunk while I was watching *Seattle Med*," I continued in her voice.

Will laughed, a full-bodied laugh that shook across the width of his shoulders and made his left-side dimple appear again.

I finished off the last of my terrible wine. I had never made it to Tate's salad; in fact, I hadn't eaten anything since the bag of popcorn I'd taken from Tate's snack pantry for lunch, and I suddenly felt tipsy enough that Will's face spun in dizzying waves. I gripped the edge of the bar counter to keep myself upright.

Will stopped laughing and put his hand on my arm to steady me. "Right. You're definitely the one who got me drunk." He gently grabbed onto my elbow. "One glass of wine. Total lightweight. I'm cutting you off." He maneuvered to help me stand. "Come on, I'll sneak you in the back before Gloria finds out you were gone."

After saying good-night to Will and inhaling Tate's salad in the kitchen, I managed to sneak back up to my room before *Seattle Med* concluded. Will had promised he wouldn't tell his mother about my snooping in her office if I promised not to go in there again without her permission. *If you have questions*, Will had told me, *ask me.*

It was a kind offer, but I still wasn't sure whether Will was a true ally. And besides, he'd already admitted he didn't know his mother very well. Did anyone? The man in that picture probably did. Whoever he was.

Lying in bed, it was all still running through my head. I thought about everything Will had told me and imagined the tiny boy-sized version of him, curled up inside the kitchen pantry while Gloria and George screamed. And it made me feel sad for him. For Gloria too, who built an entire life, a career, on her *love story* with her tragically dead husband when clearly there was another man who'd captured her heart.

I closed my eyes and tried to switch my brain off. Maybe

none of it mattered. If Gloria's whole biopic was based on lies, then why couldn't I just portray that version of her? Why did I really need to know the truth, anyway?

Because I wasn't even sure how to begin to play a character I didn't fully understand. If I wanted to truly become Gloria, then her secrets would have to become my secrets.

And that was the last thought I had before I fell asleep.

That night I had the strangest dream.

I was young again, a little girl, sitting on the floor in the dark of a closet, holding on to a little boy's arm. The smell of gas was so strong, I started to gag. I stood and cracked open the closet door, and all I could see were hazy waves engulfing an unfamiliar kitchen, running up the top of the stove, through the cabinets to the ceiling, hot and wild and free.

Annie? Where are you? I heard my mother's voice, calling me from somewhere very far away. She was so close, but I couldn't see her. I couldn't hold on to her.

The little boy could barely keep his eyes open, hold his head up right. I tried to shake him to stay awake.

Don't worry, I said, grabbing onto his arm. *I'll save you, Will.*

Will?

His name, the thought of him, awoke me, suddenly. And in the middle of the night, the dream felt so vivid; my nose still burned from the smell of gas that didn't exist.

I did some deep yoga breathing—the kind I used to calm myself before an audition—and tried to soothe myself. But my head ached from the bad wine, my mother calling for me, and I couldn't get the haunting sound of her voice out of my head.

I lay there in the dark for a long while, unable to fall back to sleep, tossing and turning for hours, sweating and unsettled.

Amelia

I WOKE UP late the next morning, remnants of that strange dream still lingering. It had taken me hours to fall back to sleep, and now I glanced at my phone and saw it was already almost eleven. You wouldn't know it from the dark gray skies out my window, though, the sound of steady rain pelting against the glass. I felt a surge of homesickness for Pasadena, for sunshine, for my mother.

But I forced myself to get up and get dressed. I made a Nespresso in my room and while I drank it, I started to read through my mother's copy of Gloria's first novel—I'd tucked it last minute into my suitcase before I'd left. I'd never read *Love in the Library* before, but it was about two college students who met in the library and then went on to have a very steamy relationship. And it was the book that had skyrocketed Gloria to fame.

I read only a few chapters and then ventured downstairs, vowing to remember to eat today and not embarrass myself. I grabbed a granola bar from Tate's snack pantry and brought it and my coffee into the dining room, where I found Will at one end of the table, a laptop and stacks of papers spread out in front of him. He glanced up when I sat at the far end, his glasses perched on the bridge of his nose. I considered telling him about my strange dream, but his expression looked so serious I decided not to. Instead, I smiled and said, "Sorry, didn't mean to disturb you."

"Not at all." He put his glasses down on the table, rubbed his eyes and sighed. "I had a few emails to return, but then I was just sitting here thinking about…" He paused for a second and looked around, but the house felt empty, quiet. I assumed Gloria was writing and Tate had gone out to the store for her morning grocery run. "…what we talked about last night," he finally said vaguely, tapping his fingers softly against the tabletop.

Was he referring to the picture on her desk? Or the fact that he believed his mother's memoir was a lie? I unwrapped my granola bar and took a bite. I barely tasted it but kept chewing, knowing I needed to eat. "And did you come to any conclusions?" I asked him, in between bites.

He stared at me for a moment as if trying to decide how or whether to answer before he spoke. "Do you have some free time this afternoon to go somewhere with me?"

"I'm supposed to meet with Gloria between one and two, but then yes, after that, I have no plans." Other than studying for the role, reviewing my lines and trying to snoop more. I was supposed to check into my hotel in Belles Woods in four days—shooting was set to begin in six, and when I thought about how unprepared I felt, nerves surged in my stomach and I put the uneaten half of the granola bar down.

Will shot me a half smile, before he stood and gathered his things. "Great," he said. "Meet me here at two, then?"

In the second chapter of her memoir, Gloria gets married. She and George eloped but she described the moment she became his wife as, *so beautiful it was surreal. Rose petals suddenly fell on us, blanketing his white tux in a sea of red. Literal hearts falling from the sky.*

This was the opening scene in the script, Gloria's beautiful elopement, and then the story flashed back—and forward—from that point on.

Cam Crawford, the actor cast as George, was an up-and-comer, plucked off a short-lived Broadway revival of *The Sound of Music*, where he'd played a well-reviewed Captain von Trapp. We had yet to meet, or talk—I'd missed the initial table read because I'd come on so last minute. But Google told me Cam was tall, like George, with what appeared to be kind eyes. I tried to picture rose petals falling on his shoulders, the joy of love I would have to somehow bring myself to understand in order to act it out in this particular scene with him. Right now, any feeling resembling love felt far away, intangible.

And as I sat waiting for Gloria, I wondered, was this even real joy she wrote about, or as Will claimed last night, a lie? How had she really felt when she married George? Was her wedding the happiest moment of her life, or was that something else, something that could be explained further with the strange picture on her desk?

Gloria's career initially took off after *Love in the Library* came out and she did an interview with Barbara Walters where she broke down crying over losing George, talking about how all the love she'd felt for him was what she'd channeled into the fictional relationship in her first novel. It was the combination of her real tragedy, and the deep unshakable love story she portrayed in her book, that had skyrocketed her to fame. But did any of that make sense if what Will remembered about her and George was true?

And now as I sat waiting for Gloria, I tried to reconcile Tom, that book's main character, with the details in her memoir about George.

I heard the thump of Gloria's cane approaching, and I looked up, and smiled at her. I expected the small frown she shot back in response and didn't let her dour expression bother me today. She sat across from me, folded her arms in front of her chest and nodded at me to begin. The clock was ticking. I had exactly sixty minutes and I was certain she was counting.

I chewed on my bottom lip, gathering my thoughts before I spoke. I was desperate to ask her about the picture I'd found, but I knew I couldn't risk letting her know I'd been snooping in her office. Instead, I'd try a different tactic.

"What did you think of the finale last night?" I finally asked her.

Her eyebrows shot up. I'd caught her off guard. "Excuse me?"

"*Seattle Med*. Tate told me you're a big fan."

Her mouth formed into what I could almost describe as a half smile. "That Dr. Ryan could walk straight into a romance novel. He sizzles on the screen."

She was not wrong. Objectively speaking, Jase was electric as Dr. Ryan. It was why, in my opinion, the show had seen so much success. "I used to date him," I told Gloria. "Jase, I mean. The actor who plays Dr. Ryan."

She nodded, her expression unchanged. "Tate mentioned that." I was glad again I hadn't revealed anything to Tate when she brought up *Seattle Med* last night.

"We broke up when he cheated on me a few months ago." I said it flatly, matter-of-factly, but the betrayal of it all still caused a tiny ache in the hollow center of my chest as I spoke.

"And that's why stories are better than real life, Amelia." She sighed dramatically. "All the most beautiful real men are self-centered jerks. But in books and on TV, we can write them the way we want. Make them gorgeous, kind and good lovers, to boot," she added. There was a hint of something in her voice now, a glimmer of excitement, that almost reminded me of the Gloria I'd watched in the Oprah interview. I understood in this moment that she truly loved what she did, creating magical love stories that weren't real.

"And Tom in *Love in the Library*?" I pressed her. "He was fictional, but he was George too?"

Gloria leaned over and picked up a small silver bell resting on the coffee table in front of her. She rang it and a few seconds later Tate darted in. "Tate," Gloria said. "I'm feeling scratchy." She ran her fingers slowly across her throat.

"One hot toddy coming right up," Tate said breathlessly. "Amelia, would you like one too?"

I shook my head. "No, thanks." The last thing I needed right now was whiskey in the middle of the afternoon. Though, I jotted the words *hot toddy, day drinking* and *scratchy* in my notebook.

"So then tell me about George," I said to Gloria after Tate ran out again. "He was the love of your life, the inspiration for *Love in the Library*. He must've been different. Kind *and* real."

Gloria didn't say anything for a few minutes. She stared at her soft pink nails, until I noticed she had the tiniest diamonds embedded in the tips of both her thumbnails. Then Tate came in with her hot toddy on a tray. She handed the drink to Gloria, who took a slow sip. She nodded at Tate, a dismissal or a thank-you, and Tate dashed out.

Gloria took a few more sips of her drink before she turned back to me. "Yes. The man I loved was both kind and real," she finally said. "But then he died."

And I noticed the way she parsed it just so. *The man I loved.* Which didn't necessarily mean she was talking about George.

Mare

1983

SHE HAD NEVER been the kind of girl who'd dreamed of her wedding.

She didn't picture white dresses, pink-clad bridesmaids, bouquets of yellow roses, or imagine the way a perfect scene would be set at a floral altar with herself, a bride, as the star. She hadn't thought about romantic proposals on the beach, or the exact right shape or size or cut of a diamond ring she might wear on her finger. She had never thought much about marriage at all, to be honest.

But then it came about as she and George sat on his threadbare couch, in his too-cold apartment. Her period was six weeks late, and her stomach suddenly recoiled at the smell of George's Drakkar Noir. She had just told George what the dour nurse at campus health had told her that morning, what she had already known in the uncomfortable crawling sensation in her own skin. Then she told him about the clinic that could fix it for two hundred dollars. George took a slow sip of his beer, and then turned and looked at her: "I don't think you should go to the clinic," he said.

She exhaled, releasing a breath she hadn't realized she'd been holding, understanding in that moment that she didn't really want to go to the clinic. At least she and George agreed on this much.

"A baby, Mare," he added softly, his voice breaking a little. "*Our* baby."

There was one truly deep-rooted thing that she and George had in common—they were both essentially orphans. His parents had died in a car accident when he was young, and he'd been raised by his cold grandmother, whom he'd cut off all contact with in college. Just like she had with her father. A baby felt impossible. But maybe, getting rid of it felt more impossible.

"We'll get married," George said, his voice suddenly infused with excitement. "We can be a family. I'll take care of you and the baby."

It wasn't a question, or even a proposal. There was no diamond, no getting down on one knee. No protestations of love or devotion. No romance involved at all. It was a practical arrangement.

And later she almost couldn't help but feel vaguely disappointed, like she had missed out on something that she had never even wanted in the first place.

"Don't marry him," Bess whispered in the dark later that night.

They had bunk beds in their room junior year. Bess was on top, Mare down below. Bess's voice floated to her from above, like it came from somewhere else altogether. Ethereal, distant. All knowing. Bess was a girl and a goddess.

"I don't have a choice," Mare whispered back.

"You always have a choice! It's the '80s for Christ's sakes,"

Bess continued, speaking louder. "If you want to have a baby, have a baby. You don't *have* to marry him."

She let Bess's words land and settle, considering them as if they were they truth. George was a senior and would graduate in three months' time. If she had this baby, she would have to leave school either way. But what would she do on her own with a baby and no degree? She had planned to teach English abroad after she graduated in another year, and then, maybe travel for a few years and work on a novel. Where did George—and a baby—fit into that? Truthfully, she hadn't much considered George at all before now. After college, Mare had planned to float away, untethered. Unencumbered. But now, a baby made everything different.

"How could I possibly do this on my own?" Mare finally whispered.

"I'll help you," Bess said softly into the darkness.

Mare sighed. Though she appreciated the sentiment, as a practical matter what could Bess really do to help? In the end, the prospect of marriage with George felt logical, financially sound. If there was going to be a baby, Mare (or Bess, for that matter) wouldn't have money to take care of it. George already had a finance job lined up for after graduation. She whispered all of this reasoning to Bess in the darkness.

"But, Mare...do you even love him?" Bess's voice meandered from above, slow and sad, like a funeral song. She was such a romantic. But Mare already knew that real life, real love, wasn't at all like the Danielle Steel novels Bess devoured in her spare time.

"Of course, I do," Mare finally said softly.

Three weeks later, at the start of spring break, George convinced Mare they should drive all night to get to Vegas.

Just after the slow burn of dawn over the mountains, they stood outside the run-down Chapel of Love right off the Strip. The sun emerged, red and glowing, over the high brown distant hills, but the March desert morning was chilly. Mare shivered, and George asked her if she wanted his sweatshirt from the car. She shook her head. Because at least the cold was something. A feeling. Other than numbness. She relished it.

They walked inside, signed a few papers and then someone handed Mare a single red rose to hold. It was wilting, the petals' edges torn. It may have been pretty once, but now it was dying, withering slowly. Any English major knew a metaphor when they saw one. Mare almost laughed out loud at that thought.

But she held it in, and she allowed George to take her hand and lead her down the tacky paisley-carpeted aisle. She clutched the rose hard enough with her other hand that a wayward thorn made a trickle of blood run warm across her palm.

Then, she and George stood together at the front of the gaudy chapel as a balding man in a sad, sequined red suit pronounced them man and wife. George leaned down and kissed her, the quick brush of his warm lips against hers both familiar and strangely distant. They had come here, driven all night, taken a few steps and now they were married. Just like that. *Till death do us part.*

"Hello, wife," George whispered, pulling back a little, after kissing her.

Wife. She had, throughout her life, been a girl and a sister, a woman and a best friend. Wife felt unfamiliar, a word that she didn't yet understand and didn't want to claim. *Wife.* She was too stunned to understand it still. She forced a smile.

Do you even love him? Bess had asked. Of course, she did. She'd just gone and married him. Of course, she loved him. What was love, anyway? It was someone who promised you something, someone who would take care of you. Help you. Be there for you. Those were all things George was doing for her right now. If that wasn't love, then what was?

"I'm hungry," George said, letting go of her. "Should we eat?"

Her stomach churned, and she wasn't hungry at all. But she nodded and followed him inside the all-you-can-eat buffet next door.

Amelia

"WHERE ARE WE GOING?" I asked Will as he turned out of Gloria's winding driveway and off onto the long, empty evergreen-lined main road.

A smarter woman than I probably would've asked this question *before* she'd gotten in his car. But strangely, I already trusted Will. (He'd kept my secret snooping from Gloria last night.) And besides, it was nice to escape the isolation of that quiet house. Wherever it was he was taking me would be a welcome change of scenery.

"My office," Will said. "Is that okay?" His voice sounded kind, like he was ready to make an illegal U-turn if I asked him to go back.

I nodded. I kind of liked the idea of seeing where he worked, knowing more about him, whether it led to any new information about Gloria or not. "What's at your office?" I asked.

"Nothing," he said calmly, as he made a right turn, following the sign that pointed toward I-5 south/Seattle.

"Nothing?" I repeated, confused.

"I just mean it's quiet there. I set up a FaceTime with my aunt at three thirty so we could ask her questions, and I didn't want to do it *in* my mother's house. We could go to my apartment in the city, but I thought you might feel…awkward there. A coffee shop seemed out of the question because people might recognize you…" His voice trailed off.

Clearly, he had put a lot of thought into this. I appreciated that, even though I didn't often get recognized in public these days, and I was pretty sure we could've gone to the bar we went to last night and been perfectly fine. But the fact that Will had overthought this made me like him more. "Sounds like a good plan."

"And I thought," Will added carefully, "we could eat an early dinner in the city after. Do you know Seattle well?"

Unless you counted *Seattle Med* (which I did not), I didn't know Seattle at all. I shook my head. "Nope. I went once with my mom when I was little, and we went to the Space Needle. Well, the story goes that she *tried* to take me up in the Space Needle and I had a full-on meltdown on the street and refused to budge. Or so my mother liked to say. I have no real memory of it." My voice caught on the edges of the word *memory*. I was repeating a story my mother liked to tell, a story that, in essence, had disappeared along with her, like all my others. Annie, her childhood, gone just like that. Even when I repeated it now, like this, who was left to know if it was true?

Will smiled and shook his head. Then he broke out into a full-on laugh that shook his shoulders and seemed to vibrate through the car.

"Are you laughing at me right now?" I said, eyebrows raised.

"No, I'm laughing because my mother has a very similar story to tell about me. Only it was the Eiffel Tower. On her first French book tour. There was allegedly a very rambunctious tantrum on the sidewalk. I may have uttered some naughty words." He paused to laugh again. "It's one of my mother's favorite stories to tell at Christmas parties. Otherwise known as How Will Likes to Ruin Anything Fun."

I smiled a little and tried to envision it. A young Will dragged to Paris on Gloria's French book tour. The fact that Gloria had regaled people with this story, at a Christmas *party*, no less. (Gloria did parties?) And then little Will, having a meltdown on the sidewalk rather than going up to the viewing platform on the Eiffel Tower. Maybe we were kindred spirits in a way, Will and I. "For the record, heights should be no one's definition of fun," I said. "And I'm sure all the naughty words you said were very warranted in the moment."

Will's shoulders relaxed, and he smiled again as he merged onto the highway. "Anyway, my office isn't too far from the waterfront. We can walk around Pike Place after and there's a great little Korean restaurant nearby. Does that sound okay?"

I realized having dinner with him in the city would keep me from my 6 p.m. dinner at Gloria's, and the maybe ten-minute opportunity I would have to watch her again today. But I had a feeling I might learn more on this FaceTime with Will's aunt than at Gloria's house. We had to eat dinner. And glass noodles and spicy kimchi? Yes, please.

And for the first time in weeks, suddenly, I actually felt hungry.

Will's office was on the second floor of a three-story walk-up in downtown Seattle.

"If you look up, you just might see the Space Needle," Will said as we got out of the car and headed toward his building.

I looked around but saw only the other walk-ups down the street. The rain had stopped but the day was cool and cloudy, a pervading mist seemingly hanging over the entire city. I couldn't see much of anything. "Really?"

"Nope," Will said, with a straight face. "That was joke."

"Ah, you're hysterical."

"I get that a lot." He sounded so serious, but it was very clear he did not get that *a lot*. If ever.

I smiled as I followed him up the flight of stairs to his office, and through a door adorned with the sign, Forrester, Lee and Wakeman. Forrester, so Will was not just lawyer but a partner? That was a fact I found altogether unsurprising even having known him for only a little over twenty-four hours. Will struck me as extremely competent, intelligent and driven.

He waved to the receptionist in front as we entered the lobby. She turned her attention to me and squinted, as if trying to place me, and I wondered if she'd seen *Saving Addy*. But no, she asked Will if I was here for a client meeting. (Did she think *I* was a criminal? I should've done my makeup before we left.)

"I thought you were off for the week, Will?" She leaned across her desk. "There's at least ten messages on your desk. And something urgent—"

"I am off. Something came up," Will said vaguely, cutting her off.

He kept walking, I assumed toward his office, and I shot the receptionist an apologetic smile before I followed him. These kinds of things fascinated me. These real-life/real-job moments. I'd been up for a part in a law series a few years ago for the office receptionist role. In the end, they'd given it to a former model who was five inches taller than me and probably about twenty pounds lighter, who definitely looked better in the low-cut tops they eventually dressed her in for the series. But here was Will's receptionist in real life, probably about my age, with frizzy hair in a harried bun, dressed in a thick gray wool sweater and looking like she had permanent frown lines etched around her brown eyes. She seemed frazzled and wound so tight she could snap at any moment. Now, *she* would be fun to watch on TV.

"What do you think?" Will asked, as I followed him inside his office. It was expansive, with a big wall of windows that looked out onto the dark alleyway behind the building, lined with an overfull dumpster and row of black trash cans.

"Fancy," I said, peering out the window to the alley below. "Isn't it?"

I thought about Gloria's desk, encrusted with diamonds, and here was Will's. It was a dark piney wood with worn edges, and the desktop itself was covered in stacks of papers. How exactly did the son of The Queen of Romance grow up to be Will, working in this office, defending criminals in court?

"Here." Will motioned to the sitting area with a small sofa and coffee table across the room from his desk. "Let's have a seat, and I'll get Aunt Marge on FaceTime."

I sat down and then he sat next to me, pulling an iPad from his bag. "Tell me about your aunt for a minute before you call her. Your mother's sister or your father's?"

"My mother's," he said.

Interesting because Gloria didn't mention a sister in her memoir. "Are you two close?" I asked him.

He shook his head. "I wasn't sure she'd even respond when I emailed her this morning. I haven't talked to her in a few years. We send birthday and Christmas messages every year but usually that's it."

"But she responded?"

He nodded. "Right away." He paused for a moment. "She and my mother have never been close as far as I can remember. But I stayed with her a few times when I was younger and Gloria went on tour without me. Then she and Gloria got in a fight, and I haven't seen Aunt Marge since."

"I sense this is all connected to the great Eiffel Tower meltdown somehow."

He laughed, but also nodded in agreement. "Anyway, I realized this morning I never thought to ask Aunt Marge about the past." He paused. "I guess I kind of buried my memories until I saw that picture again yesterday."

For a brief moment I felt a pang of remorse for whatever Band-Aid I'd ripped off for Will by snooping in Gloria's office yesterday. Gloria was my job, but she was Will's mother.

But he didn't seem upset—he was already scrolling through his contacts for his aunt's name. This was his idea; he'd made all the effort to bring me here and include me in this conversation. Maybe he wanted to understand the real Gloria as much as I did, for very different reasons.

A woman's face suddenly popped up on the iPad screen. She was Gloria, if Gloria were ten years older, had kind eyes and the face of a teddy bear. "Oh my gawd, William!" (Also, if Gloria had a thick Midwestern accent, and the gravelly tone of a smoker.) "Look at you!" Marge was exclaiming now. "You're all grown-up and so handsome!" Will's face, understandably, reddened. "Where is she? Move the camera so I can see her, William."

He tilted the iPad a little toward me and I smiled and waved. "Addy Hemlock! Alex was so wrong to break up with you. What was he thinking?"

Will raised his eyebrows, confused, but I chuckled. Alex, Addy's boyfriend, had dumped her at the end of season two. Then sadly, we were canceled before the writers could get them back together in season three. "I totally agree, Marge," I told her. "Alex will never find anyone as good as Addy."

Will cleared his throat. "Aunt Marge, this is Amelia Grant, the actress who is going to play Mom in the movie version of her memoir."

Marge frowned a little. "Well, of course I know who she is, William. Don't tell me you've never watched *Saving Addy*? Great show, honey," she added, clearly talking to me. "Never should've been canceled."

"Thank you," I said. "I'm glad to know you enjoyed it." This never got old. No matter who said it, where I was, how many years it had been. There was always a thrill in remembering that I had been a part of something that people had watched and loved. That I had dreamed of being an actress since I was a little girl, and I had pulled it off.

"So, Aunt Marge," Will said, his voice turning serious. All business. I imagined the walls of this office were pretty used to this. "Amelia has been trying to learn more about Mom for the role, and you know what she's like. She doesn't make it very easy."

Marge closed her mouth and frowned. "I haven't talked to Mare in over ten years." What was it that Gloria said to me just yesterday, that no one had called her Mare since George had died? That Mare had disappeared along with him. *Mare.* Even the name sounded foreign now, like a person neither Will nor I had ever met.

"That's okay," Will reassured her. "The movie is about how she met my dad in college. Her love story with him, and then how he died, and she started her writing career."

"I'm trying to understand her relationship with George so I can get the role right," I added. It didn't seem like Marge planned to talk to her sister anytime soon, so I didn't think I had anything to lose now by being honest. "Was George really *the love of her life*?" I asked her, thinking about how Gloria had spoken in those exact terms earlier this afternoon, and how I wasn't altogether sure she'd even been talking about George.

Aunt Marge pressed her lips together tightly and didn't move. For a second I thought she was frozen, but then she put her hand to her head, like it suddenly ached. "I didn't know George very well," she said slowly. "Mare met him in college, and they eloped, and you were already born, William, before I even met him for the first time," she added. "I saw him only a handful of times before he died. You probably remember more than I do."

Will shook his head. "I just have a vague memory of them fighting. And that's not at all what Mom wrote about in her memoir. Do you think she really loved him like she says she did?"

Marge shrugged. "I don't know," she said.

"There wasn't anyone else?" Will prodded. "No other man she was in love with?"

Marge didn't say anything, but bit her lip, like she was trying to remember or trying to decide if she should say anything more. Finally, she shook her head. "I don't remember another man. No one I ever met or heard about. But you know we were never close, so that doesn't mean there wasn't one..." She paused and pressed her lips together, and then after a moment she added, "I do remember a woman."

"A woman she was in love with?" Will asked. I turned to look at him, but his face was blank, so I couldn't get a read on what he was thinking.

"They were very close friends," Marge said. "She came out here to help take care of you for a few weeks after your mother's accident. You don't remember that, William?"

He squinted like he was trying very hard to recall it, but then he shook his head. "My mother doesn't have many close friends," he said.

While I said, "Her accident?"

"She was in a car accident when I was really little," Will clarified.

Marge nodded in agreement. And I wondered how much she had left out of her memoir. Certainly, she had not mentioned a close friend, nor a car accident, which must have happened during the time period of her memoir if Will was *really little*.

"What was her friend's name?" Will asked, still sounding skeptical. It was not at all hard to picture him as a trial lawyer, the way he was currently grilling his aunt with a quiet sort of tenacity, while I was getting lost in my own rambling thoughts.

Marge shook her head. "I can't remember... I only met her a few times, thirty years ago. She was a tiny, pretty thing. Bubbly. God knows why she was friends with Mare." She closed her eyes for a moment, then chuckled softly to herself.

"And you don't know what happened to her?" Will asked.

"I never heard about her again, after George died." Her voice caught on the final few words. *George died.* Like it was something she couldn't, or shouldn't, talk about, even all these years later. "You know what, I shouldn't have said anything at all." Marge's voice came through slow with doubt. "It was all so long ago… And I don't think this has anything at all to do with the movie. Do me a favor, William, don't tell Mare we FaceTimed, okay? I don't want to upset her." She paused and clucked her tongue. "What a life she made for herself, my baby sister. They're making a movie of it!" Marge smiled now. "Do a good job playing her, Addy," she said to me.

"I'll try my best," I promised.

But as Will disconnected us from FaceTime, I somehow felt further from doing a good job portraying Gloria than ever.

Amelia

IT STARTED RAINING AGAIN, the sound tap-tapping against Will's office window, and he offered me an oversize army green rain slicker from the coat stand by the door before we left. I already felt chilled, so I accepted it and put up the hood as we walked back out onto the street.

"Maybe we should just go back to Gloria's house," I said, as we got into the car. It was a little after four. We'd be back with plenty of time for her dinner at six. If I wasn't going to learn anything concrete about her past, then at least I could observe her mannerisms more over dinner tonight.

"No Korean?" Will sounded a little hurt. "It's only a few blocks from here. And the rain will stop and we can walk around Pike Place after we eat."

He seemed so certain about the rain stopping, the way only someone who knew Seattle well would, I suspected. A rain like this in LA would be positively Noah's ark invoking.

"And besides," he was still talking. "I already told my mother

I was taking you into the city to meet your agent for dinner tonight. She's not expecting you."

I rolled the lie around in my head. Liza had said she was going to try to get out for the first day of filming next week, but she'd yet to confirm. That was still a few days away. And Will's version of events seemed so obviously untrue I couldn't believe Gloria hadn't questioned it. "Why did you lie to her?" I asked him, genuinely curious.

"You must have a much different relationship with your mother than I have with mine," he said.

"I used to," I said. "She died a few months ago."

"Oh shit." Will cursed softly as he parked on the street in front of the Korean restaurant. "I feel like I just put my foot in my mouth. I'm so sorry about your mom. Dinner's on me?"

Will tried to talk me into ordering a bottle of soju—he passed since he was driving—but I reminded him I was a *lightweight*. And, anyway, I felt weird drinking alone.

The last time I had *japchae* and soju it was in San Marino, with my mom. A few weeks before she died. Jase and I had made a habit of going to her house for brunch on Sundays the last few years, but once a month or so or when Jase couldn't join us, we met at Korea House in San Marino instead.

Now the warm spicy glass noodles tasted like being with my mother again, and I felt tears spring in the back of my eyes as I chewed. I blinked to keep them at bay. Maybe I did need a shot of soju.

"So the reason I lied to my mother," Will said, seemingly unaware of my flash of grief, "is because she doesn't deal well with the truth. She lies and she fictionalizes, and then sometimes I'm not totally sure she even knows what's real anymore." He skillfully picked up a piece of *kimbap* with his chopsticks and paused to eat. "She already told me to stay away from you.

I couldn't very well tell her I was going to help you dig into her past."

"Why not?" I asked him, before eating more noodles. "You're an adult. An attorney. I have a feeling you deal with much tougher people than Gloria on a daily basis."

"I guess she's always been my only family, as far back as I can recall." He grimaced. "Remember how I asked you when we first met if you were the new Tate?" I nodded and kept inhaling my noodles. I really was starving. "My mother changes assistants the way you probably change hairstyles as an actress." I frowned, trying to figure out if that was meant to be an insult to actresses or if Will just wasn't very adept at metaphors. "Tate is like her fifth or sixth assistant this year."

"But you're her son. She can't fire you," I said.

He shrugged. "I wouldn't put it past her to try." He paused and picked up another piece of *kimbap* with his chopsticks. "And yes, you're right. I'm an adult. And an attorney. But I don't want to lose her." He smiled wryly. "You must think I'm pathetic, huh?"

I shook my head. "I don't think anyone wants to lose their mother."

He sighed, as if he realized what the implication of those words truly meant for me. "I'm really putting my foot in my mouth today, aren't I?"

"You're not. You're fine." Everything with Jase happened so quickly after my mother's death that I realized I'd never gotten a chance to sit down and talk about what happened to my mother with anyone. I actually didn't mind that she kept coming up now. That she had felt, weirdly, present during this whole time I'd been out here trying to get to know Gloria.

"Your mother was amazing, and you lost her, huh?" Will asked softly. Then he added, "That must've been so hard, I'm really sorry."

I put down my chopsticks and nodded. "It was. I didn't expect it, and I still can't really believe it. She wasn't even that old. It happened very suddenly. And we were close. My dad moved across the country when I was younger, so it was only the two of us for so many years…" I bit my lip, not bothering to fight back tears. I wiped them quickly from my cheeks with my fingers.

"I'm so sorry," he said again. He reached across the table like he was going to grab my hand, but then he stopped himself. His hand stayed suspended in midair for a moment before he put it down on the table in front of him.

I wondered for a second what his hand would feel like on mine, and I wished that he had done it. It might feel nice to hold on to something, to someone. To him.

"Is that why you came out here?" Will asked. "You wanted an escape?"

"Kind of," I said. "I mean, this will also be great for my career. But yeah, my mother was a *huge* Gloria Diamond fan. She would've been so excited about me taking this part." I paused and wiped my cheeks. The tears had stopped, and now I felt strangely cold and empty. "Except I came on to the project last minute—everything feels very rushed. I'm not really in the mental space to do my best work right now. And I have no idea how I'm ever going to pull this off. I don't think I understand one real thing about Gloria yet." All of my doubts flooded out of me, until I sounded and felt breathless.

"I think you'll figure out how to pull it off," he said. "You have the script to memorize. No matter what you learn or don't about my mother this week… I'm sure you'll do great, right?"

I frowned. It always felt impossible to explain what it meant to believe in the Method to a nonactor. It was something Jase and I always understood about each other, until, of course, he took it way too far with Celeste. But now I wondered if there was something about that comfort, that lack of constantly having to explain myself that had made it too easy to stay with Jase for so long. Whether I'd actually really loved him or not. "It's hard to explain," I finally said to Will.

"Try me." Will smiled, and there was a kindness about him that showed in the small crinkles around his green eyes. I genuinely liked him. Which was pretty much the exact opposite of how I currently felt about Gloria.

"When Hilary Swank was preparing for *Million Dollar Baby*, she trained like an actual boxer for months, gained twenty pounds of muscle and even got a staph infection from a blister on her foot. Al Pacino attended a school for the blind for a few months before playing a blind character in *Scent of a Woman*. When I was preparing for *Saving Addy*, Addy was an elementary school teacher and I got my substitute teaching certificate and spent a few weeks in charge of an LAUSD kindergarten class." I paused and folded and refolded my napkin in my lap. "I've never played a real person before. I was given only six days to figure out who the hell Gloria Diamond *really* is. Her hopes, her dreams, her tics, even her lies, her secrets, have to become mine, so I can become her. Am I making any sense?"

Will nodded. "I think so? It's like when I prepare for a trial. Even if my client is guilty, and I'm arguing they're innocent, I need to know that to make the best case."

I tried to imagine Will performing in front of a jury and wondered if maybe my mother saying I should become a lawyer if acting didn't work out hadn't been that far of a stretch, after all.

"Well, anyway," Will said. "I'm not willing to give up on searching for the truth yet. Are you?"

I shook my head.

"Good. Then it's settled. We'll keep digging this week until we find something that makes you feel good about playing the part."

"Okay," I said softly, grateful that Will was here. That he'd bought me food that tasted good and that I finally felt full and happy and satisfied. "Thank you for helping me. Really, I appreciate your kindness in going along with all this."

He nodded. "I have to admit, it's not totally selfless." He paused, ran his fingers through his hair and sighed. "Seeing that picture again, remembering she ran back for it that night. Deep down, I've always felt like I'm missing something big about my past. And now that you reignited that, I want to know what it is."

Mare

IT WAS WINTER AGAIN, and the baby screamed.

It had only been a little over a year since that icy December night when the world had spun off-kilter and changed everything.

Now she and George lived in a two-bedroom town house outside of Chicago, only miles from his college apartment, and yet it might as well have been galaxies. Max was in law school in Seattle and Bess had left school when Mare did, moved out to Seattle with him and gotten a job teaching art to preschoolers. Bess called her religiously, every Sunday at 7 p.m. central time. But the last two Sundays, Will had been crying too much for Mare to talk. George had picked up the phone and told Bess to call back next week.

Motherhood was hollow. It was that dark empty space of her teen years at home with her father that she'd tried to escape from in college. But here she was again. A long and winding blackness. Day and night were never-ending and empty. She barely slept, and she was too tired to think. She couldn't remember the last time she'd showered, much less written a single word. Every shirt she owned had been spit up on and smelled like curdled breast milk, and her hands were too occupied with the baby to even touch the keys of her typewriter.

And also, there was a chasm now. Her and the baby. And George.

George lived somewhere across the Grand Canyon, where he went to bed each night, woke up each morning to a 7 a.m. alarm, showered, dressed in a clean suit and left the town house, alone. He moved around her, apart from her. Away from her. Every once in a while he would plant a quiet kiss on her forehead, coming and going, offering only a small pat on the back for Will while he clung to her neck and screamed and screamed. But George never actually reached for Will when he cried, never offered to help or tried to soothe him.

"Can you not hear the baby crying?" she'd yelled at him once in the middle of the night, tugging the covers hard enough to wake him.

"I have to go to work in the morning," he'd snapped at her, pulling the covers back, over his head. "Who do you think pays for all this?"

With his face covered, his voice disembodied, he might as well have been her father, and then she'd stormed out of the bed in disgust.

It wasn't that she didn't try to make the crying stop. She did. She really, truly did.

She read every book and tried every remedy for colic—a warm bath, a swaddle, a baby massage—but none of it seemed to work. And there she still was, pacing the narrow hallway of their two-bedroom town house, bouncing Will against her hip, trying to get him to stop crying. Occasionally, he would stop for a moment and hiccup, and she would sigh with relief, thinking, *At last!* Only then he would start again. Wailing.

"I don't know what to do for you," she said to him, when he was all of three months old. "I don't understand what you want. I don't know how to be your mother."

And in response, he screamed and screamed.

"I'm coming to visit you," Bess said one Sunday in the spring. Will had settled down for ten whole blissful minutes, and Mare sat on a chair in their tiny kitchen, slowly eating a Creamsicle and twisting the phone cord around her tired, chapped fingers.

"But it's so expensive," Mare sighed, wanting to see her friend more than anything, not believing Bess could actually afford it.

"My mom gave me a plane ticket as a birthday gift. I'm coming next month, as soon as school's out. I haven't met the baby yet. You haven't even mailed me any recent pictures." There was an edge of accusation to her voice. Bess had no idea how hard this was, and Mare was too tired to try and explain it. Would the baby still be wailing endlessly next month? Probably.

"I don't know, B," Mare finally said, her voice quiet and dull. "He cries a lot. You won't like him very much."

Bess burst into laughter. It vibrated through the phone, high and sweet, such a familiar and yet distant sound that Mare felt it as a physical pain vibrating in her chest. "Of course I'm going to love him, silly. He's yours. He's a part of you."

But even as Bess said it, Mare didn't quite believe her. The baby still felt like something foreign, a tiny bald red screaming alien. He didn't feel like hers at all.

"Surprise," Bess called out, her arms outstretched, as Mare opened the door a few weeks later. Will was slung low across her hip. He'd finally found his thumb and had stopped crying, for the moment. He sucked on his thumb vigorously now, eyeing Bess and Max standing on the porch with great suspicion.

She had known Bess was coming, but not Max. *That* was the surprise? "You're both here." She stated the obvious and reached her free hand up to smooth back her hair, which was in a messy ponytail, frizzy wisps all around her eyes.

Max's eyes rested on Will for a moment, and then moved to Mare's face. He smiled a little. And god, his eyes. They were so blue. She'd forgotten the way they'd pierced her. She leaned down and kissed the top of Will's head, just so she could look away.

"Let me hold him!" Bess wiggled her outstretched arms and leaned to take Will. She cooed over him and kissed his head. Will sucked his thumb, suspicious, but didn't scream when Bess took him, and Mare exhaled with relief. She glanced at Max, and he was still staring at her, watching her. She wished she had put on nicer clothes, or brushed her hair, or for god sakes, taken a shower.

Then she felt George's arm around her, behind her, pulling her against him. Mare had been watching Max and hadn't even noticed that George had walked up from behind. He hadn't touched her in weeks. Or was it months? And now his arm clung tightly around her waist. "Max, I didn't know you were coming," George said, an edge to his voice. He rested his chin on Mare's head, and she squirmed a little in the tightness of his embrace, but George didn't let go of her.

Max's eyes trailed from Mare's face to George's arm, and he frowned for a quick second before he looked straight at George, held his hand out. "George, man, it's been a while. How've you been?"

George stayed perfectly still for a moment and Mare held her breath. But then he let go of her, so he could shake Max's hand. "Can't complain," George said. Of course, he *couldn't complain*. He left the house each day and didn't have a screaming baby clinging to him all hours of the night. "Come on in." George finally ushered Max and Bess off the porch, and inside the dimly lit foyer of their town house.

Now that Bess was holding the baby, Mare's hands were empty. And she didn't quite know what to do with them. She fidgeted a little, unsure how to be.

"I'll go call in a pizza for us," she finally said, if only so she could have something to do with her hands.

At 3 a.m. the baby screamed.

George grunted and rolled over, pulling the covers tighter around himself, and Mare sat up and sighed. She remembered Bess and Max, sleeping on the air mattress in the nursery, and picked Will up from the bassinet next to her bed quickly, trying to quiet him.

He latched onto her breast, and fussed and popped off, and he cried again as she bounced him and walked into the kitchen to fix him a bottle. It was the only remedy (aside from his thumb) that had worked to help his colic: formula. Deep down, she understood what this meant, that her own baby was rejecting her. That the milk her body made for him made his stomach hurt. That it was she alone who made her child deeply unhappy. And perhaps if she wasn't so tired, she would've also been sad. But in the moment, she was happy to have found a solution, any solution. Thank god for formula.

She tested the bottle on the inside of her wrist now and then popped it in Will's mouth. He suckled, drinking hungrily, and she strapped him into his baby chair on the floor.

"Do you need any help?" Max's voice startled her in the dark stillness of the kitchen, and she jumped. "Sorry." He put his hand on her shoulder kindly, and she froze. "I didn't mean to scare you. I heard the baby crying."

"I'm sorry that he woke you." Mare finally had the sense to speak, to take a step toward the stove, away from him.

"Babies cry," Max said, and he shrugged. "Can I do anything to help so you can go back to bed?"

His voice was imbued with such kindness, and she bit her lip. Suddenly she wanted to cry too. It would be different to have a baby with Max than it was with George. She understood that in this moment, implicitly. That motherhood alongside Max would not be a dark and never-ending tunnel but a bright blue lightness, the color of Max's eyes. Jealousy for Bess coursed through her, almost electric, and she shivered, feeling ashamed.

Max took another step closer to her, put his hand on her shoulder again. "I can sit and watch him, and you can go back to bed," he offered.

She shook her head, but he didn't move his hand. And for another moment they stood there, close enough to feel each other's breath escape their chests.

"It's so good to see you again," Max finally whispered, breaking the silence.

After months of feeling numb, feeling trapped inside Will's screams, and the black indistinguishable spaces of both day and night, Mare's face warmed. She felt something again, standing this close to Max. His kind offer to help. His hand on her shoulder. *Him*. "It's good to see you too," she said, still not moving. And then Will dropped his now-empty bottle and let out a little cry, and she remembered herself again. "And Bess," she added, finally stepping away to go unstrap Will from his baby chair. "It's so good to see you both."

She slung Will against her hip and turned around. Max had followed behind her. He stood so close to her, she could barely breathe. "Why don't you let me take him for a little bit so you can get some sleep?" Max said, holding out his arms for the baby. And it felt like the kindest thing anyone had ever said to her. She couldn't help herself then, she started to cry.

Max lifted Will from her arms, and she let him because she couldn't stop crying. She sat down at the kitchen table, rested her head against the cool wood, and cried until she was so exhausted, she fell asleep like that.

She woke up a few hours later, when the orange light of dawn seeped through the kitchen window. She lifted her head, rolled her aching neck and stood. It was so quiet, she felt instantly alarmed, until she walked into the living room. There Max was, lying on the couch, Will sprawled out on top of him, both of them sound asleep.

She knelt and stroked Will's pudgy baby cheek. He really was beautiful when he slept, when he was quiet, when he finally seemed at peace.

And then she couldn't help herself. She stroked Max's cheek too. Traced his cheekbone lightly with her fingertip. His eyes opened, and she lifted her hand, but he reached up quickly for it, caught her fingers midair, brought her hand back to his cheek. There was the hint of stubble and she rubbed her fingers against it gently.

In the soft orange glow of morning, his blue eyes took on a more golden tint. "Mare," he said her name softly. She watched his lips move, and she was so close, she remembered the way it had felt to be in college, to be free, and young, and alive. She remembered the way those lips had touched hers and how she'd felt like fire was coursing through her. Like she might burn up with Max. But now it was so easy to understand how she might simply fade away without him. "Mare," he said her name again. "I—"

She moved her fingers to his lips to stop him from finishing what he was going to say. Whatever it was would ruin this moment. His breath was warm, and instead of talking he kissed her fingers softly.

Then, Will stirred and let out a little cry, and Mare jumped and pulled her fingers back from Max's lips. She reached for Will and lifted him off Max's chest. He was warm, and when she kissed the top of his head he smelled like Max's earthy cologne.

Max sat up, reached for her arm, and then he said her name one more time.

"I don't think we should ever see each other again," she whispered in response.

Amelia

"WHAT WAS WILL like as a baby?" I asked Gloria the next afternoon as soon as she walked into the library at 1 p.m. and sat down across from me on the couch. I had three days left here, three more chances to figure her out in our one-hour conversations. Today I was thinking I would shift focus away from George, away from my thoughts about the photograph I'd found and would try instead to figure out what Gloria had been like as a young mother, which was also an important part of the role.

And besides, my line of questioning about George had so far gotten me nowhere. I'd woken up this morning and finished *Love in the Library*. It wasn't my favorite book of hers—it was more sex than character development or plot, like in the beginning of her career someone had told Gloria to throw together some steamy scenes and call it a day. But the one interesting thing I'd noticed was that Gloria's dedication read as almost exactly what she had said to me yesterday: *For the one I love, always*, and that someone—my mother, I guessed—had once taken a pen and drawn a small heart around these words. I imagined that she, like the rest of the world, had been taken with Gloria's real-life tragic love story when the book had first come out. Which only reenergized me to dig deeper, understand Gloria more. Somehow pull off my own transformation in the next seventy-two hours.

Gloria frowned now at the mention of Will's name and rested her cane against the bottom cushions. She crossed her ankles and leaned forward, like she was setting herself up for another TV interview with Oprah, not an informal get-to-know-you session with me. Except unlike when she was on Oprah, now she was dressed in casual clothes, no wig, just the slightest hint of red lipstick. The only sign of anything remotely glamorous were the massive diamond studs in her ears that felt out of place with the rest of her. Were they two carats or three? "Will?" she repeated slowly, like she was taking a moment to remember. "Well…exactly what I wrote in the book. Will was the perfect baby. Never cried," she said.

I didn't know much about babies, but I did still remember the summer my half sister, Melody, was born. She cried all night. That was the longest two weeks I'd ever spent with my dad as a kid. And was what made me think, as a teenager, that I might never want to have kids of my own.

"But you were very young when you had him. That must've been challenging?" Will was born when she was twenty-one. I could barely figure out how to light the gas stove in my mother's kitchen to make canned soup when I was twenty-one. Much less have imagined having a baby to take care of day and night.

"It was a different time then," Gloria mused. "Women had babies younger back in the '80s." I nodded. That felt somewhat true. My mother had me when she was barely twenty-five. "But yes," Gloria added softly. "The truth is, it was hard. I didn't have a mother growing up. I didn't know how to be a mother myself. At first."

I was shocked at what seemed like the first honest piece of information from her. I knew from my research that her mother had died when she was very young and that she became estranged from her father as a teenager, but hearing her speak about the absence of her own mother now hit me right in that hollow, grieving center of my chest. At twenty-one, Gloria had basically been a motherless child trying to figure out how to become a mother herself. I felt an inkling of something real for her, sadness. Longing. And that felt like something I could actually use.

"But I loved Will from the moment I first met him," Gloria continued. "Men leave you, Amelia," she added, and I nodded, feeling a wash of betrayal over Jase again. "But a son's love is for always."

I thought about the dedication again. "'For the one I love, always,'" I said. "Your dedication in *Love in the Library*. It wasn't for George? It was for Will?"

Gloria grimaced a little, leaned forward and reached for her bell, ringing it only once before Tate magically appeared as if out of thin air. "Tate, I'm feeling chilled."

Tate nodded and then reappeared again only a minute later with a giant brown fur coat three times the size of Gloria's tiny body. I looked away as she wrapped Gloria in it and tried not to worry about how many animals might have been killed for such a monstrosity.

"Anyway," Gloria said, after she waved Tate away. The coat practically consumed her now, and she had it pulled up to her chin so I could barely read her expression. "You were saying, Amelia?"

"The dedication in your first book. Was it for Will?"

"I'm done talking about that book. Ask me something else."

I chewed on my bottom lip, wondering what I could possibly ask her that would get me anywhere. "Do you have any pictures of yourself in the 1980s?" I finally asked her. "It would be really helpful to *see* you at that time." It would be great to see how she did her hair, how she dressed. What expression she wore on her face as a new mother and a new wife.

After Will and I got back from dinner last night, I'd stayed up late, watching more YouTube videos of Gloria. I'd found a conference she was keynote speaker for in 2005, but that was as far back as I could find on the internet. Will must've already been in college by then; George was long dead. That platinum blonde, diamond-clad Gloria was not at all the same Gloria that I would be portraying in the movie. At least I didn't think she was.

"Pictures…" Gloria shook her head. "Aside from what's in the book, no. Almost everything I had from that time got destroyed the night George died," she added softly.

That made sense. *Almost.* I thought about the picture on her diamond-studded desk. The picture Will said she ran back into the gas-filled house for. The man in that picture who decidedly wasn't George, and the lightness that was captured on her face in that particular moment when the photograph was taken. But of course, that photo wasn't in the book, and I couldn't just ask her about it without giving away that I'd been snooping.

All I remembered seeing in the book was her wedding photo with George and also one of Will as a baby, sitting by a Christmas tree. "So where did you get the ones for the book?" I asked her.

"My sister had a few," she said.

Her sister. *Aunt Marge.* I smiled and made certain my face didn't show any recognition or give away that I spoke with Marge yesterday. Gloria had no idea. At least, I didn't think she did. "Your sister doesn't have any other photos of you from that time?" I asked her.

Gloria burrowed her chin even deeper into the fur coat and I remembered what Will said, that they weren't close. Still, somehow Marge had the wedding photo and the photo of Will.

"Every single photograph from that time in my life made it into the book," Gloria finally said into the collar of her coat, so that her words came out almost muffled.

And even if I hadn't already known for a fact she was lying, I would've felt certain she was now from her tone.

At two o'clock, after Gloria dismissed me, I wandered into the kitchen in search of a late lunch and found Tate in there already prepping dinner in a slow cooker.

"Brisket," Tate clarified, as I peered over her shoulder. "I'm doing a kale salad on the side for you," she added. "Oh, and I picked up some yogurt and fruit for you this morning. They're in the fridge if you want them for lunch."

I smiled a thank-you and opened the fridge to pull out the yogurt and bowl of strawberries. I took a seat on a barstool at the counter, and as I popped a strawberry in my mouth, I thought about how Will said Tate was Gloria's fifth or sixth assistant this year. I suspected that was part of the reason she seemed to be trying so hard. She was worried about getting fired.

"How did you come to work for Gloria?" I asked her now, as she pulled a spoon out of the drawer near her and handed it to me for my yogurt.

"I just graduated in December, and I was struggling to find a job. English major." She shrugged. As a theater and dance major myself, I got it, and I nodded. "My creative writing professor knows Gloria, and she recommended me when Gloria was in a bind and needed an assistant two months ago. Anyway, Gloria agreed to do a trial run with me and I'm still here." Tate let out a little nervous laugh and pushed her glasses up the bridge of her nose. I realized how young she truly must be, if she'd graduated college a few months ago. Even younger than I'd initially thought. And, also, weirdly about the same age Gloria had been when she'd had Will.

I pointed that out to Tate now in between a few spoonfuls of the yogurt. Then I asked her if she had anything to say about Gloria that she wanted to share with me in confidence.

Tate grimaced, but then she leaned across the bar and lowered her voice. "I had to sign an NDA to take this job." *Of course she did.* "But my professor who knows Gloria—they've been friends for years. At least, I think they have been." *Friends.* There it was again. Gloria had actual friends. I thought about what Aunt Marge said, that there was a woman she remembered Gloria being close with. Could this be the same woman, Tate's professor?

"Do you think she would mind if I reached out to her?" I asked Tate.

She hesitated for a second, and glanced around the empty, quiet kitchen, as if she was afraid Gloria was about to pop out of the pantry and fire her on the spot. More likely, she would tinkle her little demeaning bell, say a few unkind words and usher Tate away with a flick of her diamond-clad wrist. But the only sound to be heard now was the gradual bubble of the broth in the slow cooker. "Just don't say you got her name from me, okay?" Tate said softly.

Back up in my room, I fired off a quick email to Emily St. James, associate professor of English at the University of Washington, asking if she'd be willing to talk to me for a little bit about Gloria in preparation for the role. I didn't mention Tate, but told her instead I was interviewing all of Gloria's Seattle-based friends in the few days leading up to when filming would start.

Few days. The short timeline sank in my chest after I hit Send on the email. I had learned all my lines before I'd left Pasadena but it wouldn't hurt to keep them fresh, and I rummaged in my bag for the script. I noticed the sun had finally come out, and I decided I would take the script outside, get some fresh air and some sunshine.

I found Will out on Gloria's back deck, his khakis rolled up midcalf and his shoes off, his bare feet resting up on a chair, his laptop on the table in front of him.

"There you are," he said when I walked outside, like he'd been looking for me. Though his relaxed pose didn't make me think he'd been looking very hard.

I held up my script. "It seemed nice out. Figured I'd review my lines out here, but I can go somewhere else if I'll be bothering you."

"No, please, have a seat." He gestured to a chair across the patio table from him, and I sat down. "I came to look for you earlier, but Tate said you were meeting with my mother." He paused, lowered the lid of his laptop and leaned across it so he was closer to me. "The um…person we spoke with yesterday texted me this morning. She found a box in her attic with some things she thought might interest you. She's overnighting them to me."

Gloria had said that the pictures in her memoir had come from her sister's house, and I guessed that much was the truth. Maybe there was more there she hadn't wanted to tell me about, or didn't even know about herself. "A box?" I questioned him. He shrugged and I supposed she hadn't told him much more than that.

"It should be here tomorrow," he said.

My phone suddenly dinged with a new email, and I glanced down. Emily St. James had responded quickly: I would love to talk to you! Do you have time for a drink later? I'm a huge fan of Margaret Moon!!

Amelia

MY FIRST PAYING acting job was a small supporting role in a low-budget tragicomedy film. I played a mousy vampire/college student named Margaret Moon, who went on a blind date with the intention of murdering the guy for his blood, but then chickened out and ended up dying in the middle of act two. The movie bombed and spent less than two weeks in theaters. It was made right on the tail end of the vampire craze, and between filming and when the film was released, zombies became the new vampires. In the entire history of my career, no one had ever told me they'd loved me as Margaret Moon. Before Emily St. James.

I found myself relaying this weirdness to Will as we waited to meet Emily at the Ba(r) close to Gloria's house later that night. Emily, eager to chat and to meet *Margaret Moon* in person, had offered to drive out here to me.

Will and I had both just endured a very silent dinner of brisket and kale salad with Gloria. I'd watched her slice through the tender meat with her fork, douse it in ketchup, frown at the kale salad on her plate and skip it altogether. Will had spent the meal averting his eyes from me, I'd assumed trying not to let on to his mother that we had made any sort of connection. The room had been so silent, I'd been thankful for the sound of Jasper's little claws clicking on the floor as he'd run under the table hoping for scraps. After that, I was honestly in need of a glass of wine, even a bad one.

"So it's possible Emily St. James is a vampire herself, and she's meeting us for nefarious reasons," Will said now as we grabbed a table in the corner. The bar was even more empty tonight. We were the only ones here.

"Sure, sounds reasonable."

Will leaned in close to me, across the table. "The bigger question is, where can *I* see you as Margaret Moon? I'm intrigued."

"You can't. It's not streaming." I wasn't *entirely* sure that was true. But my face reddened at the thought of Will watching me in my first and most embarrassing role. It was in my pre-Method days, and far from my best work. I didn't want that to be the first time Will saw me acting. "You should check out *Saving Addy*, if you really have any interest in watching me act. I mean, it's also fine if you don't."

Will laughed and pulled out his phone like he was about to search but we were interrupted by the bartender asking us what we wanted to drink. I decided to try my luck with the local sauvignon blanc tonight and Will ordered a beer on tap.

And just then Emily walked in, saw us, waved and walked over. She looked about Gloria's age, but her hair was a natural wispy gray, tied back in a messy ponytail, which made her seem simultaneously older and younger than Gloria. Will put his phone down and stood up to pull out a chair for her. The bartender asked her what she wanted, and she said she was sure whatever I was having would be great. *Great* hadn't been my experience the last time I'd been here, but I didn't say that.

"Thank you so much for meeting me here," I said instead.

"Are you kidding?" She grabbed my hand and clasped it tightly between her own. "What an honor it is to meet you. We watch *The Sharpest Bite* in my book-to-film class every semester and you are just a delight as Margaret Moon."

Will bit his lip and looked like he was trying very hard not to laugh. I narrowed my eyes at him, and he turned his attention back to Emily. "Sorry, I should introduce myself," he said. "I'm Will, Gloria's son. I hear you know my mother, but I don't think we've ever met."

"Nice to meet you, Will."

This didn't sound like the same woman Marge had been talking about, the one who had taken care of Will after Gloria was in a car accident. Certainly, that woman would've met Will before.

"How exactly do you know Gloria?" I asked.

"Oh gosh…we met at a writers' conference here in Seattle so many years ago. You were a baby, Will. I remember she'd left you at home with your father, and it was her first week away from you and she kept worrying about that." She paused as the bartender set down our drinks and she took a slow sip of her wine. She didn't grimace, so I took a sip of mine. It wasn't too bad! "Anyway," she continued. "We met at this conference— we were paired up as critique partners—and then we stayed in touch over the years. Even after she became *The Gloria Diamond* she was kind enough to blurb my first novel."

I made a mental note to google exactly what that novel was later. Then I tried to digest everything she had just said. That once, Gloria was a struggling writer. That Emily had met her when George was still alive, which was the time period when I would be portraying her. And also, that she was *kind*?

"So what was Gloria like at that time?" I asked. "Anything you can share, any details you remember, could help me play her in the movie."

Emily smiled widely at the mention of the word *movie*, and I could practically feel her excitement radiating in the shimmer of her pale brown eyes. "Well, she went by Mare back then," she said, once she caught her breath. I nodded. "And she was quiet. Very unassuming. But she had an edge to her. She was cool but she wasn't trying to be. Do you know what I mean?"

"Not really," I said, but then I thought about my friend Jemma from college, who was a theater and dance major with me, but whom I never got super close with because she was always somewhat aloof. Well-dressed and pretty and quiet enough that I couldn't tell if she was silently judging me or if she was just shy. I could see Gloria having been like that too. "Well, maybe, I do," I added. "Clarify *edge*."

"I got the sense she was… I don't know, hardened somehow. Or maybe that was just the vibe she wanted to give off back then? She wore ripped black jeans and a black T-shirt and a lot of black eyeliner. And I remember being shocked when she said she had a baby because she didn't look like one bit like a *mom*."

Will frowned, and I felt a little sorry for him. Gloria was a lot of things, but in spite of her telling me how much she loved Will, it sounded like she had never been very maternal. Not in the years he was throwing a tantrum at the Eiffel Tower, not now. But then I remembered what she'd said about not knowing how to be a mother at first because she'd never had one herself, and I felt sad for both her and Will.

Emily took another sip of her drink and thought for a moment before she spoke again. "Also, I don't know if this helps you. But I find it interesting. Back then, her work was very dark. Nothing at all like the Gloria Diamond books."

"Dark?" I raised my eyebrows. That seemed to fit with the black clothes and black eyeliner vibe. After having spent the last few days with Gloria I could weirdly picture this being more fitting than her Queen of Romance title and her obsession with diamonds.

Emily nodded. "She was working on a literary novel about an abusive family at that time." Emily shook her head. "I remember it to this day. Her writing was so gorgeous, haunting really. It made me cry."

"I wonder how she went from that to writing romance novels," Will mused.

Emily shrugged. "I think after your father died and she moved out here, it shook everything up for her. Sometimes as novelists we write what we know and sometimes we write to escape what we know."

I understood that, felt that as an actress too. Sometimes I took roles to escape and sometimes I took roles to understand. With Gloria, it felt like both. I didn't believe in the afterlife, yet, it felt like this role had a straight line to my recently dead mother. I could still remember the warmth of my mother's smile when a new Gloria Diamond book would come out and she'd rush to Vroman's to buy it. I felt tears welling up again just thinking about it and I bit them back, determined not to cry in front of Emily, or Will again.

"Oh!" Emily exclaimed, digging through her bag. "I almost forgot, I brought a few pictures."

Pictures. Jackpot!

She pulled two worn Polaroids from her oversize purse and handed me the first one: a young Gloria, dressed all in black as Emily had said. Her hair was, what I assumed to be her natural color, a light brown, the color of honey. She wore it in a high ponytail, big bangs teased up and framing her forehead. She had her arm around a very young Emily, who in contrast to Gloria, wore a hot-pink oversize sweatshirt.

"This is great," I said. I asked her if she minded if I snapped a photo with my phone to study later and she shook her head. When I was finished, she traded me for the other photograph. This one was a group of maybe ten of them in what looked like a bar. They stood in front of some very '80s wood paneling, in two rows, a few of them holding on to frosted mugs of beer. "Were these all the writers at the conference?" I asked Emily.

She pulled up a pair of readers from a bejeweled chain around her neck, and then reexamined the photo. "Yes," she said. "All except this one. This was a friend of Gloria's who we ran into at the bar that night."

She pointed to someone in the back row, next to Gloria. Half his face was covered by a taller guy in front of him, but he looked vaguely familiar. I turned and met Will's eyes, and his raised eyebrows told me he was thinking exactly what I was. This kind of looked like the man in the photograph I'd found on Gloria's diamond-studded desk.

"Do you know his name?" I asked.

Emily thought about it. Then shook her head. "I don't remember. It was an old friend of hers from college, I think. And we just happened to run into him at the bar—actually I think he might've worked there—and then he joined us for drinks. There were a lot of drinks that night." She laughed, and then she took a small sip of her mediocre wine as if to emphasize her point.

"And you and my mother…you stayed close after that week?" Will asked her.

Emily shook her head. "I wouldn't say *close*. We certainly have kept in touch here and there over the years. We both ended up back here in Seattle by some weird fate, but we don't see each other often." I guessed that explained how she had never met Will. She stopped talking and finished off her mediocre sauvignon blanc. "I'm so excited for her success, though. A movie about her life!" she added cheerily. Then she turned and smiled at me. "And Margaret freaking Moon."

Mare

1985

MARE WOULD TELL herself for the next thirty years that what happened that summer in Seattle happened by accident. Accidents were, by their very definition, out of one's control. Unable to be stopped. Unexpected. Unintentional.

Two cars run into each other, and then there's a collision no one intended. All the broken bones and crushed metal in the aftermath can't be helped.

Two people run into each other in a bar and there's too much beer. And then, can anyone really be responsible for what happens next?

In an accident, injuries are sustained. If you're lucky everyone gets out alive. But not everyone is lucky.

Was it fair to say they ran into each other that night, that summer in Seattle?

It wasn't like they'd made a date. But. Bess had told her where

Max was bartending to get through law school. She knew the name of the bar and the exact distance (.6 miles) from the weeklong writers' workshop before she'd even applied or been accepted. So what if she was the one to suggest to the others that bar for drinks every night? She never meant what happened to happen. It wasn't like she'd really planned it.

"Mare?" Max's voice from behind her was unmistakable. It shocked her. Excited her. Then she decided she was imagining it. It was loud inside the bar, crowded. All the writers crushed into two booths in the corner, and Mare sat in a chair at the end of one, listening to her new friend, Emily. Emily liked hair bows. *A lot.* She had a collection—and that was what she was telling Mare about over beer. She owned seventy-seven in all, but had brought only six with her for the weeklong writers' retreat. Tonight, she wore an electric-pink one that matched her similarly colored fuzzy sweatshirt.

Mare was sipping her beer, and had for the moment, for the first time in months, forgotten about Will. She was untethered. Not a mother. Not a toddler-chaser. She was a woman again. A girl, really. A writer. And the freedom of that sizzled through her, allowing her to smile, even over chatter about hair bows for heaven's sakes!

And that's when she heard it. Her name. His voice.

"Mare? Is that really you?"

She turned, and there he was. Exactly the same Max. Exactly the same blue, blue eyes. Even in the dim yellow light from the Tiffany lamp on the table, his eyes were the color of summer sky.

She stood up, and he enveloped her in a hug. The earthy scent of him, the warmth of his wool sweater against her cheek. What if she just never let go? What then?

He let go first. "Mare! What are you doing here?"

She laughed, his surprise, his joy, delighting her now. "I came for a writers' retreat."

"In Seattle? And you didn't tell me?"

She knew Bess had gone home for the summer, back to California to spend some time with her mom, and she had been uncertain as to what Max was doing from Bess's letter about it. She hadn't asked. She hadn't definitely known he was here still. (She hadn't definitely known he wasn't either.) "I thought you were with Bess in LA," she lied now.

"No, Bess and I—"

Emily cut him off. "Hello, I'm Mare's new friend, Emily." She stood to shake Max's hand.

"Sorry," Mare said, though she was not sorry at all. Emily was fine to have a beer with. But Max was *Max*. "I should've introduced you."

"Why don't you pull up a chair, have a drink with us?" Emily said before Mare could stop her.

"I don't want to intrude on...your writer's stuff," Max said softly. But his eyes traced the contours of her face and said something very different. They didn't want to let her go. In fact, they wanted to intrude very, very much.

"The more the merrier!" Emily said, and she slid over, making room for Mare on the bench so Max could take the chair.

Max sat, and his eyes stayed on her face, and maybe she already knew what they were asking, what they wanted. Maybe she already knew that here, away from her son and her husband, feeling young and free again, she wouldn't be able to stop it.

A few beers and hours later, she stumbled out onto the street, holding on to Max. Emily had gone back to their hotel in a cab with some of the other writers a little while ago. But Mare had lingered behind for one last beer with Max, telling everyone she would catch up later.

As they had sat at the table, just the two of them, Max had

asked her a question, one simple question, that in her daily life George never thought to. When she and George talked at dinner, it was usually all about him, the pressures of his job, his day, his life. "How are you doing?" Max asked her. "Really?"

He didn't ask about Will, or even about how her writing was going. He just asked about *her*.

"Good." She answered him quickly with a lie that wasn't entirely a lie. In that moment, away from her real life, back to writing again, she realized she actually did feel *good*.

"Good," he repeated. "Last time I saw you, you seemed so… sad." He took a slow sip of beer. "I was worried."

Outside on the street now it was chilly, damp, misting, and his words still lingered over her. Max had been *worried* about her. She shivered, from the cold, from the thought of it, and then he put his arm around her. She didn't pull away. Warmth was necessary to human life, there was nothing wrong with that.

But Max tugged her closer, and they walked slowly, toward her hotel. They didn't say anything, but he still clung to her, until they got to the last red light, and she waited to cross the street.

Max pulled her into a hug, pulled her against him. Held on to her so tightly she imagined what life would be like if she could crawl inside his sweater, his skin, live inside his body and be with him all the time.

The light changed; she was free to cross the street. And yet neither of them moved.

"I don't want to let you go yet," he said into her hair. She didn't want to let go either. But then she thought about Bess. Tiny, cheerful Bess. It was fair to say that she loved Bess, more than George. More than Max. Bess was her mother and sister, her best friend and her cheerleader—all the things she'd never had growing up. Margery was years older, and had been out of the house by the time Mare was ten. Her mother died when she was too young to remember, and then it was just her and her father. And well. She wasn't going to think about him again.

"I can't." She forced herself to pull away, abruptly.

"I know," Max said, running his hand through his hair. "You're married."

She shook her head. Because it wasn't that; it wasn't George that made her pull away. "You're with Bess," she said.

"No," he said emphatically. "Didn't Bess tell you? We decided a few months ago we were better off being friends."

She shook her head. Bess hadn't told her, and now she considered whether Max was telling her the truth. But then she tried to remember the last time Bess had mentioned Max in her letters. Mare was always waiting for it, wanting it. Tiny tidbits about him from afar. And now, she realized, the last thing Bess had told her had been about his job at this bar, months ago. But if they had decided they were better off as friends, why hadn't Bess mentioned that to her?

Max put his arms back around her, pulled her back to him. The light changed to red again, and then she couldn't go across the street, walk away from him, even if she wanted to. Here she was, feeling more like herself than she had in years, and maybe it would be okay to hold on to that a little longer. To take him at his word about Bess too.

"Just this once," she finally whispered into his chest, and maybe that was a promise. Or maybe it was a dare. And either way, she was pretty sure it was swallowed up in the sounds of the road noise. "Just this one night," she repeated.

Amelia

AFTER EMILY LEFT, Will asked if I wanted another drink. I didn't really, but I wasn't ready to go back to Gloria's house yet either. Will nodded in agreement when I told him that, and then he motioned to the bartender for the check.

I had only two days left at Gloria's after tonight and then I would move up to a hotel closer to set to prepare for filming to begin. And that thought felt both freeing and terrifying now. I would be able to breathe again, being in my own space. But I still felt completely unprepared for this role.

As we waited for the check, I pulled up the photos on my phone that I'd taken of Emily's Polaroids, and traced my finger across Gloria's face in the shot of her and Emily. "Do you remember your mother being this woman?" I asked Will.

He shook his head. "I was probably like one or two when that picture was taken," he said. "So no."

"And later...she didn't look like this?"

He shrugged. "What's the first memory you have of your mother?"

I thought about it for a moment. I'd always had this hazy recollection of going too high on a swing set in an unfamiliar backyard, what I assumed to be the house I'd lived in with both my parents before they divorced. But my mother was never in that memory. The first real, solid memory I had of her I was seven or eight. "The second *Father of the Bride* movie was filming in our neighborhood. I was in second or third grade," I said to Will. "My mother and I were riding bikes down the street, and then she stopped and talked the director into letting me be an extra." I laughed, and I could still remember it. Or some retold version of it. My mother on that old blue bike with a basket that she rode, for many years to come. The exterior of the house on El Molino, only a few streets away from ours, that would heretofore be known to locals and tourists alike as the *Banks' house*. The excitement bubbling up inside of me as I got to be on a real movie set. My mother likely did it for her own selfish reasons, namely her obsession with all things Diane Keaton. But that was something that didn't occur to me at the time. Only when I rehashed the story much later, as an adult.

"So is that why you became an actress?" Will asked. He reached for the check as the bartender put it down. "Your mother got you that spot as an extra?" I pulled a twenty out of my purse but he shook his head and waved me away. "My treat," he said. "You'll get the next one." Would there be a next one?

I reluctantly put the twenty back in my purse and chewed on my bottom lip. Is that why I became an actress? It was as good a reason as any, and the answer I always gave in interviews, when I was asked how I got my start. It was a cute way to explain it, and nearly always elicited a laugh, even if not entirely true. "I don't know," I said to Will now, not wanting to lie to him. "I always say that in interviews but…" I shrugged.

Now the retelling of that story and the image of my mother

on her bike is more vivid to me, more than my memory of actually being on set that day. And the truth of when I first wanted to become an actress was somewhere fuzzy, just beyond that—maybe it was being the child of divorce and having to spend exactly two weeks each June pretending I was happy at my dad's house in New Jersey, or maybe it was getting cast as Eliza Doolittle in my high school's production of *My Fair Lady* my sophomore year. Or maybe it was the Introduction to Acting class I took freshman year of college, and my professor who told me I had something special. "The truth is," I told Will now, "I don't know if I can explain *why* I became an actress. It sounds sort of silly to say, but I just kind of feel it in my bones."

"I don't think that's silly," Will said kindly, and I appreciated it coming from him, someone who seemed to deal much more solidly in facts than me.

"And, I should add, that my mom *really* wanted me to go to law school."

Will laughed and shook his head. "Maybe it's me, but that doesn't seem like it would've suited you."

"Nope. You're pretty spot-on there." I laughed too. "Now you," I added. "What's the first real memory you have of your mother?"

He thought about it, signed the credit card slip and put the pen down before looking back up at me. "I was going to say it's that night," he said. "When my father died. Her running back into the house to save that picture." He paused for a moment. "But, I don't know if that's right? I have this other hazy memory of being really sick once, and her holding on to me in the middle of the night. Clutching me tightly and rocking with me until I fell asleep. But it's so vague I don't even know if it ever happened or not."

I nodded, because it felt similar to my hazy swing-set recollection—either a memory or a dream, I was never totally sure. "It probably did happen," I told Will because he suddenly looked sad, and I wanted to reassure him.

"Maybe," he said. "Or at least I like to tell myself it did, like it's some weird proof that deep down, she actually cares about me."

Twenty minutes later, Will pulled up in front of Gloria's house, shut off his car but didn't move to get out right away. He turned to look at me. "I'm not ready to go back in there yet either," he said. "It's kind of dark…but can I show you something in the woods?"

It wasn't raining tonight, and I remembered Tate's promise that I was unlikely to be murdered by either wild animals or creeps in the woods. In fact, the sunny afternoon had turned into a mildly warm and clear evening. I peered out the windshield and a yellow moon hung low in the sky, round and bright. "It's not *that* dark," I said. "What do you want to show me?"

We both got out of the car and then Will jogged around to my side. He took my hand with one of his hands, while holding his phone, the flashlight on, with his other. "Hold on to me and watch your feet. Gloria would murder me if I caused you to twist an ankle right before the shoot."

I laughed but did what he said. I held on to him and trod carefully to a path off the side of the driveway that led into the woods next to and behind the house. I thought about the line from Gloria's book again. "This is where you *ran feral* as a child?" I asked him.

A laugh caught in his throat and then came out more like a small cry of disgust. "If by 'ran feral' you mean coming here and reading R. L. Stine books, then, yes."

"Here?" I questioned. But then Will stopped walking, and shined his flashlight upward, straight in front of and above us. There in between two trees sat a large and elaborate wooden tree house. Will had a tree house where he read books as a little boy? My heart swelled for him, picturing him running out here as a kid with his books. Then I wondered, was there any line in Gloria's memoir that wasn't a lie?

Will tested the bottom rung of the ladder now with his foot, and when it seemed stable he gave me a hand to climb the five wide steps up to the top. Then he climbed up behind me and brushed off a spot on the floor with his hands. "I was thinking we could sit for a few minutes, but now I'm seeing how dirty it is. I haven't been up here in years. What do you think?"

I was just wearing jeans and a sweater, and, anyway, I knew there were laundry services at my hotel near set. I plopped down, not worrying about dirt, and looked around. It was a protected space, quiet and cool, and somewhere in the distance I heard the hoot of an owl. Through the slatted walls, a burst of moon shone in, landing on Will's face, lightening him, making him look younger, more vulnerable than he had since I'd met him.

"It's amazing up here," I said. "This must've been pretty great to have as a kid."

He nodded and hugged his knees to his chest. "It was. I could come up here and be in my own little world. Away from everything. School. My mother." He looked at me for a moment, shook his head, and then started to laugh. A deep laugh that shook his shoulders.

"What?" I asked him. "What's so funny?"

"I'm trying to picture twelve-year-old me's face if I were to tell him that in twenty some years he'd bring a beautiful woman up here."

A beautiful woman. Not an actress. Not *Margaret Moon.* Or *Addy.* Or a young Gloria Diamond.

I felt my cheeks turning hot and I was glad now it was mostly dark. Is that really what Will saw when he looked at me? It felt so simple, and yet, it felt like it had been so long since anyone had just seen…me. The real person, not a character. Not an

actress. *A beautiful woman.* "You flatter me," I finally said, trying to keep my voice light, teasing.

"Well, it's the truth," Will said softly, his tone completely
serious.

Even in the semidarkness I could feel his eyes on my face,
and I turned back to look at him again. He smiled at me. I
smiled back, and we sat there in the quiet not saying anything
for a few minutes. I closed my eyes and took a deep breath
and the scent of pines in the warm night air felt so soothing. I
understood now how Will had truly grown up right here, in
this place, and how it was he'd turned out the opposite of his
mother in nearly every way.

Then I felt his hand on mine. It was warm, and his touch
was soft, gentle. Tentative.

"Would it be ridiculous if I said I liked you?" Will let the
words linger softly in the night air, and even with his hand on
mine, for a moment I thought he was joking. It almost sounded
more like something a twelve-year-old boy would say, than a
man. An attorney. The Queen of Romance's grown-up son.

I opened my eyes again, looked at him. He wasn't laughing
or even smiling. His features were as stoic as when I met him
a few nights ago and he thought I was a trespassing intruder.
"It would be ridiculous, right?" he repeated softly.

"Probably," I finally answered him. But I didn't move my
hand, and I didn't move my eyes from his face.

"And it would definitely be ridiculous if I kissed you right
now, wouldn't it?" Will said. He shifted a little closer and
moved his hand up to my face, stroking my cheek gently with
his thumb.

"Definitely," I said softly, as I moved my face closer to his
so our lips were almost touching, but not quite.

He ran his thumb across my lips, slowly tracing them, and I
thought he really was about to kiss me. His lips were an inch
from mine, and I could feel his warm breath against my face.

My heart thudded against the walls of my chest, and I worried it was loud enough for him to hear. Everything about this moment felt organic, uncontrolled. I wasn't acting or trying to play a role. I was just...feeling the warmth of his skin close to mine and the pounding of my own heart.

But instead of kissing me, Will continued talking. "Amelia. I shouldn't have brought you up here." Lawyer Will had come out. "I don't know—"

"Will," I cut him off. "Stop talking."

And then I leaned in that final inch and kissed him.

Mare

1985

IT WAS ONE thing to say *just this once*. To pretend that the night was a slip. A true accident that would never happen again.

But it was another thing altogether to wake up the next morning in Max's bed.

Mare's eyes fluttered open, and for the briefest moments she didn't know where she was. There was a window by the bed, and she found herself staring at a slate gray sky. The world felt upside down and different. Happy and new and incomprehensibly quiet.

Then she felt his hand on her bare stomach, reaching for her, pulling her closer to him and she remembered again. Tumbling into this room with him last night, tearing at each other's clothes, like they were obstacles that had been in their way for a million years. Their mouths on each other. Their hands on each other. *Max.*

She sat up quickly, and wrapped the sheet around her chest, suddenly modest in the light of day. Though the baby was almost two, she hadn't lost all the pregnancy weight. The flesh around her stomach was still soft and puffy, with purple trails of stretch marks. She and George had only been together a handful of times since the baby was born. And she and George had never been together *like this*.

"Hey." Max touched her bare shoulder gently. "You don't have to get up. It's early."

But she did. The writing workshop had ended yesterday. She had a flight home this morning. She might have already missed it. "What time is it?" She looked around but couldn't find a clock. So she jumped out of his bed, wrapped herself fully in the sheet and began gathering her things from the floor. Where was her purse?

Max got up too, pulled on his boxers and strode over to her, putting his arms on her shoulders to stop her from moving. "Whatever you're doing, wherever you're going, please, wait a minute." His voice was soft but steady.

"My flight…" she stammered.

"I know you're married, and I know this is complicated." Max's voice was controlled, certain. "But I have been in love with you since the afternoon I first met you in the library. Please don't just walk out of here. Let's talk first."

In love with her, since that afternoon in the library? Is that what this was? *Love?* She remembered Bess asking in the darkness of their tiny dorm room if she loved George, and she'd lied and said she did. Love was only a word. An empty and ultimately meaningless word. It could be anything. Or nothing at all. Her entire life up until now had taught her that.

"Max," she said his name softly. "We both had too much to drink last night."

He shook his head. "I only had one beer." Had he? Had he

been sipping from the same glass all night and she hadn't noticed. "I was completely sober last night," he added.

"I wasn't," she said. Because of course if she had been, she wouldn't have ended up here, naked, with Max. Not because she regretted having sex with him. But because now that she had, it felt impossible to go back to how it was with them before, when she kept him at an arm's length.

Now that she had made this mistake once, she knew that she really could never see Max, ever again. And at that thought, it took everything in her not to cry.

"Look me in the eyes and tell me you don't love me too." Max gripped her shoulders, but even his grip was gentle, warm. Like his hands only knew how to take care of her, not hurt her.

She closed her eyes for a moment, then opened them again, and looked at him. "I don't," she said petulantly.

"You don't what? Say it."

I don't love you. The words rang in her head, but she couldn't force them to come from her lips. "I can't," she said softly.

And that's when she spotted a clock on the wall, in the tiny kitchen a few paces away. It was nine thirty. Her flight was at nine. She'd already missed it.

Amelia

I WOKE UP the next morning to the sound of my phone ringing, the special tone I set for Liza a few years ago, the chorus of the theme song from *Saving Addy*.

I'd been dreaming something strange, or something wonderful, something hazy about Will... And my first thought as I reached blindly for my phone was about the way I had felt last night, kissing him in the dark in the tree house. My second thought was, why was Liza calling me so damn early?

"Amelia, I didn't wake you, did I?" Liza's voice rang through, cheerful as always. No matter what news she had to deliver, or reason for calling, or what time of day it was, Liza always sounded extremely caffeinated and overly hopeful.

"No... I uh...not really," I stammered. Clearly giving myself away. *Great acting.* "I mean, I was just getting up anyway." I pulled the phone back to check the time. It was after nine. It wasn't all that early. I really should be getting up.

"Good, okay. Well, *small* change of plans." She said the word *small* so emphatically it instantly made me nervous, and I swallowed hard. "Gloria wants to go up to set today instead of Saturday, so I wanted to let you know, I moved your hotel reservation back and I'm sending a car for you at noon."

Noon? Like three hours from now? But I was still supposed to have two more afternoon sessions with Gloria. And Will and I had parted last night talking about sneaking out for another drink after dinner. I was supposed to have two more days with him too.

"That's fine, right?" Liza hummed cheerfully. "You've gotten whatever you needed from Gloria by now and you're all set?"

"Um…" I was still too half-asleep to land on an appropriate lie, and instead of saying anything I finally just sighed.

"All good, right?" Liza repeated.

"Can you have the driver come at two instead?" I finally said something that made sense. "Gloria and I are supposed to meet at one and I still have some questions for her."

Liza was silent for a moment. "That's odd. Her assistant was the one who said noon."

Clearly, this was deliberate. I had a weird creeping sense that somehow Gloria knew about what had happened in the tree house last night. But how could she? When Will and I had come back into the house it had been quiet and dark, and I'd been certain both she and Tate were already long asleep.

"Well, call Tate back," I told Liza now. I wandered to the mirror across the room as I talked. My hair was a mess, and I brushed it away from my eyes with my fingers. "And tell her I need to meet with Gloria again today before we leave. And tomorrow too. She and I can meet at the hotel. I need a few more sessions still to prepare."

"Will do," Liza said, and though I fully expected Tate and Gloria to argue with her, I knew that she had been around in this business long enough to handle them and figure it out. "I'll be up there next week to check on you in person, but text or call if you need anything before then, okay, Amelia?"

I nodded, forgetting she couldn't see me, and I leaned closer to the mirror. I hadn't done my makeup in a few days and my cheeks looked a little pale. What exactly had Will seen last night when he'd called me *beautiful*? It couldn't have been a glamorous, made-up kind of beauty like Jase had always found attractive. It was like Will saw something else in me, something unvarnished and real, that I hadn't even remembered existed.

"Oh, and one more thing." Liza was still talking. "Cam's agent reached out and wanted your number. Okay if I share it? He said Cam wanted to meet up with you before the shoot to go over everything. I think he's getting in today, so you'll have some extra time for that too."

Cam, who was about to play George, the alleged love of Gloria's life. The man I was going to have to pretend to be so madly in love with that I built an entire career on it. Of course, I wanted to meet him before the shoot. "Yeah, please give him my number," I told Liza. "And tell them I want to meet up with him too."

I took a shower and got dressed and then packed up my things to be ready to leave this afternoon, purposefully waiting a good forty-five minutes before I went downstairs and had to face Tate, hopeful that Liza had worked out all the details in the meantime.

But the kitchen was empty, and the entire house felt quiet. I grabbed another yogurt from the fridge, and as I sat at the breakfast bar and ate, I pulled up Emily's photos and looked at them again on my phone. I wanted to know more about Emily St. James's books and I googled her. It appeared her novels were literary mysteries. And the cover quote from her first novel, *Darkness*, told me Gloria Diamond found it "stunning, searing and suspenseful."

"Good morning." Will's voice surprised me—I hadn't heard him walk in—and I dropped my phone on the bar counter. "Sorry, didn't mean to startle you." He smiled, and I stared at his lips for a moment, remembering what it had felt like to kiss him in his childhood tree house last night. I felt simultaneously embarrassed and thrilled to be seeing him now in the light of day.

"Morning," I finally said softly and returned the smile. Then I picked up my phone and handed it to him so he could see what I'd been looking at, his mother's quote on Emily's book.

"*Darkness*," he said, raising his eyebrows. "Interesting. Emily struck me as more of a lightness and rainbows kind of person."

I laughed, but I agreed that was a pretty spot-on way to describe her. It seemed funny the way a writer could be nothing at all like her work. Writing itself struck me as somewhat close to acting. Pretending to be someone you never would truly be in real life.

"Anyway, I'm getting ready to take my mother up to the set this afternoon," Will said. "And I have to run to the office first. But should I add my number to your contacts? We could…" His voice trailed off, as if suddenly he lost the courage to say exactly what we could do later.

"Please, go ahead, add it," I said.

He smiled and entered it into my phone. Then handed my phone back to me. *William Forrester*, and for "company," he wrote *Gloria Diamond's son*. I bit my lip and tried not to laugh.

"I'm staying at the same hotel as all of you for the next few days," Will said. "I need to go back to work next Wednesday but I'll be there through this weekend and for the first day on set on Monday for sure."

He presented it all factually and yet, the idea of him being there comforted me more than it probably should. If Will was there, he would keep helping me try to figure Gloria out. And more than that, I felt excited at the prospect of spending more time with him.

"Sounds good. I'll text you later," I said. "Maybe we can get a drink after dinner?" I suspected the hotel bar would be a large step up from Ba(r) down the road, and that had been our original plan for tonight.

He smiled again, and then looked around. But Tate seemed to be out, and I assumed Gloria was locked away in her office, writing. He leaned toward me, and I thought he was going to kiss me. But then he lowered his voice and spoke instead. "What I'm picking up at my office is that box my aunt overnighted."

I'd almost forgotten about that, but he had mentioned it yesterday. Before we met Emily, before we sat up in the tree house and kissed like teenagers. "You'll let me know if there's anything interesting in there?" I said.

"Of course." He looked down at his phone, unlocked it and then handed it to me. "Maybe you should give me your number too?"

I was packed and ready to go and sat on the couch in Gloria's library, nervously chewing on the skin around my thumb by 12:55. This felt like the end of a whole lot of nothing. But really, it was only the beginning.

My last project was the indie film I'd wrapped up the week before my mother died. I'd played a supporting role, a young woman named Wanda, the best friend character, who was dealing with anxiety. It wasn't much of a stretch. One, because it was a pretty similar role to Addy (Liza was starting to get worried about me being typecast). And two, I was a young woman myself, dealing with my own anxiety on and off for years.

But this role, Gloria Diamond, would mark the first time I would ever play a real person. A living, breathing (extremely critical) person whose life felt so far from my own. What I was hoping to get from her now, before we left her house, was just the smallest crumb of understanding. An emotional ledge to start from. She loved George. Or she loved this other mystery man? And if that was truly the case, then why did she lie in her memoir? And why did she stay with George? Was all of that for Will?

I held her memoir in my lap and flipped through the pages one more time. The book ended just after George's death. Gloria and Will fled to Seattle and Gloria wrote her first romance novel staring off into these woods.

I heard the thump of her cane, and I looked up in time to see her hovering over me, frowning. She was dressed casually in leggings and a plain black sweater, no wig, no makeup. "Your agent demanded this meeting. Now I'll be stuck in traffic," she said tersely before sitting down across from me and folding her arms in front of her chest.

I remembered that Tate told me she didn't drive, and I suspected Will was driving her and wouldn't complain about the traffic, but I bit my lip. "I'm sure Liza explained that I don't feel quite ready for the role yet. I'd love it if you would share more about the real you." I said it kindly, but spoke firmly, channeling my best inner badass bitch. (Which Wanda also very much was, in spite of her anxiety. Or maybe because of it. Thank you, Wanda.)

"You have my memoir," Gloria said, her voice rising in frustration. "The entire story of my young life. What more could you possibly need?"

I pulled out my phone and pulled up the photo of Emily, Gloria and their crew of writing friends at the bar. I showed it to Gloria now.

She looked at it, narrowed her eyes and then pulled her readers from the top of her head to examine it more closely. "Where did you get this?" she asked.

"I interviewed one of your friends yesterday, and she brought it to show me."

"One of my friends?" She laughed a little and raised her eyebrows, and I wondered if she didn't really consider Emily as much of a friend as Emily considered her.

"Anyway, this photo is helpful because it gives me a visual of what you looked like during the time period I'll be playing you."

"Wonderful." I thought her voice was imbued with sarcasm, but then, I wasn't entirely sure.

"It is," I said. "So, can you tell me a little more about the people you're with here? Who's this?" I put my finger on the half of the man's face next to her so she could see what I was asking.

She frowned and looked away. "I don't remember," she mumbled softly.

It's not that I wanted to out her if she had been in love with someone else. I wasn't going to reveal it in interviews. I only wanted to understand her. I wanted to understand how I was supposed to feel about George when I was playing her. Was I playing the role of a wife who truly loved him, or that of a wife who was only pretending to truly love him? And if she was pretending…why?

"Are you sure you don't remember?" I prodded. "I'll keep this just between us, whatever you tell me. I promise," I added.

She didn't say anything for a moment, and I held my breath, hoping she was about to tell me the truth. But then she shook her head. "I don't know," she said. "One of the other writers at the retreat. It was over thirty years ago. Do you expect me to remember everyone's name?"

Emily had remembered very specifically that everyone in this picture had been attending the writers' retreat except for one. That he was Gloria's friend from college. She was lying again, and I sighed deeply and rested my head in my hands. Maybe I really shouldn't have taken this role, come out here. I could call Liza back and see what else had been coming in for me. Probably several other offers for *young anxious woman* roles. I could practically do that in my sleep.

"Why does this matter so much to you?" Gloria asked me. "It's not a part of the movie. And now we've met and talked, like you wanted to, so what else is there to say?"

Like Will said over Korean food the other night, even if he was arguing his client's innocence, he had to know if the person was guilty. I thought about offering Gloria Will's comparison now, or trying to explain the Method to her, but I didn't think any of that was going to get me anywhere. And besides, it wasn't guilt or innocence I was worried about. I just wanted to be able to feel the real Gloria in my bones when I played the part.

"Who are you really?" I finally asked her. "Who *were* you?"

"I could say the same to you, couldn't I, Annie?"

The sound of my real name felt so shocking, so unexpected that I let out a small cry. I covered my mouth with my hand. It had been months since I'd heard my real name out loud. Only my mother used it. Even my dad had switched to calling me Amelia after I'd asked him to years ago. My mother, though, had refused. *You can be anyone you want for your job, for the world*, she had told me once. *To me you'll always be my Annie.* I bit back tears thinking about that now. "Why did you call me that?" I asked Gloria.

She frowned for a long moment. Then she said, "I know how to use the internet, you know. Annie Gaitlin is your given name, isn't it? Amelia Grant is your stage name."

I nodded.

"'Annie, Annie, your heart shines like a star,'" Gloria sang softly.

I closed my eyes and heard that same line in my mother's voice. She would sing it to me when I was little, a chant, a chorus. And it was one of the last things she ever said to me when she'd hugged me goodbye the weekend before she died. A swan song.

It was a line from a popular song back in the '80s, and what she told me had inspired my name because she'd heard it playing on the radio in the operating room in the minutes before they'd knocked her out and taken me from her womb. She'd woken up with a baby girl, humming that song in her head, and then she said she immediately knew my name, *Annie*.

"My mother used to sing that to me," I finally said to Gloria. "And she was the only one who still called me Annie."

She bit her lip and stared at her hands. Her nails were a freshly manicured pale purple, and now there was a tiny diamond on each nail tip so her fingers truly sparkled. I guessed she'd had them done this morning, for the shoot. "I'm sorry," Gloria said softly, after a moment. And for once, she sounded and looked like she was genuinely sorry. "I shouldn't have said that."

"It's okay," I said, though I didn't feel okay. I felt my mother's loss again, sharply, acutely, in a way that made my stomach start to ache. "It's just for a minute when you sang that line, I felt like I heard a ghost."

She looked back up and she nodded. "If you really want to know how it felt to be me moving here, writing my first novel, it was exactly like that," she said.

"Like what?"

"Like hearing so many ghosts," she said softly. "I just couldn't let them go."

Mare

1985

TO BE A fiction writer was to be a liar. But in small doses, in her imagination, in words on a page. Those lies didn't really exist when no one else read them but her.

But to be in love with someone other than her husband, it was like living in a tunnel made of lies. The walls were narrow, the tunnel long and dark. She was trapped in there, and yet, she didn't quite want to find a way out. The darkness hugged her. It was soothing and blinding, and she couldn't see beyond it. She didn't want to.

After she flew home from Seattle in a tangle of half lies (telling George only that she had overslept and missed her flight), Max started calling her on most weekdays during his lunch. She'd wrangle Will into his high chair and let him throw his Cheerios around the kitchen with glee, while Max's voice came through the line, making her heart swell.

She wasn't doing anything wrong, talking to him. Not really. He was a friend, and she swallowed back guilt when she thought about all the long-distance charges racking up, that he couldn't afford. But she was a new person this fall, waiting for the phone to ring right around two each afternoon. Talking to Max. Hearing his voice, bright and hopeful, even across all the miles between them.

"I'm flying out there in a few weeks," Max said one afternoon in late November. "Figure out how to get away for a few days and come meet me."

She giggled on her end of the line while eating the crusts from Will's peanut butter and jelly sandwich. Max was in his last year of law school, and he didn't have the money or time to fly to her. For a few days.

"I'm serious," Max said. "I called the travel agent and booked a flight after finals end. It's nonrefundable."

"You can't possibly afford that," she said matter-of-factly.

"I don't care. I miss you," he said in response. "I want to see you."

And it was in that moment that she truly understood, it hadn't been *one night*. Or just talking on the phone. Max was going to move mountains to be with her; he wasn't going to let her go. And this made her feel something new, a lightness that bubbled up inside her chest and threatened to burst out as a scream of joy. Was this feeling…happiness?

But then she thought about Bess, and that knocked the wind out of her. Bess had still failed to mention that she and Max had broken up. She was back in Seattle for the school year, and her letters came weekly, as did her Sunday phone calls, but she hadn't mentioned Max one way or another. Mare hadn't had it in her to ask. Maybe, deep down she didn't want the truth.

Max was a man, and in her life experience, men were notoriously untrustworthy. And yet, if Bess weren't to confirm that explicitly, maybe Max was the exception. Maybe Max really was different. Good. Kind.

"I don't even know if I can get away," she finally said.

But that too was a lie, closing her in her little tunnel. She *could* tell George she was going to visit her sister, bring Will to Margery's for a few nights, and go off and do whatever she pleased. George would never know the difference. Margery would never say a word—she didn't even regularly speak to George. Mare and Margery weren't that close, but Margery had been calling lately and asking when she could see Will. Her own kids were already teenagers and she claimed she missed this stage. (God knows why.) It was called "terrible twos" for a reason.

"Come on," Max said. "The tickets are nonrefundable. You won't make me spend the nights alone, will you?"

She would not make him spend the nights alone.

Three weeks later, Max's finals were done, and he got on the flight he'd booked to Chicago. Tuesday afternoon, while George was still at work, Mare buttoned Will into his puffy snowsuit, and then drove the hour to Margery's house. George and Margery both believed she was going to a writers' conference in the city, and when George had grunted about the possible expense she told him she'd been accepted on scholarship, and that Margery would take care of Will for free. And once he didn't think it was going to cost him anything, in time, energy or money, he didn't say another word about it.

It was snowing lightly, and Margery had a fire going when they arrived. After Will toddled into the house, chasing after Margery's golden retriever, Margery tried to get Mare to come inside too and have a cup of coffee.

Mare felt a flicker of something in her chest. Remorse? Shame? She couldn't quite put her finger on what it was, but then she thought of Max, probably already at the hotel he'd

booked, only twenty minutes from here, and excitement fluttered in her chest. Whatever she was feeling was about her relationship with her sister, not about him.

"I just can't today, Marge," she said. "The writers' conference starts in a half hour and I'm already running late. I owe
you. I'll be back for Will Friday afternoon, okay?"

"Not even a quick cup?" Margery's voice turned with what
sounded like disappointment. Mare shook her head. "Well,
maybe when you pick him up then?" Margery added softly.

"Sure," Mare said, and then she hesitated for a second before doing something she normally wouldn't do. She leaned in
and gave her sister a quick hug. "Thank you," she said. "You're
saving me this week."

"Saving you? Oh, you really are dramatic, aren't you?" Margery laughed. "Go write your book, baby sister. William and I
are going to have a great time without you."

She knew what she was doing. She knew exactly what she
was doing.

But still, when Max was waiting for her in the hotel lobby,
when she saw him sitting there on a couch, reading the *Tribune*,
reclined, relaxed, his legs casually crossed, she couldn't quite
remember how to breathe. He'd come all the way here. For
her. This wasn't a slip. An accident. A brief indiscretion that
could be swept away and forgotten about. This here, it was a
choice. Like Bess had told her once in the darkness, *You always
have a choice.* Maybe it was wrong, but she was choosing to do
it anyway. She *wanted* to do it anyway.

She watched him for a moment as he flipped through the
newspaper, and she tried to imagine what it would be like to
wake up in the mornings and find him sitting just like this
in her kitchen. She felt a new lightness inside of her at that
thought.

Then he noticed her, smiled, and folded and dropped the

paper on the table in front of him. He stood and walked to her so quickly, his arms were around her, holding on to her, in what felt like warp speed. He kissed the top of her head and then held up their room key.

Neither of them said a word as he took her hand and led her down the hall, to the elevator. They held on to each other's hand in silence still as it rose to the fifth floor, as they got off and walked to room 508. Then he opened the door with his key, closed and locked it, and she leaned back against the door and smiled at him.

"Hello," she finally spoke, suddenly feeling shy.

He responded by leaning in toward her, his elbows on both sides of her shoulders against the doorframe, and then his mouth was on hers, kissing her. His kiss was hungry, needy, warm. And she felt the heat from it spread quickly from her lips across her neck, rippling down through her body.

After a few minutes he pulled back, and they were already both breathless.

"We have three whole days," he whispered, finding his voice after a few seconds. "We don't have to rush."

"But we don't have to stop either," she said.

And then his lips were back on hers again, slower, sweeter. Softer. Which somehow made her want him even more.

Time stopped for the next few days, but it also strangely sped up. They didn't leave the room; they barely got out of the bed. Their clothes were in a pile on the floor, and they didn't need those either, mostly, except for when Max called for room service and he would get dressed to answer the door and she would go take a shower. The world was still, but the minutes galloped by.

Three days later, she clung to him in the plush king-size bed, pulling his naked body tight against her own. She loved the feel of his skin against hers. He was always warm, and she never felt cold when he was this close to her. "I don't want us to ever leave here," she whispered.

"I don't want to leave," he said.

His blue eyes were close enough to her own that it felt like she could swim in them, dive, get lost. Never come back up for air.

He stroked her cheek gently. "I should tell you something about the reason I came out here," he said.

The words sank heavy in her chest. She had been waiting for the other shoe to drop this whole time, and whatever it was he had to tell her now, she felt certain, here it was.

But then he said, "I had an interview. A firm in Chicago. I'd start in June after I graduate and pass the bar, if they'll have me."

In six months from now, Max might be moving back here? "A job? Here in Chicago?" she repeated, almost in disbelief.

He nodded. "It's a good job. A really good job. I could take care of you. And Will."

She bristled a little, resenting the implication that she needed to be taken care of. Though, it was somewhat the truth. She had no income to speak of, and what current skills did she have, other than managing to keep a toddler alive? But the thought of Will brought her back to reality again. Right. She had a child. With George. "I don't know," she said softly.

"I mean," Max clarified. "I'll make enough money to support you both. Will will go to school soon, and then you can write, like you've always wanted to. And," he added, "I don't want to be apart from you anymore."

She didn't want him to get out of this bed and get dressed, much less fly back to Seattle. And yet the thought of putting things in motion, to *leave* George? It felt like a mountain that even Max wouldn't be able to move that easily.

She was still thinking about what Max said, about not wanting to be apart from her, and the way his lips had felt on hers as he'd kissed her goodbye in the hotel lobby, as she drove through the snow to Margery's house an hour later. His kiss had lingered, and then his hands on her arms had lingered, and then when he finally did step back, he came right back to her, kissed her again. It was a goodbye and a promise and a *see you again soon*, though, where or when she didn't exactly know. "I'll call you on Monday," he said as he finally let her go.

By herself, back in the car, driving slowly to avoid swerving on the slick roads, everything all around her seemed too bright white, strangely surreal. It was a new world, a different world than the one she'd driven in three days earlier. A world in which she tried to envision herself with Max, for the long term. Was it really possible?

She remembered the cup of coffee she had promised her sister on her return, and she thought now about telling her everything. She had trusted Margery with Will. Maybe she could trust her with the truth about her heart too?

But before she could get out of the car, Margery ran out the front door. She wore winter boots over leggings and a Cubs sweatshirt. She hadn't even put on her coat. And where was Will? Panic rose in Mare's throat as she quickly got out of the car.

"What's going on?" Mare asked.

"Will got sick last night, and I couldn't get ahold of you."

Mare hadn't told her sister the truth about where she'd been staying. Why hadn't she told her that? What kind of a terrible mother was she? Guilt rose up her chest, to her throat, and came out in a small scream she muffled with her gloved hand. "Sick? What happened?"

"He had a really high fever," Margery said. "I gave him some Tylenol but it wouldn't come down. I tried calling a few hotels in the city, but I didn't know which one you were at and I couldn't find you." Margery's voice broke, and she looked like she was about to cry. "I didn't know what to do so I finally called George."

George's name sank heavily like a stone between them, and Mare wondered what her sister suspected about what she had been doing this weekend.

"Where's Will now?" Mare asked.

"George came and picked him up in the middle of the night. He's with George."

It felt like Margery had punched her. George barely paid any attention to Will. He would have no idea what to do with him, with a fever no less.

"I thought maybe George knew how to get ahold of you." Margery sounded apologetic now, her tone pleading, like she understood this had all gone very badly, even if she didn't quite understand the why or how of it. "I told George he didn't have to come all the way out here in the middle of the night. But he hung up on me and before I knew it, he was here, taking Will with him. I tried to call him a few times today but no one answered at your house."

"Shit," Mare cursed softly, unable to stop herself. There was a train rolling through her tunnel of lies, and in an instant, it would crush her. "I have to go," she said, getting back into the car.

Then she backed out of Margery's driveway way too fast, her wheels spinning out on the slick roads.

Amelia

THE ROOFTOP BAR at the gorgeous boutique hotel in Belles Woods was an indoor/outdoor establishment with walls of retractable glass looking out into the evergreens and a small stream surrounding the property. It was another beautiful night tonight—not even a hint of rain, and one of the glass walls was fully open to a patio. The air felt warm and sticky, like the summer nights I remembered from visiting my dad's house in New Jersey as a kid, and I breathed deep, enjoying the thick scent of pines.

I grabbed a table outside and ordered a glass of wine, a rosé that felt fitting for this warm night, and that tasted so crisp it practically felt decadent as I took a few sips. Cam had texted me while I was on the drive up and I'd offered to meet him up here at six. I hadn't heard from Will yet but was hoping we could still grab a drink later too.

I glanced at my phone now, already after six—Cam was running a little late. But I sipped my wine and didn't mind waiting. I'd ordered a room service veggie burger for dinner and had eaten it quite peacefully in my sweats in the spacious suite Liza had reserved for me. It was beautiful and much too large for one person—with a full living and dining room and a giant marble bathroom with a steam shower and a soaking tub (that I planned to take full advantage of later). I'd never been put up in anything so nice for filming before, but then again, I'd never been cast in a role as big as this one. All afternoon I'd been trying to tamp down the anxiety filling up my chest in the space where excitement should be.

Right before coming up here to meet Cam, I'd gone over my script again as a refresher. As I'd read over the first scene we'd be filming on Monday, I closed my eyes and then recited all my lines back perfectly. I knew them already. I just didn't *know* them. How was I really supposed to feel, how exactly was I supposed to say these words? What did it really mean when I told *George* I loved him as he carried me over the threshold to our new house? I was hoping that meeting Cam was about to make me feel the role more viscerally, in a way I hadn't quite been able to connect with it yet through my interviews with Gloria.

"Hey, Amelia?" Cam's voice brought me back to the real world, the rooftop bar and my glass of rosé. I looked up, and Cam Crawford hovered above me, exceedingly tall and excessively handsome. He was dressed casually in jeans, a hoodie and a baseball cap, but when I looked up at him, he smiled brightly, revealing perfect white straight teeth and perfectly symmetrical dimples on both cheeks.

"Oh, hey." I stood and held out my hand to shake, but he grabbed me instead in an unexpected hug.

Then he laughed and stepped back. "Sorry, I'm a hugger. That okay? I mean we're about to be married and all, right?"

I laughed too, though mostly to hide my discomfort. I was *not* a hugger. And definitely not with a man I'd just met. But Cam was trying to be friendly, and he seemed nice and down-to-earth enough for an actor. "Have a seat." I gestured to the chair across the table from me. "Order a drink."

He nodded, then flagged down the waitress and ordered a club soda with lime, which made me rethink my rosé, especially when he mentioned he was trying to avoid alcohol to stay in shape for the role. Then he added, "You look great, though. Don't let me stop you."

Was that a dig at me, or a backhanded compliment? Or was he being totally sincere? I couldn't tell and I took a bigger sip of my wine. "So, anyway, you just got up here?" I asked him.

He nodded. "Yep, landed in Seattle this morning. And I heard you've been spending some time with Gloria Diamond the last few days. How was that?"

How was that? Weird. Interesting. Completely frustrating. "It's been great," I lied. "She's really great."

He nodded and smiled. "So I thought we should get to know each other before our first day on set, so it's not awkward." He laughed and took a slow sip of his club soda.

We were beginning filming on the set for Gloria and George's house, which would start with Gloria and George moving in and end in two weeks with the total destruction of the house/set the night of George's death. One of our first scenes next week included us having sex by the fire. I'd never done a full-on sex scene like that before and Liza had glossed over it, saying everyone would make sure I was comfortable and still somewhat clothed. I'd been so focused on trying to figure out Gloria, it hadn't occurred to me to stress over the sex scene until right now.

"I'm coming from the stage," Cam added. "So this is still new to me. But I read up on you and you subscribe to the Method?"

I had a flash of Celeste's naked breasts, Jase with her in our bed. Him telling me it was all Method. Was this now a *thing* men were saying?

"We are not having sex," I said flatly to Cam.

He held up his hand. "That's not what I meant!"

My face reddened, because yes, Cam was not Jase. Jase was Jase, and Jase's Dr. Ryan role had changed him into some unrecognizable asshole. But I wasn't sure who Cam was yet, and now *I* looked like the asshole. I tried to laugh it off. "I know," I said. "Of course. I was joking."

"Oh. Right. Ha." He laughed now too and took another sip of his club soda. I bet he wished it were something stronger now. "What I was trying to say was, we're supposed to be married. Desperately in love, right? And we don't even know each other." I nodded. He wasn't wrong. "Maybe we could run lines tomorrow. Get more comfortable around each other?"

Before I could respond, I heard what sounded like the thump of Gloria's cane behind me. *Gloria had come up to the bar?* I turned and there she stood, dressed in black leather pants, a diamond-studded black tank top, her full blond wig and lipstick the color of cotton candy. She was holding on to Will's arm, frowning deeply. Or maybe not frowning. Maybe, I should know by now, that was the natural turn of her face. Like she was perpetually sucking on a sour lemon. Tate walked up behind her, caught my eye and smiled. "Amelia, you made it!" she exclaimed, like it was really a possibility that I might not have.

"I did, indeed," I said. "Cam, this is Gloria. And her son, Will, and her assistant, Tate. Everyone this is Cam Crawford, who will be playing George."

Cam stood, and he truly was a hugger, because he had his arms around Gloria just like that. Will looked at me and raised his eyebrows and I bit my lip and tried not to laugh.

"Oh my, look at you," Gloria said when she disentangled herself from his hug and looked up, examining his face carefully. Cam had maybe the smallest resemblance to George: height, coloring, dimples, and I supposed hair and makeup would do even more to make him George-esque. But it occurred to me how strange this must be, for Gloria to be staring in the face of her dead husband, or some version of him from thirty years ago. What had she said to me earlier about *ghosts*?

"Gloria—may I call you that?" Cam asked and she nodded. Her face upturned the slightest bit in something that might even resemble a smile. "Your story is amazing. I'm so honored to be a part of this film."

"That's wonderful, darling," she said in a tone that was all warmth.

Here was the Gloria I'd found on YouTube. Sitting with Oprah. Giving a keynote speech. Where had she been the last few days as I'd been trying to talk to her about her life?

"Really." Gloria put her hand on Cam's arm. "I'm so happy you can be a part of it. I know you'll do George proud."

Cam smiled and then grabbed a few chairs from the next table. "Sit with us, have a drink, please."

"I'd be delighted," Gloria said. "A bottle of Veuve on me."

And then in that moment it occurred to me, maybe Gloria wasn't a particularly mean or even unfriendly person. Maybe, for whatever reason, she just didn't like me.

Mare

1985

"WHAT THE HELL were you thinking?" George shouted at her as she opened the front door. His voice cut through the dimly lit foyer, abrasive and angry. She closed the door behind her and wiped her snowy boots on the mat.

"How's Will?" she said calmly, removing her boots. "Margery said he got sick."

"What kind of a mother are you?" George approached her now, but he still hadn't turned on the lights. She saw him as a shadow, large, hulking. Looming. "You have one job, to take care of this kid and you can't even do that."

Tears pricked in her eyes, and she bit her lip to keep them at bay. It wasn't so much that George sounded mean. It was that his words rang so very true. What kind of a mother was she? She'd left Will for days to go be an adulterer. Of course, George didn't know that. At least, she didn't think he did.

"Where is he?" she asked. She went to move past George, back toward Will's room, but he grabbed her arms, held on tight enough that it hurt. She struggled to break free, but he held on to her tighter.

"There weren't any writing conferences in the city this week. I checked." George spoke more softly now, the words vibrating across her hair, into her ear. She felt them almost more than she heard them. And a shiver rippled through her. "Where the fuck were you?"

"I told you," she said. "It was small. A tiny group that branched off from Seattle." God, the lie popped out so easily. It didn't even feel like a lie.

He gripped her arms tighter and shook her a little, like that alone would set the truth free. "I don't believe you," he said.

She pinched her lips together for a moment. Then she said, "Let go of me. I need to see my son."

But he held on for another moment, before he finally released her with a shove hard enough that she stumbled, tripped over her boots and fell back against the door with a thud.

The noise was enough to startle Will and he let out a blood-curdling scream. She got her footing and pushed past George. If he shoved her again, well, then she would shove right back. She wasn't a little girl anymore. She didn't take this kind of crap from a man just because he was bigger than her. George was supposed to be her husband, not her father.

She ran into Will's room. He sat in his crib in only his underwear and sucked his thumb, and even from the small slant of light from the hallway she could tell he was sweaty, listless, his curls matted and tangled. She heard George walking behind her, but she went to Will and lifted him up. His skin was so hot. She put her hand on his forehead, and he felt like fire.

"He's burning up," she turned and said to George. "Did you give him anything? Did you take him to the doctor?" George shook his head. And she didn't know if that meant he had done neither one. "Not even Tylenol?"

She remembered something she'd read in one of the baby books that if a baby's temperature reached over 105 degrees it could cause brain damage. That's why you gave them a fever reducer, so it didn't get that high. And if it didn't come down you were supposed to go to the emergency room.

"I didn't know what to do," George said meekly now.

"You're his father." She spat his own words right back at him. "Where the fuck were you?"

After she bathed Will in a lukewarm bath, and then wrapped him loosely in a towel, he put his thumb in his mouth and leaned his head against her chest. She sat in the wooden rocker in his room and rocked slowly back and forth and back and forth, and finally she felt his breathing slow against her. He fell asleep. The room was quiet and still again, and she exhaled, closed her eyes too and kept slowly rocking.

It had only been hours since Max had kissed her goodbye in the hotel lobby and yet it felt like it had been weeks. Months. The three days she had spent with him were a different life, a different world, a fantasy. *This* was her real life. Tears burned her eyes and spilled down her cheeks, and she didn't even have a free hand to wipe them away.

She heard George's footsteps approaching the room, and she shifted her shoulder to wipe her face on her sleeve, trying not to wake Will. Not wanting George to see her crying more than she wanted Will to sleep. She dried her cheeks, and then kissed the top of his head. He moaned a little, shifted, then sucked harder on his thumb.

"You're right, I'm his father. He's *my* son," George spoke softly, urgently from the doorway now. His words were so calm, they chilled her a little, and she wrapped her arms tighter around Will. "I don't know what you're up to, but if you ever try and take him from me, I swear to god, I'll kill you."

Amelia

"WHY DO YOU think your mother dislikes me so much?" I asked Will.

I was still puzzling over this a few hours later. Our little rooftop drink had broken up when after a full hour of Gloria practically gushing over Cam, I'd finally yawned and excused myself. I'd texted Will and told him to stop by my suite once he was free. It took two more hours before I heard a soft knock on the door.

I had opened another bottle of wine while I'd waited for him, and reviewed my script again, and by the time Will showed up, I felt a little tipsy. Or maybe just more relaxed than I'd felt all week. All month really.

I'd handed Will a glass, and he'd poured a little wine for himself too, sat down with me on the large couch in my suite. "I don't think she dislikes you," he said, answering my question. "Not more than she dislikes anyone else, anyway." But he frowned a little as he said it, and it felt like he could see what I meant, even if he didn't want to admit it out loud.

"She loves Cam. Like really *loves* him."

He nodded and took a sip of his wine. "I question her judgment daily."

"I mean Cam seems fine. But why does she like him so much better than me?" I heard the whine in my voice, and even as I spoke, I realized I sounded like a petulant child. But that didn't stop me from continuing. "I just spent a few days with her, and I have been trying so hard. She's been ice-cold to me. But she was hugging Cam and buying him Veuve?"

Will laughed. "If there's one thing I've learned in my life, it's that Gloria doesn't make sense. Don't try to make her rational. She's not."

I frowned, but maybe that was the truest thing I'd learned about Gloria all week. Romance itself was not rational, and wasn't Gloria known as The Queen?

Will inched closer to me on the couch, put his hand gently on top of mine. "For what it's worth, I like *you* much better than Cam."

I laughed and turned to look at him. It was much brighter in this room than it had been in the tree house last night, and I could see every inch of his face clearly: the smallest bit of stubble on his chin that told me he hadn't had time to shave today, the little lines that crinkled around his eyes when he looked at me and smiled. I looked at his lips for a moment and remembered the way they had felt on mine last night. It had been thrilling to kiss him up there in the tree house, somewhere secret, in the dark. But I realized, it would be thrilling to do it now, here too in the open. Just because it was him. It was probably the worst idea in the world to like the son of the woman I was supposed to be portraying, and yet, here he was. Here I wanted him to be.

He smiled, moved his hand back and shifted down the couch

a little so we were no longer touching. "Your room is really, really nice," he said, and he laughed a little nervously. "I have a regular tiny room on the first floor."

I wondered if Gloria had a suite—she must—but then I suddenly didn't want to bring her up again, not right now. Maybe it was the wine, or maybe it was that Will had been so kind to me this week, and it had been so long since a man, since anyone, had been that genuinely kind.

"Will," I said his name softly. He put his wineglass down on the coffee table and looked back toward me.

"Oh, right, you wanted to know about the FedEx box from my aunt," he said. I did want to know about the FedEx box from Aunt Marge, but that wasn't exactly where I'd been going with this. Still, I nodded. "I have it in my room. I meant to go down and grab it on the way up here but then I forgot. I'll show you tomorrow. It's just a few pictures of me and my mother from when I was little and an old worn teddy bear I don't recognize. But according to the note Aunt Marge included it was mine when I was little."

"I wonder why that was in her attic?" I mused. Will shrugged. And, anyway, it didn't seem to matter for my purposes. "I would like to see the pictures, though, if you don't mind sharing."

He nodded. "Of course. Unfortunately, I don't know how much it'll help you. They're from about the same time as the photos Emily showed us, I think. My mother looks about the same." His phone suddenly chimed with a text, and he glanced at it and sighed. "Speaking of the devil."

"Gloria?" I asked. He nodded and stood. "Wait—are you leaving? Already?"

"She left her eye mask in my car, and she needs it to sleep. I suppose I should go get it for her and let you get some sleep too."

That was the last thing I wanted him to do, leave, or let me get some sleep. But I nodded slowly.

"I'll text you in the morning and we can find a time for you to look at those photos," he said as he walked toward the door.

"Will—" I said his name again, and he stopped walking and turned back to look at me. *Come back when you're done. I'll be waiting here for you. Stay the night.* All of those lines ran through my head, but then I bit my lip.

"What?" he asked.

"Sleep well," I finally said.

He smiled. "You too."

I woke up late the next morning, with a dull ache above my eyes. Too much wine. Cam probably had the right idea about cutting back and trying to look his best right before the shoot.

I'd been having a weird dream, just before waking. But once my eyes were open I could remember the dream only in fragments. I was in my mother's house in Pasadena, but then it wasn't familiar at all. It was in fact a stranger's house, a stranger's kitchen, but my mother was there, cooking up a pot of her famous beef stew on the stove. *Annie, you have to eat more,* she said. I tried to remind her I was a vegetarian now, but no matter how many times I said it, she couldn't, or wouldn't, hear me.

I got out of bed and shook the strange remnants of the dream away. I wandered into the living room—the half-drunk bottle of wine I'd been sharing with Will last night still sat open on the coffee table, and I recorked it and put it on the bar. Then I opened the blinds in the living area to reveal another gray and rainy day. I missed LA, the sunshine. I knew a lot of people who hated LA, but I'd spent almost my whole life there, and no matter where I went, how far or for how long, LA always felt like home. Maybe I would fly back next weekend to check on the Pasadena house and Sebastian the cat.

I glanced at my phone, and I hadn't really missed anything while I was sleeping. A text from Cam asking what time I wanted to run lines, but I ignored that for now. Nothing from

Will yet. It was almost noon, and I wondered if he'd forgotten about the photos. No, more likely Gloria had kept him busy.

And then I remembered that Gloria and I were still supposed to meet at one today, at my request. No one had specified where, so I texted Tate and asked her.

Penthouse, she texted back quickly. Don't be late.

This was my last chance to get something real out of Gloria. I would most definitely not be late.

Amelia

THE PENTHOUSE SUITE was three times the size of mine and reachable only by a small, old-fashioned birdcage elevator that shook as it rose steadily from the lobby. I swallowed back nausea and pressed the buzzer when it reached the top. And then Tate came and opened the door.

They were all sitting just inside on a giant plush sectional: Gloria, Will and even Jasper, who was adorned today in a little red diamond-studded collar, and who couldn't help but let out a low growl when I approached.

Will shot me a look but I couldn't tell exactly what he was trying to say, whether it was *sorry* or *good luck*, and then he quickly looked away from me, picked up Jasper and announced he was taking him for a walk with Tate.

"Have a seat," Gloria said to me coldly, after they piled into the elevator. She was more dressed-up today than she had been during the day in her own home: a black pantsuit, a full face of makeup, her wig. It was almost astonishing how much the bigger head of hair made her look more like a bona fide star and less like a cranky older woman.

I sat down next to her on the couch. "This hotel is beautiful, right?" I said, keeping an air of cheeriness in my tone I didn't feel. Why was Gloria so much nicer to Cam than to me? Did she deep down really just dislike me? And why did that bother me so much? Why did I even care if she liked me or not?

She ignored me and glanced out the window. It was still raining, and it occurred to me that Will might not get very far on his walk with Jasper, though, maybe Jasper was used to the rain.

"You liked Cam a lot," I said. "Does he remind you of George?"

She turned back to me and shrugged a little. I noticed her bell sitting on the coffee table in front of her. (She had actually packed it and brought it along?) But Tate was out with Jasper. Gloria wasn't going to get out of answering my questions by ringing it now.

"Was that weird?" I continued to push. "I mean, it must be. To see an actor who's going to play the love of your life who—" I stopped myself before saying "died," realizing how that might sound insensitive. "Who is no longer with you," I added.

"Cam is gorgeous and he seems like a real sweetheart," Gloria said, sounding oddly cheerful for her. "How lucky we were for him to agree to the role."

"Why do you love him and hate me?" I blurted it out before I could stop myself.

"Why would I hate you?" Gloria said calmly, coolly, her voice giving her away. She absolutely did hate me.

"I have no idea," I said softly. I really didn't know. Why wouldn't she answer any of my questions but spent hours last night fawning over Cam? It wasn't that she was nervous about the movie as Will had suggested a few nights ago. It was very specifically something about me. "If I said something to offend you, or did something wrong, I wish you would tell me so I could apologize and fix it."

Gloria stared at me and didn't say anything for a moment. Then she said, "When you make that face, you look exactly like him."

"Look like who?" I put my hand to my cheek trying to figure out what face she meant. A look of confusion? Was I frowning?

"You know, I watched all your movies and your series," Gloria said. "You're very good. You're a talented actress." She paused and examined her still-perfect purple diamond nails. "I know you think you do, but you don't need anything from me. Play the part as it's written. I have no doubt you'll do it very well."

My mind was reeling from the compliments, from her confusing comment that I looked like *him*. And from the fact that maybe she was right. I was good at my job. Jase had gotten me into Method just like he'd gotten me into vegetarianism. I could eat a burger, even if I didn't exactly like it. Maybe I could pull off the part of Gloria as written in the script too, play devoted wife to Cam/George whether it was true or not.

Gloria looked up again and she was staring at me, her eyes locked on my face so steadily, I shifted, uncomfortable. "Who do you think I look like?" I tried again.

She bit her lip and didn't respond at first. "Your father," she finally said softly.

My father? It had been a few weeks since we'd talked, but last I heard he was taking my half sister, Melody, to tour colleges this summer. Or had that been last summer? Now I honestly couldn't remember. In his life in New Jersey with Melody and my stepmom, he worked as an engineer for public transit. He hardly read books, much less romance novels. "How do you know my father?" I asked Gloria.

She stared at me for another moment and then she shook her head. "I told you, I looked you up on the internet."

But that made no sense. She had been studying Gaitlin's face online to see how closely it matched up with mine?

The door to the suite opened, and suddenly Tate barged in, off the elevator, before I had a chance to ask anything else. "Sorry to interrupt," she said. "We forgot Jasper's raincoat."

"Oh, poor baby can't do with getting wet. I'll get it." Gloria stood so quickly, she almost fell, and then she leaned on her cane for a few seconds to steady herself before thumping off toward what I assumed was the bedroom. Her cane was plain, dark wood, and it occurred to me now that unlike so much of the rest of what she always wore and had with her, her cane was not a prop. She truly needed it to get around.

"Sorry to barge in like this," Tate lowered her voice and said to me. "Jasper acts like a little bitch if he gets wet."

"Tate, why does Gloria use a cane?" I asked.

"Oh, the cane?" Tate's tone shifted. My question had caught her off guard. "Well... Will would know better than me. There was an accident, a long time ago. I think her leg got crushed and she's used a cane ever since."

"An accident? You mean...the night George died? Or the car accident when Will was little?" I whispered, not wanting Gloria to hear me from the other room.

Tate thought about it for a minute. "I'm not really sure," she finally said. "Like I said, Will would probably be the one to know the details."

I nodded. That was, at least, a knowable answer. I would ask Will later.

Gloria thumped back in, carrying a tiny yellow raincoat. "Make sure you put his hood up." She held it out toward Tate, and I noticed that the hood was rimmed with a tiny row of diamonds.

Tate nodded and took the coat. "I know. I will."

Then Gloria turned back to me and frowned. "Amelia, something's come up and I'm afraid I'm going to have to cut our meeting short. Tate, see her out on your way back down."

Before I could protest, she was already walking back toward the bedroom. But I noticed the way her hand was shaking now as it tightly gripped the top of her cane. Maybe what Will and Tate had originally said about her being nervous had actually been true. Did *I* make her nervous?

And then I felt this rush of disappointment, that I hadn't been able to put her at ease, talk to her, truly learn about her over the past six days. Suddenly it felt like I'd already failed miserably in playing my part before we'd truly even started.

Mare

1986

IT HAD BEEN a pattern throughout her life, that whenever someone told her she couldn't do something, she couldn't want something, that only made her want it more. When other people said *no*, she only heard *try harder*.

Her father told her she wasn't smart enough to go to college, and she proved him wrong by getting a full scholarship. She flew away and never spoke to him again, for the entire rest of his life.

When George told her that he would *kill* her if she left him and took Will, in her head she thought, *Just go ahead and try.* George was a finance guy, a numbers man; he liked rules and order. And he didn't like confrontation. Though he would often complain to her about his job, about the entitled jerks in his office he was forced to kiss up to, he would never once dare do or say anything about it at work. And if he thought she was going to stay with him, that she was going to listen to him because he'd threatened her with a useless, empty threat? He was out of his fucking mind.

What she thought instead was, she would leave him now for sure. And she would take Will too. And no matter what he said, George would never really have it in him to stop her.

Max didn't get the job he interviewed for in Chicago, but then he did get one in Seattle. He told Mare he would save up, buy a house and there would be space for all of them. All she had to do was figure out the best way to leave George. All she had to do was run away to Seattle. And he would be there, waiting for her.

So Mare steadily planned their escape. Every week she bought a little less at the grocery store and put a few dollars aside. She wouldn't tell George a thing, and then one morning, when she had enough cash saved, just after he left for work, she would take a taxi to the airport. She would buy their plane tickets in cash and get on a flight. By the evening, when George would come home from work, she and Will would already be across the country. What would George do then? He would call Marge. Or he would call Bess. And so she didn't tell either one of them what she eventually planned to do either.

Her plan had holes, sure. For one thing, this wasn't a way to divorce him. And she could run away as far as she wanted, but even in Seattle, George would still technically be her husband. For another, what would she do if he agreed to divorce her but sued her for custody of Will? She'd recently rewatched *Kramer vs. Kramer* on television one evening when George was working late. And Meryl Streep's character had been haunting her ever since. It was one thing, she now realized, to love a man and to live without him. But it was another kind of love that she felt for her son. How could she possibly be apart from him?

And then, there was Bess. Every time she thought of Bess, every Sunday she talked to Bess, she had to swallow back a lump in her throat. Bess had never told her what Max had, that they had broken up. And when Bess told her instead that her mother was ill, and she was moving back to California to take care of her, Mare guiltily sighed with relief. Because California was far from Seattle, from Max. And if Bess were in California, then she couldn't be there with him. Even if she wanted to.

One crisp fall day in October, her doorbell rang in the middle of the afternoon. Will was almost too old to nap, but sometimes he did anyway, and today was one of those days. Mare put a pot roast in the oven for dinner and then had made herself a cup of coffee. She sat with her notebook at the kitchen table, jotting down half a story, or a dream, while he slept.

As soon as she heard the chime of the bell, she jumped and ran to the door, hoping it hadn't woken Will. But then she heard him talking to himself from his room, and she opened the door and sighed.

Max stood there, kicking at a few stray orange leaves with his boots. He looked up as the door opened and smiled.

"What are you doing here?" She grabbed him and dragged him in from the porch, lest one of the neighbors should see. She slammed the door shut behind him and he leaned against it, pulling her to his chest in a hug. Her heart pounded from being this close to him again, from being thrown by his sudden appearance too.

"I missed you too much," he whispered in her hair. "I just wanted to see you."

The unexpectedness of it, of him in her house, like this, caught her off guard, and she pulled out of his hug and stared at him. "I don't understand," she said. "What are you doing?"

"I wanted to surprise you. I bought a house," he said. "It's outside of Seattle, but not too far. And there's plenty of room. There's even a tree house out back for Will." Max worked in estate law, and he continued on to explain how he'd heard about this house in foreclosure at the office, that it needed some repairs, but he'd bought it for a song, free and clear with a little money his grandmother had willed to him when she died.

"I still don't understand," she repeated. "If you bought a house in Seattle, why are you here now?"

He laughed, and grabbed her in another hug, and this time she eased into the warmth of his body, the feel of him against her. Her limbs evaporated and she couldn't let him go, even if she wanted to. "To convince you to come back with me," he whispered into her hair.

The thud of Will's little feet running in snapped her back into the real world, and on instinct, she jumped away from Max's grasp. She had kept Will in the crib, though he was much too big and he climbed in and out as he pleased. Now he stood in the front hallway, before them, naked except for a pair of Superman briefs, sucking his thumb.

Max dropped down on the floor on his knees to meet Will eye to eye. "Hey, Will," he said gently. "Do you remember me? I'm your mom's friend, Max."

Will eyed him suspiciously, glanced at Mare, who nodded a little in confirmation, but then continued sucking on his thumb.

"I brought you a present," Max said. He unbuttoned his overcoat to reveal a small brown teddy bear he'd had hidden in the pocket underneath. He held it out in front of him, and Will stared at it but didn't move.

"Go ahead." Mare nudged her son's shoulder gently. "Take the stuffie and go get back into your crib and rest some more."

Will reluctantly took the bear, held it to his bare chest, but he didn't budge from his spot on the floor in front of them.

"You can go sit in my bed and turn on the television." If there was one thing she had learned as a mother, it was that bribery got you everywhere. And the television in her bedroom was always the best form of bribery.

He listened then, clutched the bear in one hand, kept his thumb in his mouth and padded off down the hallway toward her bedroom. As soon as he was out of sight, Max grabbed her again in another hug.

She leaned into him for a moment, pushing away the rush of thoughts, of fear. The feeling that suddenly she was careening inside her own tunnel of lies in a car with no brakes. *This was not her plan.* She hadn't saved enough money yet to fly to Seattle. She hadn't figured out how to plug the holes so she could keep Will with her, always.

"Max, you have to go," she said. Though she clutched him tighter as she spoke, took a deep breath and inhaled the piney, reassuring scent of him. "George comes home soon, and you can't be here. Like this."

"Why not?" Max said.

She had almost forgotten. That they were all friends first. A college foursome. That Max had been here to visit before. With Bess. At the thought of Bess she swallowed hard and took a step back.

But Max reached for her and pulled her to him again. "Let me talk to George," he said. "Let's talk to him together. I know everything is complicated, but I don't want to live without you anymore. And I don't want to lie to him. Why don't we just tell George the truth?"

And what exactly was the truth? The very concept of it escaped her now.

Her truth was—if she was really going to admit it all—she had loved Max from the afternoon she first met him in the library. She should've told Bess the morning he showed up to their dorm with her wallet. And the truth was, also, she wasn't totally sure now whether she was stealing something from Bess or not. Max had said he and Bess were better suited as friends. But what was Bess's truth? And in that moment she understood that before she went anywhere with Max, what she needed to do was the hard thing she'd been dreading all along: talk to Bess.

But before she could say any of that, she heard the sound of the garage door opening. George was home.

Amelia

THE RAIN CONTINUED all afternoon, and as I made my way to Cam's room to run lines, raindrops pounded against the large glass windows of the hotel stairwells, and then a loud clap of thunder landed hard enough for the building to shake. I jumped from the noise and stopped on the stairs to catch my breath.

Cam said he also had a suite with plenty of room to spread out, but a floor above me, on the third floor. I felt a little awkward coming here at his invitation, but I wasn't about to suggest we run lines in the lobby or the rooftop bar amidst other random people, and the rain prevented us from finding a more public but quiet space outdoors on the hotel grounds. It seemed our options were his room or mine.

After I took the birdcage elevator down with Tate, I'd regrouped in my own room for a little while before walking up here. I was still puzzling over why Gloria had brought up Gaitlin. But I'd come up with no real answers, and now I clutched my script in hand, hoping that a least one thing Gloria had said today was actually true: I had everything I already needed to pull off the role, even without her cooperation.

But I felt this weird sense of dread as I reached the third floor, and I stopped walking and decided to text Will to see if he wanted to meet me after this for dinner. At least that would give me something to look forward to.

I waited a moment, but he didn't immediately text back, and then I put my phone in my pocket and knocked on Cam's door. He opened it quickly, and he was casually dressed in workout clothes and had his face covered in what looked like a Korean sheet mask.

I laughed before I could stifle it. "Am I interrupting your skin care regime?" I asked as he opened the door wider so I could step inside. It appeared Cam had an identical suite to mine, only in reverse. His windows faced the stream out front, while mine faced the woods on the back of the property.

"Give me a second to get this off," Cam said, and he jogged back toward the bathroom.

I put my hand to my own face. I was, always much to Jase's dismay, notoriously unconcerned about my body. I supposed I had good genetics, and a good metabolism. But I never dieted, aside from trying to eat healthy and vegetarian to begin with. I only worked out when forced, and I didn't do much more for my skin other than simple soap and water before bed. After Jase got cast as Dr. Ryan, he'd started going to the gym twice a day and definitely started looking down on me for not joining him. Judging from the workout clothes, I would bet Cam was in that annoying phase right now too. I understood, of course, that I was in a business driven by appearances, and yet, I loved acting for the way it made me *feel* to become someone else. I didn't have it in me to stress over all the superficial stuff, and I was lucky that I could still get away with looking good without obsessing over it.

"Sorry, I was just about to take that off when you knocked." Cam walked back in, patting his face with a towel.

"Your skin looks great," I said, only half joking. I mean, his skin looked fine, but it wasn't something I would normally comment on if he hadn't made it such a conversation piece.

"Really? Do you think so?" He walked up to the small mirror on the wall above the couch to examine his cheeks closely.

"Yep." I stifled another laugh, but he was too busy checking out his pores to notice.

I stared at him, staring at himself, and I supposed Cam was attractive in a classically handsome kind of way. But there was something about him right now that reminded me so much of Jase when Dr. Ryan first started to gain popularity. I couldn't help myself, it kind of made me hate Cam a little. I pulled my phone out of my pocket and glanced at it—still no text back from Will—before putting it down on the coffee table.

I cleared my throat. "Should we get started?" I flipped open my script. "Where do you want to begin? Filming starts when they move into their new house—scene twenty-six. We could start there?"

Cam finally stopped examining his face in the mirror and flopped down on the couch next to me. He sat close enough so our thighs were touching, and then he casually draped his arm around my shoulders.

I gently removed his arm and slid over a bit, flipping my script to scene twenty-six. But he made no move to grab his script off the coffee table and instead slid closer again and put his arm back over my shoulders.

"What are you doing?" I asked.

"We're husband and wife, right? I know my lines. I'm sure you know yours. Let's figure out how to be comfortable together instead."

I thought about how ridiculous he'd made me feel when I'd

told him last night we were *not* having sex. But now I wondered if my initial instinct hadn't been so far off base.

There was nothing about any of this that felt *comfortable* to me. And suddenly I regretted agreeing to run lines in his room alone. Rookie mistake, and I should know better. I did know better.

I shook off his arm and stood. "Let's just run the lines, okay?"

"Okay," Cam said. "If that's what you want." But he made no move to pick up his script. Instead, he stood up and grabbed me in a hug, circling his arms around my waist, holding on tight. Yesterday he'd said he was *a hugger*, but this felt over the line, even for that.

"Cam." My body flooded with uneasiness, and I tried to tug away, but he held on too tightly. He locked his arms behind my waist and dipped his face down like he was about to kiss me, but then he stopped a few inches from my lips and gave me a little arrogant smirk before he suddenly let go.

"What the fuck are you doing?" I said as I stumbled back a little bit, weightless, and grabbed onto the side table to keep my balance.

"Sorry," Cam said, and he almost did sound sorry. "I was trying to make you feel more comfortable with me, and I think maybe I did the opposite?"

I sighed, remembering that Cam was younger, newer at this than I was. "Why don't we run a scene?" I said, struggling to keep my voice calm and kind. "You get into character as George. I'll become Gloria, and lets just get comfortable together running lines, like that."

Cam nodded and finally did pick up his script. Then he closed his eyes for a moment, took a breath, cleared his throat. He opened his eyes again, shot me a smoldering look and patted the couch seat next to him. "Come sit next to me, wife." His voice was filled with urgency, longing. And maybe that was the way George would've spoken to Gloria. But I was having trouble channeling Gloria, and I stood there frozen, feeling a little nauseous and unnerved by our whole interaction.

My phone suddenly dinged with a text, vibrating against the coffee table, and I pushed past Cam to grab it.

Will: I can meet you up in the bar whenever you're free.

I texted Will back: Free right now. Meet you in 5 mins?

"I have to go," I said to Cam. "My agent," I lied. "Something urgent came up. I need to go call her and figure some things out."

Cam shrugged easily. "Sure. Text me later. We can do this whenever you want today." Then he added, "But not after nine. I need ten hours every night to look my best."

All the glass walls in the rooftop bar were closed today and awash with so much water, I felt like I was trapped inside an aquarium. I was weirdly shaken by my strange and stupid interaction with Cam—both the way he'd acted and my own inability to slip into the Gloria persona and deal with it. I sipped a glass of water and tried to calm down while I waited for Will. But my mind suddenly flooded with doubts—if I couldn't get anywhere with Gloria, and if I couldn't figure out how to play what was written in the script either, what was I even doing here? Sure, part of why I'd wanted to take on this role was the potential for it to be huge for my career, but if I did a terrible job, if critics hated me, it could actually have the opposite effect.

"What's wrong?" Will was suddenly standing in front of me. It was loud in here with all the retractable glass closed and the rain and I hadn't even heard him walk up.

I smiled at him and motioned for him to have a seat.

"You look upset. Was my mother mean to you again?" He frowned as he sat down across from me. "I'm starving," he added. "Do you want to share some guacamole?" I nodded, and just being this close to him, listening to him order guacamole as the waitress came by, I suddenly felt more at ease.

"Gloria wasn't any more difficult than she's been all week," I said when he finished ordering. "And I'm fine. Really." It was only half a lie because I did feel kind of fine, now that he was here.

"Tate said she was being weird when she went back for Jasper's raincoat. And that you started asking her about my mother's cane and she told you to ask me. I thought you knew about that?" I shook my head. "Yeah, the car accident that Aunt Marge mentioned. Her leg got crushed. She's used a cane ever since I can remember."

So the cane was a part of Gloria, a part that had remained hidden in her Oprah interview, her public persona and from her memoir? When Will had mentioned she was in a car accident when he was little I hadn't quite put two and two together, that the cane was connected. If the effects from that accident were this lasting, it seemed even weirder not to have included it in her memoir. I said that to Will now.

He shrugged. "Well, she doesn't like to talk about the accident."

I guessed that made sense. It had probably been traumatic if her injury was bad enough to be this long-lasting. And I supposed that on top of everything else, Gloria would never want an accident or an injury to define her. Besides, her cane felt drastically out of place with her Queen of Romance persona. But the more I learned about her, the more I truly was agreeing with Will about her memoir being *fiction*. Her memoir focused on *the amazing life* she had in her few years with George—when exactly in there had her leg gotten crushed?

"Anyway—" I realized Will was still talking. "Sorry I never texted you earlier. Gloria was in top form with me today." He rolled his eyes before he continued. "But, I have something you're going to like." The light glinted off the green of his eyes through his glasses as he smiled warmly now.

"What's that?" The waitress set down our guacamole in the center of the table. I grabbed a chip, dipped and nibbled slowly.

"I think I figured out who the guy in my mother's picture is."

I had not been expecting him to say that. "Really? How?"

"I recognized the knotty wood paneling in that bar in Emily's Polaroid. It's a little place in downtown Seattle called Up and Down. The walls and booths still look like that."

"Oh, I bet that aged well." I laughed a little and ate another chip. I was starving. I hadn't felt this hungry for months, since before my mom died.

"It's actually a pretty popular bar. It has that vintage/kitschy thing going on now and the drinks are still very cheap but also good. Anyway, I stopped in yesterday when I went to the city to swing by my office and I talked to the owner, showed her the picture to ask her if she had any ideas."

"And did she?" The picture had to be around thirty-five years old. Even if that man had worked there, as Emily sort of remembered he might have, I couldn't imagine the current owner would remember him.

He shook his head. "She did not. But her mom used to own the bar back in the '80s and she told me she'd email her mom a copy of the picture." He paused for a moment and smiled. "She called me this afternoon. It turns out her mom does remember him, and now we have a name—Max Cooper."

Mare

1986

"MAX COOPER, HOW THE hell are you?" George said it with a convivial smile, like here he had just come home from work and stumbled upon an old friend having a jovial and innocent cup of coffee in his kitchen.

She and Max had run to the kitchen when they'd heard the garage. She'd thrown her coffee cup in front of Max, and pulled an empty one from the cabinet to hold on to herself before sitting down across from him breathless, seconds before George walked in. What else was George to think?

"Hi, George." Max stood and shook George's hand. Mare watched the two of them lock eyes, hold on to each other a beat too long, neither one of them wanting to stop gripping first, and then she swallowed hard.

"George, Max is in the city for work, and he stopped by to say hello to us. He just got here."

Max finally let go of George's hand. He looked at her and then nodded slowly.

"And where's Bess?" George looked around the kitchen, as if maybe he thought she was hiding and was about to pop out and surprise him.

"Bess—" Max started.

"Bess is in California," Mare cut him off. "Her mother isn't doing well. I told you that." She had, in fact, told George that several weeks ago.

He nodded now. "Right, you did say that." George turned back to Max. "So work brought you out here, huh, Max? Estate law must be getting more exciting these days if they're sending you off to travel."

Max nodded to acknowledge George, yet, he was still staring at her. His blue eyes spilled over with something she couldn't quite read. Regret. Remorse. Anger. Love?

He finally looked away and focused his eyes on George. "There's a conference." He repeated her lie from last year. "I'm in Chicago for a few days for a conference. Anyway, I figured I'd better swing by and say hi while I was in town. Mare invited me for dinner."

She nodded and smiled, though neither of them had mentioned dinner until right now. Max couldn't stay for dinner. She wasn't sure she could make it through five more minutes in the same room with both him and George, much less an entire meal. "But then you mentioned that dinner at the conference tonight," she lied easily. "So we were having a cup of coffee now instead."

"But I really could skip the conference dinner and eat with my friends," Max said.

She laughed nervously and George shook his head and smiled. But color rose from under the starched collar of his white dress shirt, up his neck, through to his cheeks. And suddenly Mare could hardly breathe. "Well, then," George finally said. "Whatever brought you here it's good to see you again, Max." He paused and loosened his tie. "I just stopped home to change quickly. I have a client meeting in the city tonight."

A client meeting in the city? George hadn't mentioned that this morning had he? It was why she'd put a pot roast in the oven, which she had promptly forgotten about as soon as Max had shown up. But George wasn't always considerate enough to mention these things to her in advance. And she wasn't always considerate enough to listen when he spoke at breakfast, so maybe he had said something and she'd missed it.

George suddenly reached for her, pulled her to him tightly and kissed the top of her head. It had been a while since he had touched her, held her that close to him, but now it felt possessive, not loving. She squirmed a little, but he held on tighter for another moment.

"I shouldn't be too late," he said, finally dropping his arms. "Max, if you're still around on the weekend maybe we could play a round of golf. Catch up."

Max nodded, and Mare wondered if he even played golf. It was one of George's after-college hobbies. Something he did with the entitled jerks from his office—she'd noticed how as much as he complained about working with them, he always said yes when they invited him for a round of golf. But what was she thinking? Whether Max played or not, Max and George could not ever play together. Max could not be left to talk to George alone.

Even after they heard the garage door close again, heard George's car back down the driveway and into the street, she and Max sat across her kitchen table from each other in silence.

"You shouldn't have come here like this," she finally said.

"I think something's burning," Max replied.

Shit. *The roast.* She stood quickly and opened the oven door, waving away the smoke that billowed out into her face, causing her to cough. She grabbed pot holders, pulled the pan out of the oven and rested it on top of the stove. When the smoke cleared a bit, she could see that the roast was totally black. "Dammit," she cursed softly as tears stung her eyes from the smoke.

Max strode across the room and wrapped his arms around her waist. "It's not that bad," he said.

Maybe he meant the roast, or maybe he meant George walking in here, finding him in the kitchen. Or maybe he meant the current state of things, where she was married to George but in love with him. Where she wanted nothing more than to walk out of this house and forget about everything else in the world but Max, but she wasn't sure how to do that and still be a mother to Will. Truth be told, it *was* that bad.

"George might let me go," she finally said softly. "But he won't ever let Will." She thought about feverish, crying Will that night George had taken him from Marge's and they hadn't been able to find her. George understood fatherhood more as a title that gave him some sort of status he'd always longed for than as a practical job that required love and care. Will needed her. "And I want to be with you," she said to Max. "I really want to be with you. But I can't leave Will," she added.

Max kissed the top of her head softly. "Of course, you won't leave Will. He's your son." He paused for a moment to think. "There's a good divorce attorney in my office. I can talk to her next week and see what she thinks about the best way to ensure you get custody. We're going to figure it out, okay? I'm patient. I can wait."

She nodded, though she didn't quite believe what he was saying was possible. But she appreciated the kindness in his tone, his commitment to trying. "Max," she said his name softly. "I—" But she couldn't finish. *I don't think it's possible. I don't want you to waste your whole life waiting for me.* Or maybe, she was about to say, *I love you.*

"Why don't we go out and get a pizza for dinner?" Max said before she could figure out how to finish her thought. "My treat."

★ ★ ★

It started to rain as they sat inside the pizza parlor a few blocks away from her house. A howling, drenching fall rain shook gold and orange leaves from brittle branches, soaking them across the road, and making them as slippery as ice.

She watched the drops pound the glass of the door behind them, not trusting the stillness. It wasn't even five o'clock and they were the only ones at the sleepy Italian restaurant. But for some reason, she didn't quite believe that George wasn't about to burst in through those doors at any second and cause a scene. Still, theoretically, she was doing nothing wrong. Nothing she couldn't even tell George about later, if he asked. She was eating a slice of pepperoni pizza with her son, his new teddy bear and her friend from college.

She looked away from the door, back to Max, and now he was making silly faces across the table. Will started laughing. That pure innocent sweet child bubble-laughter that felt like confection, and for the smallest moment made her heart swell with joy. She laughed too, and Max reached for her hand under the table and squeezed it gently.

Imagine, the squeeze of his hand seemed to be saying. *When you move to Seattle, we'll have this all the time, together. We'll be so happy.* She imagined. She wanted it so much that it made her stomach hurt.

She put her slice of pizza down on her plate and turned to look at Max. *I love you*, she mouthed to him now. And that might have been the truest words she'd ever said to anyone in her whole entire life. It was so simple. And yet. It just was. *She loved him.* She'd loved him since the moment she first met him. She would love him for the rest of her life.

The waitress walked by and dropped their check on the table, and Max let go of Mare's hand, pulled his camera from the pocket of his coat and handed it to the waitress before she walked away. "Can you take our picture?" he asked. He turned to Mare. "We don't have any pictures of us."

"What a cute little family," the waitress gushed, as she fiddled with the camera, looking for the flash.

Mare realized her hair was a mess, and she tried to brush it away from her eyes, comb it with her fingers. But Max reached up and caught her hand. "You're beautiful exactly the way you are," he said softly.

"Should I get your son in too?" the waitress asked, pointing to Will, who was now trying to feed the teddy bear a slice of pepperoni.

Max put his arm around Mare, and pulled her closer to him. "No," he said. "Just get one of the two of us."

Then they leaned their heads together close and smiled, and she snapped the picture.

Amelia

GUACAMOLE TURNED INTO a glass of wine. And wine turned into ordering salads for dinner, and then dinner turned into lingering for a little while longer over coffees. And by then it was dark, the rain had stopped and an eerily clouded moon shone in through the glass ceiling of the rooftop bar.

We had left the topic of Gloria and of Max Cooper behind somewhere right after we finished the guacamole. I'd tried to google Max on my phone, but it was such a common name— I didn't get very far before I gave up. Will said he could get his assistant to try a public records search at the office on Monday.

For the time being we put Max and Gloria aside, and by the time the salads came, conversation turned. Suddenly we were just…talking. About ourselves. Will was telling me about how he decided to go to law school because he (weirdly) loved reading law briefs when he took an introduction to law class in college at Stanford. (Of course, he went to Stanford.) He may have grown up surrounded by romance novels, raised by the

Queen of Romance, but he said that very few of his friends or colleagues actually knew this fact about him. And that he had always felt grateful for his mother's *ridiculously flashy* pen name and the anonymity it gave him away from her. Law briefs were his comfort read, not love stories.

I listened, slowly sipping my wine, soaking up his quiet honesty, and I wondered if part of what he liked about spending time with me was that I actually knew he was Gloria's son. And that I liked him, not in spite of or because of Gloria, but because Will was Will.

But I didn't say any of that out loud. Instead, I found my own quiet honesty coming out of me as I finished off my wine. I told him about how I truly thought I had made it big when I'd been cast as Margaret Moon, and how in the ten years of ups and downs since, I'd realized how I was in this career for the long haul. Hard work, day after day, year after year, part after part. Rejections and small successes, followed by setbacks, more rejections and then, more and slightly bigger successes. "Sometimes it felt like I was slowly chipping away at an iceberg with a spoon," I told him.

He laughed. "A slow build is much better than an overnight sensation," he said with certainty.

"If you say so," I laughed too. "I would've been more than fine with being an overnight sensation."

He shook his head. "Too boring. Doesn't suit you."

I smiled, and then I found myself asking him if he'd dated anyone recently. He told me how the prosecutor he'd dated for four years had broken his heart about six months ago when she'd suddenly moved out of their apartment over her lunch break and then sent a text to tell him it was over.

"Ouch," I said. "I'm sorry. That sucks."

He shrugged. "I mean, at the time, it kind of did. But I realized in hindsight it was more of an ego blow than anything else. Now, honestly, I can't even remember what I liked about her to begin with."

I nodded, understanding because I felt a similar way about Jase. I was really mad when he cheated on me right after my mother died and it felt like the world as I knew it had entirely fallen apart. But once I'd moved out of our apartment, the truth was, I hadn't actually *missed* Jase much at all. I told Will now that I wasn't even sure what had kept us together for ten whole years. Except maybe it was just sharing our acting failures, our small triumphs, our commitment to our work, the Method. "But as soon as Jase's career took off, he wanted someone younger and more plastic than me," I said. "Could he be any more cliché?"

"Actors." Will rolled his eyes. "Present company excluded, of course."

I laughed, but then I told him I kind of agreed with him. And I spilled the details of my weird moments in Cam's room before coming up here tonight.

Will cursed softly under his breath in response. "I thought he seemed like an ass yesterday. I'm sorry."

"Why are *you* sorry?"

"My mother brought you both here, and somehow that makes me feel responsible, I guess." Even though Will had seemingly disconnected from her in his adult attorney life, the real him, the one I felt I was seeing right now before me, was so intricately connected to her that he was in Belles Woods for the filming, apologizing for something completely out of his control.

I shook my head and grabbed the check off the table, happy I was finally able to treat him this week.

"Let me give you some money," he said, reaching for his wallet.

"Nope. This one's on me," I insisted firmly. "And you have no reason to be sorry. I'll deal with Cam. I've dealt with far worse." Sadly he was not the first actor I'd ever worked with who'd made me feel uncomfortable. "At the end of the day, acting is a job, like anything else. Sometimes your coworkers suck."

"Well, to be fair, some of my coworkers suck too," Will said. "And for what it's worth, I still think you chose wisely for your career."

I laughed again and stood up from the table.

"I'll walk you to your room," Will said as he stood too, and then we walked toward the elevator together.

I was about to tell him that he didn't have to walk me to my room, that it was totally unnecessary and I was perfectly capable of walking to my own room. But the truth was, I was enjoying his company too much to say that, so I kept my mouth shut as the elevator slowly descended to the second floor. We got off and walked down the hallway together and then we stopped in front of the door to my suite.

He turned to face me, and we stood there, staring at each other for a moment. The light in this hallway was dim, Will's face shadowy. I thought again about kissing him in the tree house and that suddenly made me smile.

"I guess… I should…go," Will said softly, though still neither one of us moved.

I glanced at my watch. It was just past eight. Tomorrow was Sunday and totally unscheduled for me. All I planned to do was run through my lines one last time as a final refresher. "It's still early," I said. "If you want to come inside… We could watch something…?" My voice trailed off as I remembered when he told me he didn't watch much TV. "A movie maybe?"

"Do you even watch movies?" Will asked. I thought he might be joking but his voice sounded totally serious.

"Why wouldn't I watch movies?" I asked.

"It's not like an occupational hazard for you or something?"

I shook my head. "How weird do you think I am? I love movies."

"Right. I was thinking it would go one of two ways. You'd either love them or you'd hate them."

"You're overthinking," I said. But I took that response as a yes, pulled my key card out and opened the door.

Will followed me inside and shut the door behind him. Then he stopped there for a moment, leaned back against it, as if he wasn't sure about following me inside any farther. So we stood by the door, staring at each other until he averted his eyes first and then stared at his sneakers.

I put my hand on his arm, and he slowly looked back up at me. "We don't have to watch anything, though," I said softly.

He gave me a half smile, and I knew he knew exactly what I was saying. He lifted his hand, like he was going to touch my cheek, and then stopped himself midway, leaving his hand suspended in the air. "Is this the world's worst idea?" he whispered, like if he spoke the words any louder he'd have to admit they were true. In a whisper it could still be a question.

I bit my lip. Getting involved with the son of the woman I would be portraying in a movie, having sex with him tonight, felt at best like a misguided choice, at worst an unmitigated PR disaster for Liza to deal with should anyone find out. But standing here so close to Will, I didn't have it in me to care about any of that. I just genuinely liked him. No acting, no pretending. I liked Will in a real honest way, as a person. For the first time in a very long time, I wasn't thinking about my career at all. I was actually allowing myself to feel something entirely truthful.

"So what if this is a bad idea?" I finally whispered back to him. "I like you. What's so wrong with that?"

His face softened and he moved his hand the rest of the way to my cheek now, stroking his thumb gently over the arch of my cheekbone. "I like you too," he said.

We both smiled and stood there for another moment, as if

what we were about to do next was so tenuous, that whoever moved first might accidentally break the whole thing apart.

"Okay," he finally said softly. "Ground rules."

I nodded. Lawyer Will was out again, and he was honestly sexy as hell. "Ground rules," I repeated. Then I added, "Everything that happens tonight stays in this room."

He nodded. "My mother never finds out."

"*No one* ever finds out," I said.

"If you wake up and hate me tomorrow, you won't quit the film."

"I'm not going to wake up and hate you tomorrow," I said.

"But regardless, you won't quit the film."

"I won't quit," I echoed back.

"And—"

I cut him off by standing up on my toes and kissing him once softly. Then I whispered softly against his lips, "No more rules."

Mare

1986

THE RAIN CONTINUED HARDER, wind scattering the gold and orange leaves across the parking lot, the asphalt as slippery as ice.

They hadn't thought to bring an umbrella. (Had rain even been forecasted? How could she keep track of such mundane things these days?) And as they got out of the booth and walked toward the door of the restaurant, Max handed her his camera and asked her to shield it from the rain in her purse. She tucked it deep inside her giant leather bag. When she looked up again, Will had already pushed open the glass door himself and stepped out into the rain.

"Will," she called after him. "Hand. There's cars." She held out her hand and waited for him to comply, as he usually did. He understood those simple things at the age of three. *Hand*.

Cars. Danger. But instead of listening this time, he laughed and shook his head, and kept on walking.

The lot was eerily empty save for her Buick wagon parked a few steps away, and any danger seemed more imagined now than real. But still. He had to learn to listen. "Will," she commanded him, stretching out her arm. "Hand."

He ignored her and stepped off the sidewalk, out into the lot, giggling at the wash of raindrops on his face. Then he kicked through a puddle, splashing. It was too cold for puddles, and the fall wind whipped across the lot, making her shiver.

"Will," she tried again, but she heard the way her voice sounded. Desperate, exhausted. Defeated. Could he already intuit somehow her plans for their escape, to take him from his father and everything he'd ever known so she could be with Max? Of course he couldn't. He was a toddler. "Will!" She yelled his name sternly.

He stopped walking, turned and stared at her. He continued to ignore her outstretched hand, but then, he didn't move any farther into the lot either. He jumped up and down in the same puddle, splashing almost defiantly.

Max took her outstretched hand instead, laced his fingers easily in between hers. Then he leaned in close, whispered in her hair, "Give me your keys."

"And where are you taking us?" But she didn't wait for the answer before opening her purse and digging through the giant bag for her car keys. There was so much junk in this bag. Tissues and Cheerios and Will's favorite dinosaur board book, Max's camera, and where were those keys?

She was still rifling through her purse, and so she heard it before anything else. The sound of a motor. Then tires squealing, sliding across the leaves.

When she looked up, the car was already too close. Max had let go of her hand to step into the parking lot and push Will away from danger.

Maybe she screamed Will's name or maybe she didn't.

Maybe she ran to grab him or maybe she didn't.

Then suddenly, somehow, she was on the ground. Red and gold leaves swirled near her eyes, through her tangled wet hair. She heard the sound of tires careening through wet leaves as the car didn't even stop and sped off into the rainy night.

Amelia

I AWOKE IN the middle of the night with a start.

I'd been dreaming that strange dream again: I was trapped inside a closet with a younger Will, my mother's voice calling for me in the distance, but it was hard to get out, hard to find her. *Don't worry*, I promised Will. *I'll save you.* But the truth was, I didn't know how. I was lying.

I opened my eyes, and there was actual Will, breathing softly and sleeping peacefully right next to me in the bed. I sighed and instantly felt calmer. Then I realized I was naked underneath the covers, and from what I could see with the sheet half draped on top of him, Will was too. Maybe I would've felt embarrassed if he'd also been awake, but instead, the shadowy shape of him in the darkness made me smile. He'd been worried I would hate him in the morning, but if anything, I felt the opposite.

It was almost strange the way I had felt so comfortable with him last night, at dinner, here in my room. Even after clothes came off, and the lights were still on, I hadn't remembered to

think about what my body looked like, or what he was thinking as he saw me naked like I did with Jase. I didn't think about
how to act. I was only thinking about how much I liked him
and how nice it felt to be with him. How good his hands felt
against my skin. Even now, hours later, I felt no embarrassment
or regret. I just felt…happy.

There had been no discussion of this in the ground rules.
What if I woke up the next morning and wondered if I was
in love with him? What if I realized I wanted more than one
night? Much more. What then?

I reached up now and gently touched his face, and he murmured a little in his sleep, reached for me and pulled me toward
him as if on instinct. And then with my head in the crook of
his arm, I drifted back into a dreamless sleep.

I woke up again hours later. The curtains were open a little to
the balcony door near the bed, and sunlight streamed in, blinding me. The side of the bed where Will had been was empty,
but I put my hand in the imprint of where his body had lain,
and it still felt warm.

I grabbed my robe, wrapped it around myself and wandered
into the living room. Will was sitting on the couch, drinking a
cup of coffee, and I sighed, happy that he hadn't left, run away,
while I was still sleeping.

"Good morning," I said softly, and he turned at the sound
of my voice.

He stood up. "Oh, I can get out of your way, if you want?"

I shook my head, walked over to him and put my hand on
his arm. "You're not in my way. Sit down. Drink your coffee."

He smiled and sat. "I made you a cup too." He pointed to the
counter in the dining area, where there was a coffee bar with
a single-serve coffee maker. "It should still be warm. It hasn't
been that long. But I can make you another one."

I walked over, grabbed it and took a sip. "It's perfect," I said, and we just stared at each other for a minute until we both started to laugh.

"This is awkward, isn't it?" Will said when he finally stopped laughing. "I should've snuck out in the middle of the night."

I shook my head, and I walked over and sat down next to him on the couch. "No, I'm glad you're still here." I took another sip of my coffee and then put it down on the table in front of me, next to his cup. "And maybe it's a little awkward, but only because I really like you and I really liked last night, and I don't want to mess this up." I paused. "But don't worry, all ground rules still apply."

He chuckled and reached for my hand. He turned it over and stroked my palm softly with his thumb. "Okay, then I have one more rule. Starting now, we're about to lie to everyone else about what's going on with us. But let's not ever lie to each other, okay? If you want me to leave, tell me to leave."

"I don't want you to leave," I said.

"I mean it in a theoretical sense. Ever. Not just this room, this morning."

After Jase, the idea of honesty felt nice, refreshing even. "Okay," I said. "Then same for you."

"Agreed," he said. I heard his phone buzz against the coffee table, and he reached for it, read the text and frowned.

"Gloria?" I said softly, and somehow even saying her name in here, sitting with him like this, I felt like I was certainly breaking one of the ground rules we had established. I just couldn't put my finger on exactly which one.

"Yeah." He sighed. "She wants me to walk Jasper, and she tried calling my room and when I didn't answer she became convinced I was dead." His phone buzzed again in his hand and he glanced at it, then rolled his eyes. "*Dead or hungover.* She amended."

I couldn't help it, I laughed.

"She should be having Tate walk Jasper. I don't know why she has an assistant at this rate."

I remembered what he'd told me about the number of assistants she'd already fired this year and I hoped she hadn't found out about Tate leading me to Emily and fired her. Everything had seemed perfectly fine yesterday.

"You should go," I said to him. "We can text later and meet up tonight. I have to work on my lines today anyway." Shooting would begin tomorrow, and the thought of that made butterflies erupt in my stomach. Was I really ready to *become* Gloria Diamond? I definitely did not feel ready.

I looked back up and Will was frowning. "You're working on lines...with Cam?" he asked.

I was not dying to run lines with Cam, though I also knew I probably should. I'd pushed my simmering doubts from last night away the whole time I'd been with Will, but now they were bubbling back up. I had to figure out some way to get a handle on what I was doing before tomorrow. "Don't worry," I said to Will, though it felt kind of nice to think that maybe he was anyway. "I'll suggest we meet in the garden or somewhere public outdoors." Will's frown creased deeper. "I can handle myself," I said. "Really."

He nodded. "I know. You know what you're doing. I don't mean to imply you don't." He gently kissed my forehead and then stood. "And that reminds me. I was going to show you those pictures my aunt sent last night but then we..." His voice trailed off, and I smiled, remembering exactly what we had been doing instead of thinking or talking about Gloria or the pictures his aunt sent. "Anyway, they're in my room. I'll take some pictures of them with my phone and text them to you before I forget."

I nodded, but my brain still felt fuzzy, warm, thinking about last night. I did want to see the photos, but more, I wanted to cling to Will and whatever we had started for a few more minutes. So I stood and grabbed him in a hug, wrapping my arms around his waist and leaning my head into his chest.

"I'll see you later," he finally whispered into my hair, though he didn't let go yet either. "Promise."

I picked up my script after Will left, but it felt impossible to get into the Gloria mindset given how I was currently feeling about her son. Any former loyalty I'd felt toward the Method had kind of just flown out the window. I tried not to think about it all too hard—that I was supposed to be playing a young Will's mother, and I had also slept with actual adult Will in my bed last night, because it felt confusing and made my head start to ache. And it occurred to me I might've truly fucked everything up in the last twenty-four hours.

But weirdly, thinking about Will again only made me smile. I loved acting, but it felt very clear to me now that what I said to Will last night was true: it was a job. A job I had worked my ass off to get this far, and I wanted to continue to do well, of course. But it was still a job nonetheless. Everything had been so entwined with Jase, our shared commitment to the Method— life and work, love and careers. Looking back, I couldn't even remember the last time I'd felt like my real, honest self with Jase. Maybe I'd been putting on a show for so many years, on set and off, I'd almost forgotten that my life and my work could be separate.

But Will had things to do today and so did I. Whether I was ditching the Method or not, I still needed to finish preparing for filming tomorrow. Or else I needed to call Liza and tell her that I couldn't do this at all. But I swallowed back that thought, and I forced myself to text Cam instead. We arranged to meet in an hour in the hotel's garden.

Then I put the script down and went and took a shower, hoping the steam would clear my head, help me get into the mindset to work. But standing naked under the hot water, all

I could think about was Will's warm hands running across my body last night. And that didn't help matters.

I turned the water off and wrapped myself in a towel. And then I heard my phone dinging from the other room. I dried off a little and walked out of the bathroom to find it. Will— he'd sent me the photos from Aunt Marge, and a text that said, **As promised. Text you later. Last night was amazing. X**

It *was* amazing. If I could just shut out all the other noise and focus on that, I realized I felt happier than I had in months. Years. I smiled at that thought and then I clicked on the photos to scroll.

The top one was Gloria, from about the same time in her life as the pictures Emily had, exactly as Will had said. She was eating a piece of pizza, smiling, though she wore a dark green sweater (not all black) that matched her eyes. Her hair was down and hit a little below her shoulders, and her bangs were teased up in an '80s arch. She looked happy here in a way I hadn't see her in most of the other pictures, or in real life.

Then there was another photo of her taken from behind from a distance, that same night, maybe, as she was wearing the same green sweater. And she was holding on to a little boy's hand. But in the picture you could only see their backs. Still, it must be Will?

And then I scrolled to the next picture, only this one wasn't of Gloria at all. It was another woman, and I gasped at the sudden and unexpected sight of her. She was standing in a colorless room, her head tipped back in laughter, her long honey-colored hair pleated to the side in a braid, her stomach round and swollen.

This woman, this beautiful, pregnant woman, was unmistakably my mother.

Bess

1986

IT WAS NEVER a good thing when the telephone rang in the middle of the night.

It had happened to her last spring when her mother fell. A doctor's voice stretched and clinical across the miles, and she'd gotten a cab straight to the airport at 4 a.m., gotten on the first flight to LAX.

Now it was happening again. The ringing jolted her up out of bed. But all she heard when she first picked up the phone, groggy, still half-asleep, was the sound of a man sobbing. And she thought at first, it was a wrong number. Or a middle-of-the-night prank.

Then he said her name: "Bess. Bess. Is that you?"

She still couldn't place him for a moment. But then it hit her. She was suddenly wide-awake and panic gripped her chest, making it hard to breathe. "What's wrong, George?" she asked.

"Bess," he said her name again, in between a sob.

"Is Mare okay?" Her voice shook with alarm, with confusion. George certainly wouldn't be calling her if Mare *was* okay.

Then he explained, his words jagged and tear-filled, that there had been an accident, a hit and run. Mare and Max were in the hospital.

"Are they going to be all right?" Bess asked. That was her first question—though, later, it would occur to her to ask why they were together. Why Max was even in Chicago at all when he lived in Seattle? But in that moment, truly, all she could think was that Mare had to be okay. She just had to be.

"I don't know," George whispered across the line, his voice so soft, it was like he couldn't admit all the possibilities to himself.

"I'm leaving right now. I'll be on the first flight." She rested her hand against her swollen belly, feeling the reassuring bumps of the baby's tiny feet kicking. "They're going to be fine," she insisted. "They have to be."

It had been a long, bizarre seven months. Her mother's fall became a terminal cancer diagnosis, and she had quit her job in Seattle to move back to Pasadena where she had become more of a nurse than a daughter or an artist. She'd started casually dating Gaitlin, a grad student at Caltech, whom she'd met at a bar on Lake Avenue after drinking too much pale ale one night. He was nice enough, a good distraction from her boredom and depression, but it wasn't anything serious, and she hadn't even mentioned him to Max when she'd returned to Seattle to pack up the remainder of her things.

Then, she'd discovered, there was this baby, growing, moving inside of her.

It was a strange kind of a secret she had been keeping from Mare, so obvious to everyone around her in Pasadena now. Her dying mother, who swore she would live long enough to meet her grandchild, though that seemed somewhat unlikely. Gaitlin, who said foolish things about getting married when he graduated in May, and she'd nodded along to oblige. But as she had told Mare once—it was the goddamn 1980s; a woman could have a baby on her own for heaven's sakes. She'd told Gaitlin she'd think about marriage to placate him. (She had not, in fact, thought about it once since he'd brought it up when she'd first told him about the baby.)

But Mare didn't know that Bess was pregnant. And for some reason, Bess hadn't been able to bring herself to say it over the phone. It wasn't that she was ashamed. She wasn't. It was more that telling Mare would make it all more *real* somehow. Or would seem to invalidate everything Bess had ever felt for Mare. Maybe Mare would even talk her into marrying Gaitlin, after all. Or maybe Mare would tell her to call Max instead. She was pretty sure she would never be able to talk to Max again after what she'd said to him that last night she was in Seattle. (And she could not share that with Mare, not ever.) So all of that was why the word *baby* had sat on the tip of her tongue at the end of every phone call she'd had with Mare for months. But she had not yet uttered it aloud.

And so, when she walked into the waiting room of the intensive care unit of Mercy Hospital, and George lifted his head from his hands and looked at her, his eyes wandered straight to her belly, and then his face turned pale. "Shit," he cursed softly under his breath and averted his eyes. Even after all these years she still didn't truly know him well enough to know whether he was judging her for being unmarried and pregnant in the first place or judging himself for dragging her out here like this. The latter seemed too kind for George, so she suspected it was the former.

But she was always a people pleaser, so she smiled at him, put her hand on his shoulder. "It's okay. I'm okay," she lied, because nothing at all felt okay. "How are you doing? How are *they* doing?"

George didn't answer right away, but then he looked back up and slowly shook his head. "I'm sorry," he said softly. "I'm so, so sorry, Bess."

His words hit like a punch that instantly took her breath away. It was a feeling she would feel again, a few years later, the sudden gaping hole inside of her, the empty space where the person you loved more than anyone in the world had once resided. "No," she insisted. "I won't believe it. Mare *has* to be okay."

George frowned, looking confused and he didn't say anything for a moment. "Not Mare," he finally said. "Max."

Amelia

I STARED AT the photo of my mother for a long time, unsure what to do next. I was still wrapped in my towel, but I didn't make any move to get dressed or do my hair either. I just sat on the edge of the bed, zoomed in on my mother's face in the photo and ran my finger slowly across it. It was almost surreal, seeing her so young, and in this most unexpected of ways.

Gloria must've known my mother. Otherwise, it made no sense how this photograph would've ended up in a box in Marge's attic amongst what Marge said were Gloria's things. But if Gloria had known her, why hadn't she mentioned it to me? And was my being cast in this role a coincidence, or had Gloria somehow orchestrated bringing me here *because* of my mother?

I had so many questions, and absolutely no answers. All this past week I'd thought I'd needed to know the real Gloria Diamond so I could understand how to do my job. Now I suddenly wanted to know her to understand how this all related back to my mother.

I thought about texting Will, but my finger hovered over my

phone for a moment, unsure what to write. Certainly, he didn't know about my mother and Gloria having some connection, or he would've mentioned it. At least, I was fairly sure he would've.

Instead, I scrolled through my contacts until I hit Gaitlin. I hadn't talked to my dad in weeks—I couldn't even remember if I told him about this new role. He'd been checking in every few days after my mother first died, saying he was worried about me. But once I'd acted well enough a few conversations in a row, we'd gone back to our once-a-month text exchange.

I hit the icon to call him now, and then almost immediately regretted it as he picked up right away.

"Hey, honey. Why are you calling? Everything okay?"

Gaitlin, as usual, cut right to the chase. Not even bothering to hide his surprise about me calling him out of the blue on Sunday afternoon. And I nodded, forgetting for a moment he couldn't see me. "I'm good," I finally said.

"You used to see your mom every Sunday, right?" Gaitlin said softly, and I was surprised he both knew that and thought that was why I was calling him now. "You must be missing her."

I was, but that wasn't why I was calling him. I cleared my throat. "Did I tell you I'm out in Washington state right now, about to start shooting a biopic tomorrow?"

"Oh gosh, a biopic, honey. That's great."

I vaguely wondered if Gaitlin even knew what a biopic was, but that was altogether besides the point now. "I'm playing Gloria Diamond. It's based on her memoir—*Diamond in the Rough*. Do you know it?"

"Sounds familiar," he said unconvincingly.

"You don't know who Gloria is?" He was silent on the other end of the line. "So I guess you wouldn't have any idea if Mom knew her?" I sighed.

"Hold on a second, honey. I'll walk to my computer and google her."

It was almost ridiculous to think he would know anything about my mother, except for the fact that my mother was clearly pregnant in this photograph. She had only been with Gaitlin for a few short years, and this would've definitely been one of them. And Gloria had said something about how I looked like my father yesterday. They must've all known each other.

Then I remembered—Gloria wasn't yet Gloria back then. "Actually, she would've been Mary Forrester then," I said. "She didn't go by Gloria until later."

Gaitlin still didn't say anything, and I imagined him inside his cluttered office, searching for his reading glasses on his desk so he could read Gloria's Wikipedia page.

"Queen of Romance," he said. "Sold over a billion copies worldwide." He whistled lightly under his breath. "This is gonna be a pretty big role for you, isn't it?"

In a different situation, I might've appreciated that Gaitlin was genuinely trying hard to be a dad to me right now. But I felt more impatient than grateful. "Mary Forrester," I repeated. "Do you remember how Mom might've known her?"

He was silent for another moment. "I'm sorry, honey. You know we weren't together very long. I didn't really get to know her friends." He paused and then he added, "There was someone from college I think she stayed in touch with."

"College? Mom didn't go to college." It was one of the reasons why I'd thought she was so keen on law school for me. As an artist, she used to say she wished she'd had the backup of a degree. She was somewhat successful as a freelancer, but even I knew from a very young age that there was nothing steady about her chosen career and income. And she was grateful Gaitlin always sent the child support on time. She was prone to overusing the words *safety net* whenever I used to try and talk to her about wanting to be an actress.

"No." Gaitlin sounded adamant now. "She went to college a few years. She just didn't ever graduate."

I frowned, uncertain how Gaitlin could be so sure when he could barely remember anything else about her. It felt unfair that he knew this one detail about her that I never had. And more unfair that she was no longer here for me to ask her—about any of it. College. Gloria. Where she was in that picture, why she was laughing and how it ended up in Gloria's sister's attic to begin with?

A fresh wave of grief crested in my chest, and tears stung in my eyes. I blinked hard, not wanting Gaitlin to hear me cry and start worrying about me all over again. I breathed slowly in and out and regained my composure. "Where did she go to college?" I asked him, now wanting all the details he had.

He was silent again on the other end of the line.

I sighed. "You don't remember, do you?" If Gaitlin was my best remaining source of information about my mother, I was pretty screwed.

"We dated for a very short time. You were born, and then we were married for all of three years." I already knew all this, of course. Now he said it more as an apology than anything. But I couldn't blame him. He and my mother just weren't meant to be together, and as a result I'd grown up across the country from him. I doubted he knew much more about me than he knew about my mother. Which was, to be fair, by my age at least half my fault.

My phone buzzed with a text, and I suddenly remembered I was supposed to meet Cam. Certainly by now, I was late. He was probably looking for me. And here I was still in a towel—I'd never even combed my hair after the shower.

"I really have to go," I said. "But thanks for trying to help."

Gaitlin sighed, and then I felt bad for calling him in the first place. "Good luck on the movie. Do you need me to send you any money?"

My heart softened toward him. He was trying so hard. "The studio is paying for my accommodations. And I'm really good. But thank you for offering."

He was quiet for another moment and then he added, "I'm real proud of you, you know, honey."

And even if I knew next to nothing else about Gaitlin, this much I did know.

Mare

SHE HEARD THE vague steady noise of a beeping heart monitor. The sound of someone being alive. And then she realized, that someone was her.

She opened her eyes, and Bess was there, sitting in a chair by her bed, reading a magazine, her arm resting across her swollen, pregnant belly. Mare blinked because surely she was dreaming this. Bess was in California, and though she hadn't seen Bess in nearly two years, they still spoke every single Sunday afternoon. Bess had never mentioned a baby. Or a man she might've been dating in California. And the first sickening thought that hit her was that Bess must be pregnant with Max's baby. That Max had lied to her about everything.

Then again, she had never mentioned her involvement with Max to Bess either. In the vaguest moment between waking and sleep, between hovering near death and coming back to life, Mare suddenly wondered if she and Bess had ever told each other the whole truth about anything.

"Oh my goodness, you're finally awake!" Bess exclaimed. *Finally?* Had she been asleep for more than a night? "I should get the nurse."

"Bess," she whispered her friend's name, or she tried, but what escaped from her sore and swollen throat came out more like a hiss. She looked around—she was in a hospital room. And yet she didn't remember how she had gotten here. Or why.

She knew she had been with Max earlier. They were in her kitchen together drinking coffee. Was that right? But everything that came after felt hazy, just out of reach. She had so many questions and couldn't find the words to ask them, or maybe it was that she wasn't strong enough to speak them.

"There was an accident," Bess was saying now, as she pushed the call button for the nurse. "But Will is okay. Not even a scratch. He's with your sister right now."

Will. How had she not remembered to think first about her son?

She nodded slowly and her head throbbed, and she remembered that last night Will had spent at Marge's, the fever that had gotten her to call George. But Bess was saying Will was there now, he was safe. Everything was okay.

"You gave us quite a scare," Bess said. "You were out for weeks."

Weeks?

Bess stood, using both arms to push off the sides of the chair and balance her unsteady weight. She had to be at least six months along. Mare tried to remember the exact month Bess had fled Seattle for California but her head was too foggy to come to any conclusions. How was Bess even here in front of her? Much less pregnant?

Bess leaned over and stroked her forehead, tucking her hair behind her ears. Then she softly kissed the top of her head.

"You're going to be okay," she said. "Thank god, M, you're going to be okay."

But if that was true then why were Bess's eyes flooded with tears when she pulled back?

Finally, Mare managed to choke out a word. "Max?" she whispered. Alone it meant so many things. Where was he now? If he was the father of Bess's baby, why hadn't he told her that? Had Bess kept it from him the way she'd kept it from Mare? Or had Max lied to her?

Bess sat back down in the chair, as if she couldn't hold her own weight up any longer. "He's gone, Mare," she said softly, the words sputtering out of her in a half hiccup.

Of course, if she'd been out for weeks, he would've gone back to Seattle. "Is there a phone?" Mare got out the words slowly. She needed to call him. She needed to ask him about Bess, about the baby, about who he'd really loved this whole time. Her. Or Bess? And what if the answer was Bess? What would she do then?

Bess reached for the phone on the end table and pulled it closer. "You want me to call George? He's at work."

She shook her head. "Max," she said again. "I need to talk to Max."

Bess bit her lip, but tears streamed down her cheeks. She let go of the phone to wipe them away furiously. "Mare," she said softly. "Max is dead."

Amelia

I WAS ALREADY twenty minutes late to meet Cam in the garden. By the time I got off the phone with Gaitlin my hair had half dried and was frizzy and completely unmanageable. I pulled it back into a bun, quickly got dressed, put on a little bit of makeup and then grabbed my script.

As I was halfway down the stairs my phone dinged with a text from Gaitlin: Mare. That was her college friend's name.

My heart thudded in my chest, and I leaned against the railing, trying to remember how to breathe. *Mare.* My mother and Gloria really, truly had been friends, once. They'd stayed in touch after college. And yet my mother, big fan that she was of Gloria Diamond novels, had never mentioned this one tiny, enormous detail? Why not?

Then I remembered again what Gloria said to me yesterday, about looking like my father. Maybe she actually had met Gaitlin, once, many years ago. So why hadn't she just told me that when I'd asked her?

I stumbled down the last step, into the lobby, but then instead of walking out back to meet Cam, I got into the birdcage elevator. I took a deep breath as it made its wobbly ascent to the penthouse, and I texted Cam, told him something had come up and that maybe we could meet later today. I was pretty sure he was minutes away from complaining to his agent and/or the director about how difficult I was, but I didn't care. There was plenty I could complain about his behavior too.

But then he surprised me by texting back. **No worries. I want to get another workout in anyway.** Well, of course he did.

My finger shook as I rang the penthouse bell and it occurred to me that I didn't quite know how to ask Gloria about my mother. I couldn't very well let her know about the picture Will had sent me or mention Will's involvement in this. But I couldn't *not* ask her about my mother either. *Gaitlin.* That's what I would say—that Gaitlin told me.

The door swung open, and Tate stood on the other side, her eyebrows raised. I was glad to see she hadn't been fired. "Gloria isn't expecting you," she said with a frown.

I nodded to acknowledge what she said, but then walked inside the penthouse anyway. "I really need to talk to her. Does she have a few minutes?"

"I wish you had called first." Tate's frown creased deeper.

Will walked out from the kitchen, noticed me and his face erupted into a smile. He put his hand to his mouth as if realizing that might give him away.

I averted my gaze and smiled sweetly at Tate instead. "Can you please go see if she can give me a few minutes this morning? I can sit here and wait until she has the time." I plopped onto the couch, knowing full well that Tate wasn't going to physically remove me from the penthouse. I was leaving her no choice. She was going to have to deal with me whether she liked it or not.

She sighed heavily, and I almost felt a little bad thinking

about Gloria yelling at her at my expense. But then she did what I'd asked, walked back toward the bedroom.

Will came over and sat down next to me. "Hey, what's going on?" He kept his voice low, barely a whisper. "You look a little pale. Is everything all right? I thought you were running lines."

I looked behind me, but Tate and, I assumed, Gloria were still in the bedroom with the door firmly closed. I opened my phone and pulled up the picture he sent. "This woman," I whispered back, "is my mother."

"What?" Now it was his turn to look a little pale, and it was obvious he'd had no idea.

The bedroom door burst open, and the thump of Gloria's cane preceded her. Will and I both jumped and turned around. She was wearing a bright red terry cloth bathrobe, no makeup, no wig, her thin hair pulled back into a tiny bun at the nape of her neck. And still, somehow, she appeared terrifying as she thumped her way toward the couch, frowning deeply.

"Amelia, I thought we were done. Filming begins tomorrow! What else could you possibly need?"

I stared at her but didn't say anything for a moment. Nothing. *Everything.*

It had been clear to me for days already that Gloria was indeed a liar but now that it felt like her lies had been hiding some connection to my dead mother, I felt it all personally, a gut punch, and it was difficult to catch my breath. "You knew my mother?" I finally said.

Her cane crashed to the hardwood floor with a loud, shattering thud, and then she gripped the side of the couch, maneuvering around it to sit down. "Why would you ask me that?" she finally said softly, once she was seated.

Will's eyes widened, and I could practically hear the words rattling around in his brain, ground rules. *Ground rules!* I shot him a look that I hoped he understood meant *calm down. I'm a professional, remember?*

I forced myself to offer a half smile to Gloria. *Young, eager actress.* No, *young grieving daughter.* I cast my eyes toward my feet. "I was just talking to my dad," I said slowly to the tops of my tennis shoes. "Telling him about playing this role. And he mentioned that my mom was friends with you in college."

"College…" Gloria spoke with hesitation now. "College was…a very long time ago."

"My mother's name was Elizabeth Gaitlin." It felt weird to say my mother's name aloud. Weirder to remember that she didn't exist here anymore, in the flesh. She was a name, a memory, but no longer a living breathing person. And I wondered if there would ever be enough time that could pass that would not make me feel a crushing heaviness in my core at that thought. *My mother no longer existed.* I struggled to keep my breathing even as Gloria stared at me, frowning, not saying anything at all. "Or I guess she would've been Masters back then," I added softly. "Elizabeth Masters."

"Bess," Gloria whispered. Then covered her hand with her mouth as if the name had slipped out of her and she hadn't meant to say it.

My mother sold her art under her legal name, Elizabeth Gaitlin. But it was almost like a weird alter ego. Because in real life, no one called her Elizabeth. And *Gaitlin* referred to a marriage she'd been in all of three years. Still, she always said she had kept his last name legally simply because it was my last name too. And even when I got rid of it, she used to say it was too late for her to change by then. But the people who knew my mother, her friends, had called her *Bess*. Gloria, no, *Mare*, truly had been friends with her.

"I knew her back in college, yes," Gloria finally said. She stared at me for another moment and then continued: "But I only put two and two together after you arrived and told me your mother had recently died. I told you I googled you. When I did that, I found her obituary. That's when I realized the connection." She paused and then she added, "I was very sad to learn what happened to Bess." Her face turned, and she genuinely did sound sad. "But I had no idea until you got here."

"So it's just…a giant coincidence, then?" It felt impossible, even as I said the words out loud. "You didn't even realize you knew my mother when I was hired for this role?"

She slowly nodded. "Just a coincidence," she said softly. I glanced at Will, and he frowned, like he too didn't believe her.

"And you didn't think to tell me, once you figured it out?"

"What good what that have done? I hadn't seen or spoken to your mother in so many years. We were girls back then. It was a lifetime ago."

"But you mentioned yesterday I reminded you of my father when I made a face. You must've met Gaitlin." Even as I spoke I knew this didn't quite add up. Gaitlin hadn't even known who she was until he'd googled her. But I supposed it was possible they had met and for some reason Gloria remembered it, while Gaitlin did not all these years later.

"A lifetime ago," she repeated softly. "We lost touch after college."

I thought about the photo Will had sent me, with my mother visibly pregnant. I was born a whole six weeks early, on the last day of 1986. That photo couldn't have been taken too much before that. And my mother surely would've already been a few years removed from college by then. I bit my lip, not quite sure yet how to call her out on this lie without giving away Will's snooping.

"But then here you were before me, just like that. Isn't it funny," Gloria was saying now. "How life is a circle sometimes?"

Is that what this was? Is that what was going on here?

And then she gestured for Tate to pick up her cane from where she'd dropped it on the floor, leaned onto it and stood. "Now if you'll excuse me," she said. "I have a spa appointment."

Mare

1986

SHE COULDN'T REMEMBER everything about the night of the car accident.

In the years that would follow, she would piece details together in her head, until she came up with the singular story she told herself again and again and again. The things she remembered: The pizza, the rain, Will's teddy bear that Max had brought him as a gift. Then the things she couldn't: It was raining so hard, they stepped out into the lot. They couldn't see. A driver lost control. But what color was the car? Why was it driving so fast? And the truth was, she would never really know what had happened in the minutes just before she and Max were hit by a car and Will was spared.

All she would know was what George would tell her. (And even though she had hit her head, she still understood that George was an unreliable narrator.) George said she and Max had been hit in the parking lot of the pizza joint, walking out after they ate. The car had sped away. The cops never caught the guy. The only witness was Will, who was too young to truly understand, and who was found standing there sobbing in the rain, clutching a teddy bear, by a poor waitress who'd been crying too hard herself to get her story straight. Max died the next morning of his injuries. But Mare was lucky. She woke up. Her head injury would leave no lasting damage. Though, her leg had been crushed and she might never walk without a limp again. But still. Luck was luck. Living was living and dead was dead.

But was she really living without Max?

That thought crossed her mind again and again in the first few weeks after she woke up. How could it possibly be true that she would *live* the entire rest of her life without ever seeing him, being with him again? Now that she had felt love, she didn't understand how a life without it was any life at all.

Then George brought Will to visit her in the hospital. He climbed up into her bed and wrapped his small arms around her neck, held on tightly. She inhaled the sweet Johnson & Johnson baby shampoo scent of his fine brown curls. And she felt it swell up in her chest, a love she felt for her son too.

"Thank god you're okay." George leaned in and joined the family hug, clinging tightly to both Mare and Will. "I don't know what I would do without you, Mare." They held on to each other, all three of them.

George finally pulled back, though Will still clung to her, and his cheeks were streaked with tears. "I'm going to try harder from now on," he said, stroking her cheek gently with his thumb. "Do better."

It occurred to her that maybe he was being truthful. Maybe somewhere inside him, he honestly felt something for her. He didn't want to lose her. Not to another man. Not to death either.

"I love you, you know," George added softly.

In response she simply clung tighter to Will, kissed the top of his head.

In her writers' workshop they would've called this "deus ex machina." Max had been suddenly and unexpectedly plucked away. And now this was to be her fate, spending the rest of her life with George, whether she loved him or not.

When she finally left the hospital, her leg still in a cast, Margery came to pick her up. As Margery rolled Mare out in a wheelchair, she handed Mare her purse, told Mare that she'd had it with her the night of the accident. And George, in the days first following the accident, had retrieved it from the hospital staff and asked Margery to keep it safe.

Once inside the passenger seat of Margery's powder-blue Chevrolet, Mare searched the contents of her own bag, remnants of an old life, the former person she used to be. She found a familiar camera in the bottom. *Max's camera.* And she asked Margery if they could stop by the one-hour MotoPhoto on the way home.

In the developed roll of film, she found the picture of her and Max together, at the pizza restaurant, right before the accident. But then, there was a photograph of a very pregnant Bess, too. And why in the world would that have been on Max's camera, if he wasn't still with her, if he wasn't the father of her baby? Mare couldn't fathom another reason. And that's when she knew that she could never tell Bess the truth about what Max had been doing in Chicago, what Max had been doing with her. Their secret, their love, would die along with him.

Amelia

LATER THAT NIGHT, I couldn't sleep, anxiety pulsing through my veins.

I was supposed to be on set, in hair and makeup, at 8 a.m. In a few hours from now, I would be transformed into a young Gloria. But as I lay in bed, Will sleeping soundly next to me, all I could think about was that picture of my mother. Why had it been in Marge's attic? Why did I feel like Gloria wasn't telling me the whole truth? And why had my mother never mentioned that she'd once been friends with her favorite romance novelist?

A swath of moonlight shone in through a slit in the curtain, illuminating Will's bare chest as it slowly moved up and down with the easy breathing of sleep. I leaned my head against it, felt the warmth of his skin, the steady rise and fall of his body against my cheek. And then my anxiety shifted. How would everything change tomorrow morning when shooting began? When Will saw me transformed into Gloria? This moment, or whatever we were sharing tonight, was certainly fleeting, and yet, I already knew I didn't want it to be.

When Will had texted me just after eight tonight to ask if I was free, and I had texted back and told him to come up to my room, neither one of us mentioned what had happened in Gloria's suite earlier in the day. Or the fact that somehow my dead mother was involved in Gloria's past. We didn't mention any of it as I'd let him in, or as I'd shut the door and kissed him.

We didn't say a word about the movie, about his mother, or mine. We didn't say anything at all; we pulled off clothes, moved to the bed, explored each other's bodies greedily as if we had been craving only this one thing all day.

Here, in my hotel room, only the two of us, a new tacit ground rule emerged: there was nothing else. No one else. Just me and Will. But how could that possibly continue for much longer?

Will shifted a little in his sleep, rolled onto his side, wrapped his arms around me, pulled me close and sighed. And then at last, my body relaxed. I leaned into him, and the pulse of anxiety slowed.

My last thought before dozing off was how comfortable it felt to be this close to him. How, for the first time in a long time, I felt like I was home.

Mare

ON THE VERY last day of 1986, Bess had a baby girl.

And three weeks later, in the middle of January 1987, two remarkable things happened. One, Mare received a certified letter in the mail from Max's former law firm, and then that very same evening, Bess called to tell Mare she was marrying a man named Henry Gaitlin that she had met in Pasadena.

"What about Max?" Mare had asked softly, twisting the kitchen phone cord anxiously through her fingers. She had not yet opened the certified letter, though she had stared at it all afternoon. Run her fingers across the return address in Seattle, remembering how Max had sat at that very same address once and called her every weekday on his lunch hour.

"What about Max?" Bess repeated.

Mare wanted to say that Max hadn't even been dead four months. That if Bess had just given birth to his child, it felt downright disrespectful to go ahead and marry another man so fast. But she bit her lip and didn't say that at all. Because then she might say what she was actually thinking, that Max had betrayed her. Maybe, Max had betrayed both of them. And she couldn't work it out yet, how much she loved him, how much she missed him, how much she hated him. Instead she said, "I can't walk well enough yet to travel out for the wedding, B." Mare was going to physical therapy three times a week, and still, even with the help of her cane she moved like an eighty-year-old woman.

Bess laughed softly. "We're not having a wedding. Just a marriage. We'll go to city hall with my mother. You don't need to come."

She remembered the way Bess had tried to talk her out of marrying George from the bunk beds in their tiny dorm room. "You love this man?" she said softly to Bess now. But she wondered how it was even possible that Bess could *love* someone she'd never even told her best friend about.

Bess didn't say anything for a moment. Then she said, "Gaitlin loves the baby so much, Mare. You should see him with her."

It felt like there was more to say, more she should ask. Gaitlin loving another man's baby didn't make him marriage material for Bess. But even the thought of saying all that felt so heavy, so much effort. And what good would it do? She hadn't listened to Bess and Bess wouldn't listen to her. So instead, she murmured some trite congratulations and a request for pictures.

Once they hung up the phone, she uncorked a bottle of Merlot and poured herself a large glass. George was not yet home from work, and Will was asleep. She took a sip of the wine and stared at the certified letter again. She didn't have to open it. She would never have to know what it might say, what message Max might be sending her after death.

But even this letter felt the way everything always had with

Max. She couldn't simply ignore it, forget it. She couldn't let it go.

And so she slid her finger under the seal, and pulled the typed letter out. She read it, not quite believing what it said. What kind of a twenty-six-year-old man makes a will?

An estate lawyer.

Then she read it through a second time, and remarkably it still said exactly the same thing. Max had bequeathed her the house he'd recently bought outside Seattle, a few months before his death. He left it to her. Not to Bess. Not to his then unborn child. To her.

Did this mean that he had loved her, not Bess, after all? Or did it simply mean that of the two of them, Max thought that she might need the house more than Bess did.

A few weeks later, a card arrived in the mail with a photograph of Bess, her new husband and the baby standing in front of city hall. Mare squinted, focusing in hard on the baby's face, trying to see if there was any hint of something familiar, of Max.

But the baby was small, pink, bald and wrapped in a blanket, revealing not much more than her chubby cheeks.

Amelia

"AMELIA...? AMELIA...ARE YOU awake yet?" Liza's voice cut into the haziness of another strange dream.

I opened my eyes and couldn't quite put my finger on what exactly I'd been dreaming about. Something about my mother, about Will. Anxiety still pulsed through me, but now I wasn't exactly sure why. And it took me a second to remember where I was and what was going on. Then it hit me. *The hotel. Belles Woods. The movie. Will.* Liza had said she was coming for filming, but how did she get in my suite?

"Someone's...here?" Will's arms were still wrapped around me, and he whispered the words into my hair, panic slowly vibrating into his voice.

"My agent," I whispered back.

"Amelia?" She knocked on the bedroom door now. "I'm coming in."

"Hold on a minute," I yelled back, unable to disguise the

desperation in my voice. "Just let me get dressed. I'll come out. Have a seat on the couch."

Will quickly scrambled out of bed, searching the floor for his jeans, picking up mine by accident, then throwing them back down. I spied his on my side and I threw them to him. "I'll get rid of her. Go hide," I whispered.

"Where?"

I gave him a gentle shove toward the bathroom. Then kicked the remaining clothes from the floor under the bed. I grabbed my robe off the back of the chair and wrapped myself in it. Will shot me a slightly panicked look before he walked into the bathroom. He was smart. The bathroom was large. He would figure something out. And hopefully Liza had emptied her bladder before she'd barged in here.

I tied the robe tighter as I walked out into the living area and plastered a smile on my face. *Excited, eager actress.* Go. "Liza, you're here!" I added a bubbly and delighted-sounding laugh to show exactly how *pleased* I was.

"Of course, you know I wouldn't miss this."

"And so early in the morning!" I exclaimed.

"I came right here after my flight landed so I could escort you to set!"

Escort me to set? Well, that was not going to work out with Will hiding in the bathroom, and surely Gloria would want him to escort *her* to set. Suddenly all the *ground rules* felt like matchsticks that had gone up in flames with one misdirected strike.

Liza plopped down on the couch and sighed. "Don't rush. I can rest here for a bit while you finish getting ready. I barely got any sleep last night."

I bit my lip as I stared at her for a moment. Liza was tall, blonde, strikingly beautiful and ageless. I suspected she was in her fifties from knowing how long she'd been in the business, but she didn't look a day over thirty-nine, and even now, fresh off a plane and lacking sleep she appeared oddly flawless. She leaned back against the couch, and I wasn't exactly sure how to ask her to leave now without also telling her the truth. That there was a man hiding in my bathroom. A man who had spent the night. And not just any man, but Gloria Diamond's son.

Liza watched me watching her carefully, and then she frowned and fired off a round of questions: "You look upset. What's wrong? The room is great, right? You're ready for today, right?"

I nodded, swallowing back what I was really thinking, that I was not ready at all, and I'd considered quitting the film more than once since I'd arrived in Belles Woods. "Everything is great," I lied.

"Are you sure? You look..." Her voice trailed off as if she couldn't exactly put her finger on what was bothering her. It was almost like she could weirdly sense Will was here.

I nodded again, adding my most convincing smile. I absolutely could not tell her the truth about me and Will. For one thing, I'd be breaking our ground rules, and for another, it felt like if Liza knew, she'd convince me that whatever Will and I had found the last few days would need to be over. "I have some um...things to take care of before we leave this morning. Some private things. Could I meet you in the lobby in forty-five minutes?"

"Oh my god." Liza lowered her voice and pointed to the bedroom. "Is *he* in there?"

"He?" My voice broke, and everything I knew about acting left my head. How the hell could she actually know about Will? And why did it suddenly feel so hot in here? I fanned myself with my hand.

"Cameron Crawford?" She whispered and raised her eyebrows. "Not that I would blame you. He's adorable," she added. "Much cuter than Jase. Did you two...?"

Ugh, Cam. He was the farthest thing from what I would call *adorable*. I shook my head. "Cam? Definitely not. And no one is in there." That lie popped out along with an easy laugh. "I just need a little privacy to center myself before today. Get in the right frame of mind."

"Align your Gloria Diamond chakras?" Liza asked.

It was hard to tell whether that was a serious question or a joke. I nodded. "Something like that."

"Okay, then." She stood up. "I'll go find some coffee. Text me when you're ready. I'll meet you in the lobby." She grabbed me in a quick hug. Then she pulled back, looked at me and smiled. "I'm so excited to see you in action today. You're going to be fabulous as Gloria Diamond."

I swallowed back my doubts again, gave her a half smile and tried to remember how excited I'd felt the morning she'd first called to tell me I'd been offered the role. I'd stared at my mother's bookshelves then and thought that *this* was what I'd needed to get me out of my funk. It had felt strangely meant to be, but now I wasn't at all sure. What had Gloria said yesterday? *Life was a circle?*

"Liza, can I ask you something before you leave?"

She nodded. "Of course."

"Why did I get offered this role?"

"What do you mean?"

"I mean, whose idea was it to offer it to me in the first place?"

"Everybody wanted you. You're perfect for this part, Amelia."

I frowned. I didn't want the agent's answer; I wanted the real answer. "But I mean, did Gloria know who I was before I got here? Did she specifically ask for me to play her? Or was it the studio who wanted me?"

Liza smiled. "Gloria asked for you. She was a huge fan of Addy, and she said she could see something in you that reminded her of her younger self. She practically insisted it be you once the role opened up last minute."

Either Liza was bullshitting me right now or Gloria was playing some kind of game that I hadn't figured out the rules to. "So she knew exactly who I was, before I showed up here?" I mused. Granted, my acting name was not my given name, but Gloria knew that too. If she had known enough to insist *I* play her, I suspected she must've known who my mother was, even before I'd stepped off the plane in Seattle. Is that why it had felt like she didn't like me right away, because of some old connection or grievance she had with my mother? But if that were the case, why had she insisted on having me for the role to begin with? None of it made any sense.

"*A lot* of people know who you are," Liza was still talking. "Addy was a *huge* success."

She was exaggerating by a *huge* amount, but I suddenly remembered Will stuck in the bathroom and realized that for now I needed to let it, and her, go. "Okay," I said, pushing her gently toward the door. "I'll meet you in the lobby. Forty-five minutes, tops."

She nodded. "If you need a pep talk before then, text me and I'll be right back up here."

She had mistaken my questions for nerves. I shook my head. "I don't need a pep talk," I assured her.

I needed something, yes, but that wasn't it.

I waited a minute to make sure Liza was truly gone, and then I knocked on the bathroom door. "You okay in there?" I called out softly. I mean, there were worse fates than having to hide in a five-hundred-square-foot marble bathroom for ten whole minutes. But I still felt kind of bad that I'd shoved him in there.

"Yeah, come on in," Will called back.

I opened the door and found him sitting on the closed toilet lid, reading something on his phone and frowning deeply.

"You sure you're okay?"

He nodded. "Remember when I said I was going to have my assistant do a public records search on Max Cooper to see if we could find him?"

"And…?" I asked. "Did you find him?"

"He's dead," Will said softly.

Dead? I wasn't sure exactly why that hadn't occurred to me. My mother was dead too, after all. But for a few seconds it took my breath away. "We're never going to know the truth, are we?"

Will looked at me for another moment, and then looked

down at his bare feet. "I don't think so," he finally said. "But I'm starting to think that maybe it's better that way."

"I don't understand." I frowned. "I thought you wanted to know about the missing pieces of your past."

"Well, I haven't told you the weirdest part yet." Will stared at me and chewed on his bottom lip, as if considering whether or not to actually tell me the rest.

"Will, come on," I prodded. "What's the weirdest part?"

"Max used to own my mother's house," he said softly.

I shook my head, confused. "What house?"

"The house you were visiting last week. The house I grew up in, with the tree house out back." He paused, as if the memory of being there in the tree house with me the other night rendered him speechless for a moment. Then he added, "It was Max's house."

"You lived in Max's house with Max?" How could that be right? Then Will would've known him.

He shook his head. "No, property records show the house transferred to my mother after Max's death in 1986."

1986? That was the same year the photographs I'd found had been taken, both the one of my mother and the one of Gloria and Max together. Max must've died really young.

I realized Will was still talking and I looked up. "She and I didn't move to that house until 1991, though, after my father died," he was saying now.

"So Max left your mother his house when he died in 1986. Then you moved into it five years later, after your father died. And Gloria has lived there ever since?" I asked. Will nodded.

I had so many more questions. For one thing, how did Max and George both die so young in the span of a few years? Why did Gloria keep so much a secret? And how was my mother connected? "Okay, so then what's our next move?" I asked Will.

He chewed on his bottom lip. "I think maybe we should stop here," he said softly. "Wherever this leads next, I have a feeling it isn't going to be good for my mother. Maybe we should leave well enough alone."

I considered what he was saying, and wondered if he was right. Did Gloria have sinister reasons for fictionalizing her memoir? Two men who died young in such a short span of time. Could Will and I discover something truly awful about her past if we did keep digging? But I couldn't believe that diamond-studded, hot-toddy-drinking, bell-ringing Gloria had once had it in her to be a murderer. Something was off here, but I didn't think that's what it was. "We've come this far," I finally said. "Don't you want to know the truth about your past?"

Will shook his head. "I've gone my whole life without it." He paused and then added softly, "My mother is a piece of work, but she's still my mother. Maybe I just need to respect that she's had a reason to lie to me all these years and leave it at that."

Will sounded so forlorn that I couldn't bring myself to argue with him any more. And then I remembered, Liza was waiting for me in the lobby. I had to be on set soon, and I wasn't even dressed. "Let's talk more about this later, okay?" I said to Will. I tried to sound sympathetic, like I understood his hesitation, but really, I felt a weird sort of jealousy rising in my chest. My mother was gone. I wished again I could just pick up my phone and call her, ask her all the questions I now had about her past. I wanted to tell Will that he should forge ahead unafraid, that he should ask Gloria *everything* while she was still here to answer him. But instead, I told him I had to get ready to go meet Liza.

He nodded, stood up and wrapped me in a giant hug, holding me tightly to him. He held on a minute longer than I'd expected him to, as if maybe he too was worried that whatever was happening between us couldn't survive whatever was about to happen next.

Mare

1988

"I BOUGHT A HOUSE," George said, casually, one April night over dinner. He spoke in the same nonchalant tone he had just used when he'd said, *Pass the potatoes*.

Mare had been staring at the mashed potatoes on her plate, picking at them with her fork. She was here at dinner, but not really here, the way she had been in the months, no, over a year, since she'd come home from the hospital. Time hadn't softened the blow of Max's death. If anything, the pictures Bess sent of her growing daughter only made it worse. The girl had her father's blue eyes. It was clear, even in the Polaroids Bess enclosed with her letters.

"Well," George prodded. "Don't you want to know more about it?"

"A house?" She made tracks through the potatoes with her fork, and again, she thought about Max. About the letter that had come in the mail from his law firm last year. She dragged her fork back and forth through the potatoes now, and she wondered, was it possible George found out about Max's house? Is that why he was talking about a *house* now? She had hidden the letter and she hadn't yet decided what she would do with the house. And she supposed, sitting empty all this time, the house might've already fallen into a state of disrepair. Was it too late now to sell it, rent it, run away to live there amongst Max's things and pretend he was still alive...?

From across the table Will suddenly laughed, and Mare looked up. He'd started copying her potato motions with his fork, and now he made inroads. "Don't play with your food," she said flatly. But he didn't stop, and she didn't admonish him again.

"About twenty minutes from here," George continued, ignoring Will altogether. "Bit more out in the burbs, in Glen Coves. On a huge lot. There's a garden for you in the backyard."

Mare had never gardened in her life. In fact, she was certain that any plant she tried to grow would die on the vine. Just like everything else she had done in her life. Leaving home. College. Max. "Garden," she huffed. "You know I practically have a black thumb." It felt easier to argue with George about the garden than about the fact that he had bought a goddamn house without asking her first.

"Four bedrooms," George was saying now. He leaned in and lowered his voice. "Maybe we can even try for a little brother or sister. We'll have room now. You'd like that, Will, wouldn't you?"

Will stopped running tracks in his potatoes, his eyes suddenly wide with concern. His father had spoken directly to him. It rarely happened, and now Will stared back at George saying nothing at all, looking a little pale.

"George," Mare said, sternly. "I like our town house." She didn't really like the town house. It was small and nothing special.

But moving felt like so much effort, and she barely had it in her to get out of bed and limp through their small place these days.

"I already signed the papers," George said, as if with one easy sentence he could remind her that married to him she had no true autonomy. She was his wife and he was the boss. And now she had nothing else. No plan. No Max. No college degree. No career. Only a house that had been willed to her two thousand miles away from here sitting empty. "We'll move in in thirty days," George said.

Thirty days? She put her head down on the table, suddenly exhausted.

George got up, walked across the kitchen and grabbed a can of Budweiser from the fridge. He popped it open and took a long swig before sitting back down. "At least try and look happy, Mare. I'm doing this for you. I do everything for you." He spoke calmly but coldly. The same old excuse he always used. Every time he complained he hated his job. It was all *for her.*

"I am happy," she lied, not even bothering to pick her head up off the table. "Why wouldn't I be happy?"

The new house was large, and Mare found it to be obnoxiously gaudy.

The previous owners had wallpapered nearly every room in different visions of gold. Gold flowers. Gold leaves. Gold monkeys in the master bathroom for heaven's sakes.

"Do you like all this...gold?" she said to George. He had signed the papers, gotten the keys and left early from work to drive her and Will out to see it for the first time. Will ran through the downstairs now, and she walked slowly through each one of the gaudy rooms, still not totally efficient with her cane. Would she ever be?

George laughed and then kissed the top of her head. "I knew you'd hate the wallpaper. But, it'll give you some projects."

"But my...leg," she stammered. She was suddenly tired again, and she wanted to sit down but there wasn't even any furniture here yet. Instead she leaned against the golden pineapples on the wall by the large kitchen window and sighed.

"The doctor said your leg is as healed as it'll ever be," George said, somewhat sternly.

It was true. Dr. Graham had said that at her last visit. But she still needed a cane to walk; she would probably always need a cane to walk. And in her head, she had gone from a person who had done whatever she wanted, to being a person who needed to hold on to something, or someone, just to barely get by.

"I can hire someone to help you do the grunt work," George said. "But the house is your oyster. Make it whatever you want it to be. Make it yours. Make it ours," he added softly.

He suddenly sounded so kind, that she felt a burst of something unexpected for him. Not love exactly, but gratefulness.

Amelia

THE GLORIA WIG the stylist placed on my head looked nothing like Gloria's hair in the few photos from the 1980s that I'd come to find of her the last few days. Nothing at all like the teased bangs of Emily's Polaroids, or even the soft shoulder-length brown waves she'd sported in that one photo with Max Cooper I'd caught a stolen glimpse of on her writing desk.

Instead, it was a platinum blonde, full, straight, shoulder-length wig, similar to her hair color and wig style now, if maybe only a few inches shorter.

I tugged at the ends of it gently as I stared into the giant mirror. I liked my '80s makeup—a nice pink lip and soft blue eyeshadow—and large gold hoop earrings in my ears, even though it all seemed like the opposite of how dark dresses-in-all-black Gloria would've looked at the time. But today's scene called for me to move into a brand-new house that George had surprised me with. In the script, and the memoir, Gloria is upbeat, elated, on this particular day. *It was life at its very best*, she had written in her memoir, *before it would all explode, literally, a few short years later.* The look they'd given me, the makeup, would certainly reflect that tone, even though I was skeptical if any of it had actually happened this way in real life at all. And now as I stared at my reflection, I thought about Will's weird revelation this morning, that Max Cooper was dead and he had willed Gloria the house she lived in to this day.

"Oh my god, you look great." Liza clapped her hands, and turned to murmur a compliment to Mimi, the very kind and talented woman who had done my makeup and placed the wig. I murmured a quick "Thank you"—she had a done a good job. I was every bit the Gloria her memoir presented her to be. Just like that. And I tried to push all the many doubts I had out of my head and center my focus on what I needed to do this morning. Who I needed to become. A cheerful, 1980s version of Gloria, who loved her husband and her life more than anything.

A knock on my trailer door interrupted my thoughts. "Everyone decent?" *Cam.*

"Come on in," I shouted, and Liza's jaw practically dropped to the floor as he opened the door and stepped inside. He wore a dark well-fitted blue three-piece suit, and with his hair gelled back and colored a darker brown, he did look remarkably like George in the wedding photo included in the book.

"Hello, wife," he said to me, with a huge smile that revealed his bright white teeth and symmetrical dimples. "Don't you look pretty today."

I watched Liza watch him, her mouth open slightly. She shot me a sideways look that said, *Are you sure you weren't hiding him in your bedroom this morning?* I rolled my eyes at her.

"Hey, Cam. You ready to go?" I took one last look in the mirror to make sure my wig was straight and then hopped down from the makeup chair.

He reached for my hand, but I quickly shook him off and opened the door of the trailer. The sun was shining today, as if Gloria herself had made a deal with the devil for the perfect weather for us to film the first scene. We were beginning with the exterior shot of George showing Gloria their new house for the first time. Then moving to the interior shot, of the George and Gloria sex scene in front of a roaring fire. I had not totally wrapped my head around that second part, which would require a wardrobe and makeup change and would not be happening until after lunch.

Once outside my trailer, Cam grabbed my arm and steered me toward set. He held on tight enough now so I couldn't let go without making a scene. I sighed and kept walking, and suddenly dreaded every moment of pretend sex with him this afternoon.

Liza had asked earlier if I needed a pep talk, and maybe I did. But as Cam and I walked onto set, it felt weirdly too late for that now. For better or for worse, I was about to be Gloria Diamond.

Whatever the hell that meant.

Exterior new Chicago house, day.

George (hands covering Gloria's eyes): I have a surprise for you!

Gloria (laughs): Another surprise? George, stop, you're too much. Why are you so good to me?

George uncovers her eyes and Gloria stares at the large two-story colonial house in front of them.

Gloria: I don't…understand.

George: It's ours, baby. (He dangles a key out in front of him.)

Gloria: You...bought a house for us?

George nods, and Gloria grabs his neck and squeals with glee.

Gloria: Oh my god, George, it's the most perfect house I've ever seen.

George: There's a garden out back. And a tree house for Will.

Gloria (covers her mouth with her hand): You know I've always dreamed of having a garden!

George swoops her up into his arms, unlocks the front door and carries her over the threshold.

But on the fourth take, Cam tripped, stumbled up the steps and accidentally knocked my head right into the doorframe.

I caught the smallest glimpse of Will standing off to the side with Gloria, just before I passed out.

Annie

1990

SHE DIDN'T LIKE CHICAGO.

She never felt warm, no matter how many blankets she asked for at night. She missed sunshine. The ocean. Her short-sleeve dresses. And her father.

It's only for a few weeks, Annie-bear, her mom told her when they'd first arrived. *Just till I can get back on my feet.*

But even at the age of almost-four, it was easy enough to tell when her mom was lying to her. Which had been happening a lot lately. And then she overheard her mom and Miss Mare talking about how they could stay as long as they liked, forever, if they wanted. *Forever?*

Forever was the longest time. It was the end of a rainbow, or the other side of the Pacific Ocean. Everything unreach-able, unimaginable.

That was when she decided she would run away. She had

her father's phone number written on a scrap of paper pinned inside her backpack, from when she would take it with her to school back in California. All she had to do was take her backpack, walk to the payphone she'd seen outside the Dominick's supermarket and call him collect. If she told him how much she hated it here, he'd come get her right away.

She decided to sneak out early the next morning. Everyone was still asleep, and she grabbed her backpack and tiptoed around her mother, walked carefully down the steps and out the front door.

Only, she had forgotten that you always needed to wear a coat in Chicago. It was snowing outside, and she couldn't remember exactly which way to turn to get to the Dominick's. Still, that didn't stop her. She did eeny, meeny, miney, moe and then turned the direction her finger told her, down the street.

She walked for a few blocks, and felt certain she was supposed to turn somewhere, so she did eeny, meeny, miney, moe again. But then it was snowing harder. Nothing looked familiar anymore. (But maybe that was because of the snow?) Had she turned the wrong way? Maybe she should go back and try again tomorrow? But which way was back again? Now she wasn't sure.

The sidewalks were suddenly slippery; she slid and crashed onto her bottom. And then she began to cry. She wanted to go home. To her dad's house in Pasadena, to her bedroom with the Strawberry Shortcake wallpaper. Her parents had let her choose the wallpaper right after she'd turned three. It wasn't fair they'd let her pick the wallpaper and then told her about a divorce and made her move out a month after they'd put it up on the walls. The thought of Strawberry Shortcake still there in her room without her made her cry even harder.

"There you are." A boy's voice startled her, and she looked up. Miss Mare's son was a few years older than her and hadn't been very nice to her since they arrived. This was the first time he'd even spoken to her.

"Did you follow me?" She crossed her arms in front of her chest and tried to scowl. But then she shivered from sitting in the cold, cold snow.

Will took off his coat and handed it to her. "Put this on or you'll catch a cold."

Did sitting in the snow make you catch a cold? She didn't know if that was true. She'd had lots of colds in California and had never once seen snow before now. But she was freezing, so she listened and put on his coat.

"What are you doing out here, anyway?" Will asked.

"Running away." It suddenly felt like a stupid plan and she started to cry again. Even if she got to the payphone and called him, maybe her dad wouldn't come for her. Maybe divorce meant he didn't come when she called him anymore. Maybe that's why her mom had brought her out here to begin with.

Will nodded and held out his hand so she could use it to pull herself up. "I hate it here too," he said.

"Why?" she asked him. "You live here." She couldn't imagine hating your own home. She wanted to go home right now more than anything.

"My mom is sad all the time and my dad scares me," he said softly.

"Why would your dad scare you?"

He shrugged. "He pretends to be nice. But then when he thinks no one's watching him, he's actually mean."

Annie wasn't quite sure what Will meant by that but she didn't ask him to explain more. "I miss my dad," she told him instead. "He's not scary at all. You could run away with me."

Will shook his head. "Kids can't run away. It's not safe."

"Are there kidnappers here?" They had been warned about this at school in California. Strange men who might offer you candy if you got into their van. But she hadn't ever seen anything like that in Pasadena. It felt like a story. Something in a book. But then, so did snow.

"There's kidnappers everywhere." Will spoke with such authority, she believed him. "So you can't run away, okay?" He stopped talking for a minute and stared at her. Then he said, "But we can be friends while you're here if you want. We can hate it here together."

She nodded, accepting that solution for now. Because it seemed like maybe hating something with a friend was much better than hating something alone.

Then he showed her how to walk on the sidewalk when it was slippery. Short steps, like a penguin.

He held on to her arm, and they were penguins together as they slowly walked back to his house. And she didn't fall again.

Amelia

I OPENED MY EYES, and Will was right there, his kind face hovering above me. "You helped me," I murmured. "We were friends."

He brow creased with worry, and he gently put his hand on my cheek. "How's your head?"

"The snow," I said. "I slipped. I wanted to run away."

"You hit your head when Cam tripped walking up the steps," Will said, frowning. "You were feeling dizzy so the set EMT looked you over and brought you here to rest for a little bit. You don't remember any of that?" His voice was thick with worry.

I squinted and looked around. *Right.* I had been on set. Playing Gloria Diamond. Where was I now? On the couch in my trailer. Will was here, but Will had been there for me in the past too. Or was that some weird dream I had after I hit my head? "I think I was at your house when I was a kid," I said softly. It looked exactly like the house on set. Had seeing it triggered an old memory? Or had I just made up the whole thing?

Will's frown creased deeper as he sat on the edge of the couch and gently put his hand on the top of my wig. "You hit your head pretty hard," he said. "Does it hurt?"

I tried to nod and that hurt so I stopped midway. "It doesn't feel great."

"I brought you some ice." He stood to go get it, but I reached for his sleeve and tugged him back to the couch. I didn't want him to move away from me. I wanted him to stay right where he was.

Then I remembered our ground rules. How had he even gotten in here? And where was Liza? "Where's everyone else?" I asked.

"Eating lunch," he said. "Don't worry. I snuck in here, told Gloria I had to make a work call. Cam is very upset that you got hurt and they're all working hard to console him." He rolled his eyes.

I laughed a little but then stopped when that hurt my head too. "Poor Cam," I said. I was not his biggest fan, sure, but I didn't think he'd knocked me into the door on purpose. The reality that this was how the shoot began sank in my chest now, and it felt like a bad omen. I wondered if it was truly too late for me to quit.

The door to my trailer suddenly swung open and Will jumped up from the couch as Liza waltzed in. "Oh thank god, you're awake." She eyed Will, then me, then Will again, and she bit her lip.

"This is Gloria's son," I said to her. "Will, have you and my agent, Liza, met? Will was kind enough to bring me some ice."

Red crept across the back of Will's neck, across his cheeks, and I knew he was probably thinking of how he hid in the bathroom when Liza had barged into my hotel room earlier.

But Liza had no clue. "No, I don't believe we have met." Liza swept toward Will and shook his hand all in one motion. "You brought ice. Are you…a doctor?"

"Lawyer," I said.

Liza laughed. "We're not gonna sue. Accidents happen." She was joking. Kind of?

Will nodded. "Well…if you're all right…" He stared at me, and I nodded slightly trying not to move my head too much. "I guess I should…get back…"

Our eyes met for a moment, and I offered him my bravest smile. *We can be friends while you're here. We can hate it together.* Had that happened once, in another lifetime? I felt almost certain it had. But if that was true, then why didn't Will remember it too?

He left, and after the door shut behind him, Liza came and sat down next to me on the couch. "How are you doing, kiddo?" she asked, kindly.

How was I doing? Confused about what was going on, why I was here, and whether or not I'd really known Will in the past. Worried that continuing with this role was going to have the opposite effect on my career we'd both hoped, if I truly couldn't figure out how to pull it off. But of course, that was not what she was asking.

"Does it hurt a lot?" Liza was saying now.

"It's just a little bump," I said softly. "I'll be fine." But then I tried to sit all the way up, and my head really did ache. I gingerly removed the Gloria wig, lay back against the couch pillow and sighed.

"Okay," Liza said. "I'm going to tell them you need the rest of the day off and then maybe I should take you to the ER."

I hated hospitals and was not about to agree to the ER unless I passed out and Liza dragged me there without my consent. And I didn't plan to do that. I remembered what Will had just told me. "The set EMT already checked me out. I don't need the ER," I insisted.

Liza stared at me, squinted a little, and then sighed. "Well, I

can at least get you back to the hotel so you can rest more comfortably."

I opened my mouth to argue with her but a break this afternoon actually sounded nice. My head really throbbed. My
hotel room and the bottle of ibuprofen I knew I had there suddenly sounded amazing.

"I mean the lengths you went to to get out of having pretend-
sex with that gorgeous, gorgeous man this afternoon." Liza
laughed.

"There's always tomorrow," I quipped, hoping I was hiding the relief I was actually feeling at putting it off for another
day. Then I added, "Hey, Liza, I think I really need to talk to
Gloria. Can you see if you can set up a meeting with her later
this afternoon?"

Liza frowned. "Work can wait until tomorrow. You should
rest."

But how was I supposed to tell her that this had nothing at
all to do with the role anymore, and everything to do with my
past, with Gloria's past? With understanding who my mother
was, who she once had been. And that now I realized, it probably wasn't my acting abilities that had brought me here at all,
but some strange intersection of all our lives I still couldn't
quite put my finger on.

Mare

1990

WHEN BESS CALLED to tell Mare she was getting a divorce, the first thing Bess said was: "Where am I even supposed to go?"

"Here." Mare answered her immediately, without even thinking it through first, without contemplating how strange it was that Bess had seen her marriage to Gaitlin as a place to live more than a man to love.

Mare had finally finished the renovations on the new house. It had taken her nearly two years, but now, all the gold wallpaper was gone, replaced with more subtle brown and blue paint tones. And somehow, scraping a thousand golden pineapples off a kitchen wall, one by one, had been a strange kind of therapy. She had made the gaudy ugly house beautiful, hers. And then she had told herself: new house, new life. Will went to school now during the day, and she was back to writing again. Max was gone, but, in her novel, he was still very much alive.

"I couldn't impose like that," Bess said, finally responding to her offer.

"There's plenty of extra room, B," Mare said quickly. "You can stay as long as you'd like."

Bess laughed, like she was certain Mare was joking.

"I'm serious!" Mare said. "You and Annie should come and stay with us until you get back on your feet."

"Live together again," Bess murmured. "Like college?"

But nothing was like college anymore, was it? That thought sank like a stone.

"Annie might like a change," Bess contemplated out loud on the other end of the line.

Annie was almost four, and Mare had yet to meet her in person. And in the latest photographs Bess had sent, Mare could see that Annie had the bluest blue eyes. Just like Max. "It'll be fun," Mare added, her voice a little stretched because maybe she was already regretting the offer.

"All right, M," Bess finally agreed. "Just for a little while."

"What do you mean stay with us?" George frowned later that night and loosened his tie, before removing it altogether and sitting down at the table for dinner.

"You love Bess," Mare said.

George frowned. "I do?"

"You used to, back in college."

"I used to love a lot of things back in college." George said it with such a pointed stare that it felt clear he was somehow denigrating her. She glanced at Will across the table to see if he'd noticed, but he seemed to be concentrating hard on dipping a chicken nugget into barbecue sauce.

"Well, I used to love a lot of things too," Mare said, throwing it back at him. That wasn't true, though. She had loved Max, and she had loved Bess, but she had merely tolerated George, even in college.

George sighed. "A few days, Mare. No more."

She nodded, but she was inwardly fuming. Who was he to tell her how long her best friend could stay in the house she had meticulously redecorated herself from top to bottom? Maybe George had signed the papers, but the house was hers now. And she would do whatever she liked.

"Be nice," Mare finally added. "Bess is getting a divorce."

George glared at her, dropped his fork on his plate, and the clatter was loud enough that Will looked up. Then George stood and stomped out of the room.

Mare wasn't quite sure what had set him off to that degree, but maybe it was that she had said the word *divorce* out loud. And he had heard it something like a promise, or a threat.

It was one thing to see Annie in the photographs, but another altogether to see her in person. *Those eyes.* It was as if Max had suddenly reappeared and was staring at her again in the form of a tiny blue-eyed girl.

Annie stood there silently in the foyer when they first arrived, and gazed up at Mare with *those eyes.* Mare looked away first. And then Bess grabbed Mare in a hug.

"Thank you so much for having us." Bess held on so tightly that her words were almost swallowed up in Mare's hair.

For the smallest moment, Mare felt responsible for everything that had happened to Bess. To Max. To her. If only she hadn't run into Max that night in Seattle, years ago, Bess and Annie and Max would all be across the country now. Max would still be breathing. Bess wouldn't be so sad and alone. That little girl would have a father. And Mare would have two perfectly working legs. All the what-ifs hit her and she swallowed hard, fighting back tears.

"How about a glass of wine?" Mare said when they finally let go of each other. "You look like you could use a glass of wine, B."

But the truth was, Mare could really use a glass of wine herself.

Amelia

LIZA, OR MAYBE it was the studio, sent a doctor to my suite to check me out. He assured me that I had no signs of a serious head injury, though I was supposed to report to the ER if I had any dizziness or vision changes or other unusual symptoms. I was already feeling better after a few ibuprofen, and almost felt a little silly for having left set and for holding up production on the very first day.

"Phew," Liza exhaled after he left, doing an exaggerated swipe of her forehead with her hand. "Crisis averted."

If Liza only knew about the personal Gloria-related crisis raging in my head right now, I wasn't so sure she'd be sighing. "Did you get that meeting with Gloria set up?" I asked her.

"Just stop worrying about Gloria," Liza said, as she ushered me into the bedroom and then walked me to the bed. "Lie down. Get some rest. Take care of yourself."

"Liza, I'm serious. I need to talk to her." I sat on the side of the bed and then immediately noticed Will's hoodie, still lying across the chair by the sliding glass door. Luckily Liza didn't seem to see it, or if she did, she didn't register it as belonging to a man.

"Okay, okay, I'll work on it." Liza sighed. "Now, I'm serious. Get some rest."

As soon as I heard the door close behind her, I got out of bed, picked up Will's sweatshirt and wrapped myself in it. It was warm and it still smelled like him, like the evergreens surrounding his childhood tree house. *We can be friends. We can hate it together.* Had we really been friends, thirty years ago? Is that why I found myself so drawn to him now?

And at that thought, wrapped in the warmth of his sweatshirt, I lay down in the bed and promptly fell asleep.

When I opened my eyes again, the room was dark, my mind empty. I must've slept the whole afternoon away, in a thick and totally dreamless sleep.

I looked around for Will, half hoping he would be here, sitting in the chair where his sweatshirt had been earlier. But the bedroom was empty, quiet. I grabbed my phone off the nightstand, but there was only a message from Cam telling me how bad he felt and how he hoped I was okay, and then a message from Liza, telling me Gloria was too busy to talk today and that I should rest and worry about the movie tomorrow.

Liza should know better than to think I would listen, and I got out of bed, felt the throb of my head again and downed a few more ibuprofen with a glass of water. I texted Will, and when he didn't respond right away, I tried to call him. But he didn't answer. And, anyway, I wasn't sure if he'd help me talk to Gloria now or not, after he'd decided this morning he was done searching for answers. I felt restless, impatient, unmoored. What else could I do but go up to Gloria's suite myself and demand she talk to me?

The birdcage elevator seemed to rattle even more than it had yesterday, and by the time I reached the top, I felt a little nauseous. Was that one of the symptoms I was supposed to watch for? Probably. But I ignored it, took a deep breath and rang the bell. No one answered, and I rang it again, twice. Still nothing. Liza had said they were busy. Why had I automatically assumed that was a lie?

Then the door swung open, and Will stood there on the other side. He looked surprised, and then seemed to register it was me standing in front of him, because he broke into a smile. "Nice sweatshirt," he said.

I had forgotten I was wearing it, and I curled my fingers into the too-long sleeves. "You left it in my room," I said sheepishly. Then I added, "I came up here looking for Gloria."

"I figured." He tapped the doorway gently with his hand. I mean, obviously. This was her suite. My face reddened a bit, but I guessed I should be thankful he'd opened the door and noticed me in his sweatshirt, not her. "They went out somewhere for dinner with Cam and the director I think? Or the screenwriter? I can't keep them straight."

I laughed. The director was a middle-aged man and the screenwriter was a woman younger than me. Will was so outside of what went on in the world of my job, it made him even more adorable. If there was a man who was the opposite of Jase in every way, that was Will. Is that why I liked him? Maybe partly. "So what are you doing here?" I asked him. "No dinner for you?"

"I get to watch Jasper." He rolled his eyes. "No, I didn't want to go anyway so I offered to let Tate escort Gloria instead while I stayed back on Jasper duty." He chuckled softly. "I was hoping to check on you in a little bit. Come on in. Come have a seat."

"I called you," I said, as he took my hand gently and led me inside to the large couch.

It felt weird to be in here with Will, in a room I'd associated so far as Gloria's. Clearly it was a hotel room, not her house, but I still felt oddly like an intruder, invading her space while she was out to dinner. *Don't touch my things.* Here I was, in Will's sweatshirt, holding Will's hand. Jasper was lying in his crate off to the side of the couch, and when he noticed me, he picked up his head and let out a half growl, the diamonds in his collar glinting in the yellow light of the end table lamp.

"Jasper, cool it," Will said. Jasper lowered his head in shame, and then Will turned back to me. "I just saw you called. Sorry, I was on the phone with the office."

"Oh, am I interrupting?"

He shook his head. "Not at all." He paused for a moment, stared at me. "I've been wanting to see you. I was worried about you after you hit your head. And I felt like the way we left everything earlier in your room was…"

"Weird?" I finished his sentence.

He nodded, but maybe that wasn't exactly what he'd been trying to say. "I just… I hope I didn't upset you this morning. I know we've been spending some time together because we were trying to figure out my mother's past. And I told you I was done. So theoretically maybe that makes us done. But—"

I scooted across the couch so I was close enough to him that I was almost sitting in his lap. "Will." I said his name softly and ran my finger across the stubble on his cheek. "I meant it when I said I liked you."

His lips curved into a smile and I slowly traced them with my forefinger. He reached up for my hand, held it, then kissed it gently. "Good," he said. "Because I meant it too."

"So that's why I'm going to tell you this," I said. "I know you don't want to look into the past anymore, but I might've remembered something this morning. I think maybe being on set, seeing a replica of your old house, triggered an early childhood memory."

Will's smile slowly faded into a small frown and I was pretty sure that meant he didn't really want to hear what I was going to say.

But I couldn't stop myself. "I think maybe we knew each other when we were younger," I said.

Though I was pretty sure I'd said this same thing groggily in my trailer this morning, it didn't seem to register with Will until right now that I was trying to tell him something real. "I didn't know you," Will said.

"Are you sure?" I asked him. "You said your earliest clear childhood memory was the night your father died, your mother running out of the house with the picture of her and Max." I paused and turned to look at him again, and his expression was bewildered. My chest ached. *Stop talking.* And yet, I couldn't. "I think my mom and I came to visit you sometime before that. It was snowing. I tried to run away and I got lost and you helped me. I think something bad happened after that, but I can't remember what it was. And maybe that's why Gloria brought me back here now?"

Will gently pushed me off him, moved down the couch, put his head in his hands and didn't say anything for a few moments.

"Will," I said his name softly. "You really don't remember me at all?"

"I can't do this," he finally said. "Please."

I stood up, and I was hit by another wave of dizziness or maybe it was grief. I felt very suddenly like I'd just lost something. I grabbed the edge of the couch to steady myself, and Will seemed to notice me struggling, quickly stood and reached for me.

He wrapped his arms around me, held on to me, held me up. I closed my eyes and leaned back into him. If this was the last time he was ever going to hug me, I wanted to remember everything about it, how warm and steady I felt with his arms around me, how he smelled like coffee and pine cones. "Ground rule," he said, into my hair. "I like you. You like me. Let's not talk about anything else but that."

It was a stupid *rule*, and I knew it would be impossible to follow. But for now, for the night, maybe I could pretend. "Okay," I finally said. "Come down to my room later when you're done watching the dog?"

Will kissed the top of my head and sighed. "It shouldn't be too long. I'll be down there in a little bit."

Back in my own room, I flopped down on the couch and wondered what I could do next on my own. My mother was gone. Max was dead. Will was out. Gaitlin was clueless.

And part of me knew that what Will had said earlier this morning was right. The past was the past, and maybe nothing good would come from digging it up. In the present, I had the job of a lifetime. I had Will (who cared if there were *ground rules* attached?), whom I really, really liked.

But there was also the strangest feeling of grief that made my heart pause every time I thought about it, that picture of my mother from Marge's attic. Whatever history she'd had with Gloria, now it felt like I *had* to understand it all in order to ever truly let her go.

I heard a knock on my door, and I jumped. Will hadn't been kidding when he said it wouldn't be long.

"That was quick," I said, as I opened the door.

But standing on the other side was not Will. It was Gloria.

Mare

1991

BESS'S VISIT WENT from one week to two. From one month to four.

Winter bloomed into spring, and then, Mare almost couldn't imagine Bess ever leaving. How had she lived life without Bess since college? How had she existed day by day, without her best friend by her side?

It was Bess who finally planted vegetables in the backyard garden, who told Mare that she would teach her how to can sauce at the end of the summer once she harvested her tomatoes. It was Bess who put the children to bed with an animated story and then snuck out to the back porch with a bottle of George's gin tucked under her shirt and two paper cups to drink it stashed in her bra. It was Bess who chose the light blue fabric for the living room curtains and then sewed them herself while Mare lay on the couch across the room, reading a book.

Mare remembered the way she lost and forgot things, and Bess put them back together. How had Mare even been whole without Bess by her side? (Maybe, she hadn't.)

By April, Bess started picking Will up from school, and Mare was taking an extended long afternoon to write after lunch. Bess even cooked dinner for everyone once she got home from getting Will. And then with her mind completely free again, Mare realized, for the first time since the accident she felt happy and strangely whole.

"Tell me about your novel," Bess said to Mare one May evening, when it was warm enough to sip George's gin barefoot on the back porch. George was not yet home from work and, anyway, none the wiser that Bess had found his stash of liquor in the basement. He was a beer guy, except on very special occasions. He'd never even taken the liquor out of the box he'd used to move it here.

"Oh, I'm not sure how to describe it yet, B." The book had existed solely in her head, and in jumbled, roughly sketched pages. Until right now, no one had ever asked her to talk about it. It was a literary mystery about a man and a woman having an affair, except that the man gets murdered. But in many ways, the man was Max, and the truth was, Mare had no idea how to piece the mystery together. Her novel, at the moment, like what had happened in her real life, made very little sense.

"Is it a love story?" Bess asked softly. Her face was a shadow, and Mare couldn't quite gauge her expression, but she felt Bess's eyes on her.

Mare shook her head. "I think it might be a tragedy."

"So it'll make me cry?" Bess sighed. "Remember in college, I always told you, you should write love stories. They're my favorite."

Mare laughed a little, remembering Bess whispering that

to her at night from the bunk bed above. "You're still reading Danielle Steel, like you did back in college?"

Bess held up the paperback of *Hollywood Wives* she had in her lap and shook her head. "Jackie Collins. It's delicious. You should read it. And then, you should write your own romance novel."

Mare shook her head, not telling Bess that she had, in fact, caught some of the miniseries on TV. The glamour, the unapologetic sex. She couldn't imagine herself being fearless enough to tell that kind of story. "I don't think I'd even know how to write any kind of love story. I'm not sure I even believe in love, B." She was thinking about Bess's divorce, about being married to George and even about Max's betrayal. "Men are all terrible," she added.

Bess reached for Mare's hand in the darkness and squeezed it. "But maybe we don't even need men?"

She was right; their friendship had survived so much. And it had been wonderful having her here these last months. "Exactly. You're never going back to California." Mare squeezed Bess's hand right back "I'm not letting you go."

Bess nudged Mare's bare toes with her own and giggled softly. "Who says I want to leave? Maybe you couldn't even make me if you tried."

"Good," Mare said, giving Bess's tiny hand one more squeeze. "So it's settled, then. You and I will be together forever."

And if there was one perfect moment before the end of everything, it was this one. Mare would think that later—Bess next to her on the back patio, the warm spring night, the warm cast of the gin rushing through her body and the warmth of her best friend's hand holding on to her own.

Mare would think, if only she could've paused things right there, right on that carefree happy night, her life might've been good forever.

Amelia

"I HEARD YOU were looking for me," Gloria said, with a frown. She rested her weight on her cane, and after I got over my shock that it was her, not Will, standing in the hallway, I opened the door wider and gestured for her to come sit down.

"I was," I said. "But Liza said you were busy."

"I am," she said pointedly, and I suspected she had come straight here from dinner, as she wore a black shift dress, embroidered with diamonds around the collar and cutout sleeves, and still had a gray diamond-studded fur stole draped through the crooks of her elbows. I pondered over how much her outfit must be worth as she took a little time to get down on the couch, and then she rested her cane against the side of the coffee table. "How's your head?" she asked me, once she was seated.

"Better," I said. "I think I'll live."

"Glad to hear it." She didn't quite sound *glad*, but she wasn't scowling either. She stared at me, like she was waiting for me to explain myself, but she was the one who'd showed up here, so I didn't say anything for a moment, I stared right back at her. "I suppose I came here because I have something I want to say to you," she finally said.

"Go ahead," I said quickly.

"Stay away from Will." Her words vibrated and then settled.

It was not at all what I had been expecting her to say, and I opened my mouth in surprise, then closed it without saying anything at all. "Will?" I finally repeated lamely. We had so many ground rules. How could Gloria possibly know anything? "I don't understand."

"You're wearing his sweatshirt," she said pointedly.

"I was cold on set after I hit my head." The lie burst out of me, sounding believable.

She stared at me and frowned. "I saw you. In the cameras outside my house last week." She spoke slowly, decisively. "The tree house. Were you cold then too?"

Cameras? Gloria had outdoor cameras pointed at Will's tree house? I felt warmth creeping across my cheeks and put my hands up to try and cool them. Gloria had already known about me and Will before we had set any ground rules. How was that even possible?

"I came here to make a deal with you," Gloria was saying calmly now.

"A deal?" Even repeating her words I felt like I was about to sell my soul to the devil, and I suddenly felt queasy.

"You've been asking me questions all week. Ask me *one* you want the answer to the most, and I'll answer it for you right here, right now. Truthfully."

Truthfully? Did Gloria even have it in her to differentiate between the truth and fiction? Then I remembered she was trying to cut a deal. "And what do I have to do in return?" I asked her.

"Stay away from Will," she said coldly. "Forget you ever met him."

I chewed on my bottom lip and curled my fingers into the

long, soft cuffs of his sweatshirt. "What if I don't want to?" I said softly. Maybe Will was right. Maybe the past was the past and the future could be something different, something that had the two of us wrapped inside a little bubble where nothing—or no one—else mattered.

"You already hurt him once," Gloria said. "I won't watch you do it again."

Hurt him? I would never do that. But then I thought about little Will, holding my hand in the snow. I would've been three or four years old back then. Had something happened that I couldn't remember now? "I don't understand. How did I hurt Will?" I asked Gloria.

"Is that your one question?" She raised her eyebrows.

I sighed and shook my head. I had so many questions, but as much as I liked Will, that one wasn't at the top of my list. I thought about it for another moment. There was one thing I wanted to know. No, I *needed* to know. "Why did you bring me here to play you? Really?"

Gloria nodded, like this was exactly the question she had been expecting, and I felt certain her answer was about to have something to do with my mother. "Max," she said softly.

Max Cooper? The man who had died, whose house Gloria lived in. The man who made Will think that nothing good could come from continuing to dig into the past. The man who Gloria had looked truly happy with in the photograph I'd found on her desk. But what did any of that have to do with me? "I don't understand," I finally said.

"Because Max was the love of my life." Suddenly Gloria sounded breathless, like she was speaking through a rush of wind. "And because you, Annie, are his daughter."

Mare

1991

"BESS NEEDS TO LEAVE," George said.

He was sitting in the dark at the kitchen table, and when his words slurred through the pitch black, Mare jumped. She'd gotten out of bed to get a glass of water and she hadn't even realized he was home yet, that he was down here. He'd called around dinnertime to say he'd be home late, and after they'd put the kids to sleep, she and Bess had been watching *Chances Are* on cable in her bedroom. They'd both fallen asleep halfway through, and Mare had been having some weird half dream about a reincarnated Max, who looked strangely like Robert Downey Jr. from the movie, and then she'd awoken, disoriented. She'd just sent a sleepy Bess to her own room and had stumbled down the stairs for water.

She flipped on the light now, and then she saw George slouching against his chair, still in his work clothes, his red tie loosened around his neck. He took a sip from his can of beer, what appeared to be the fifth of a six-pack, judging from the empty cans in front of him.

"You need to go to bed," she said firmly.

She walked over to the table and started gathering the empty cans to throw them away. But he suddenly lunged forward and grabbed her wrist. She cried out in surprise, and the empty cans clattered against the oak table.

She tried to pull out of his grasp, but he held on tight. "George," she said his name sternly. "You're hurting me."

"I mean it, Mare. Bess needs to leave. Tomorrow. Or else."

She tried to yank her arm away but he held on too tight. He stared at her for another moment and then let go of her so suddenly she lost her balance, tumbled back. She had left her cane in the bedroom and now she grabbed onto the edge of the table to steady herself. Once she regained her footing, she spat back at him: "*Or else?* Is that a threat?"

He took another swig of beer. "Maybe it is."

"You're drunk. On a Wednesday night. Why would I listen to you?" Distaste for him curled in her voice and came out sounding a little like a threat of her own. Though what she was threatening exactly was unclear, even to her. If Bess left, could Mare leave with her? She had planned to leave George to be with Max, once, but what if she left George to be on her own, with her friend? Like Bess had said, maybe they didn't need men. Though it occurred to her now they had no jobs, no degrees, two kids and no place to live between them.

"I don't want Bess to leave," she finally said, firmly. "And this is my house too."

George took another sip of his beer and seemed to consider this. "Don't think...I won't...make her." He stumbled drunkenly over his words, making this threat sound juvenile, almost cartoonish.

Mare laughed. "Okay, George," she said softly. "We'll talk

tomorrow once you've sobered up." She paused and then she added, "Having Bess here makes me happy. Don't you want me to be happy?"

"Happy?" George let out a bitter laugh. "You mean like you were when Max fucking Cooper was here?" He suddenly sounded more sober.

"Don't say his name like that," Mare said quietly. "What gives you the right?" No one had uttered Max's name out loud in her presence in at least a year, maybe two. And definitely not George. She hated the way Max's name sounded in his voice now, bitter, angry, awful. Did George look at Bess's little girl and see Max in her blue eyes too? Mare doubted he had the capacity to think past what he had been told, what was spoon-fed to him. Bess was here because of a divorce from another man. George hadn't seen beyond that. Had he? So what was he even talking about now? "Bess is my best friend," Mare finally said. "Of course she makes me happy."

"What do you and Bess even do all day when I'm at work?" George laughed a little and finished off the fifth can of beer before reaching for the sixth. "I saw the two of you asleep in our bed tonight. Are you fucking her behind my back too?"

He was so drunk he wasn't making any sense. She refused to dignify any of that with a response. "Don't you think you've had enough?" she said instead. But suddenly the word *too* rang in her ears. Had he known what was going on with her and Max? Was that what had gotten him all riled up now?

He ignored her and opened up the beer can. "I want Bess gone by the time I get home from work tomorrow." George took another swig of beer, and then he added, "Or I'll get rid of her same way I got rid of Max."

Same way I got rid of Max?

The words tumbled in her brain. She remembered nothing, knew nothing, of what had really happened the night of the accident. What was George saying now? That he had been involved somehow? But that didn't make any sense. It had been a hit and run. She saw the police report; that was how it had been classified.

Just then Bess walked into the kitchen, swept across the room and grabbed on to Mare's arms, pulling her away from the table, holding on to her tightly. "Could you help me out with something upstairs, M?"

Had Bess heard what George just said? And if so, how much? The part about George wanting Bess to leave, George asking if they were *fucking* behind his back or only the last part about Max? Her cheeks warmed with embarrassment at the thought of Bess overhearing any of his drunken ramblings.

"Oh, look. Bess is awake," George slurred.

"Hello, George," Bess said coldly. "Nothing like a little midweek beer to show what a good family man you are." If she was trying to antagonize him on purpose, she was doing it correctly. George's expression sank in a frown, and red crept up from his neck, across his face. "M, come on. I need you upstairs."

Mare allowed herself to be pulled out of the kitchen, and then she leaned her weight on her friend to walk toward the stairs.

"She always needs you," George muttered as they walked out. "That's the fucking problem."

Bess didn't say a word until they were upstairs in Mare's bedroom again with the door shut. Then Bess turned the lock on the door handle and came and sat on the bed next to Mare.

"Why didn't you tell me he was like that?" Bess finally spoke softly.

Mare could barely think straight because she kept hearing what George had said about Max. He *got rid of Max*? Could George have been the hit and run driver? He'd had a meeting in the city that night. But had he really? Or had he lied about that?

"Mare," Bess said her name sternly and Mare looked up. "Why didn't you tell me?"

"Tell you what?" Everything she had ever wanted to come clean about to Bess sat on the tip of her tongue. That she had loved Max. That she would've left George for Max. That she still was unsure whether Max had truly loved her or Bess the whole time. But she bit her lip and didn't say any of that out loud. She knew intuitively somehow if she said all this out loud she could lose Bess forever. And she couldn't let that happen.

"You didn't tell me that George was abusive," Bess whispered. "I mean I saw you two weren't always getting along while I've been here, but I didn't know he was like this."

Abusive? George was George. He liked empty, drunken threats. But he didn't hit her. Mare laughed a little. "Oh, Bess, he's just having a bad night. Really. It's not a big deal." But even as she spoke, she knew she sounded like one of those sad women on the afternoon talk shows she used to watch in the year after her accident when she could barely bring herself to get out of bed. George wasn't a very nice drunk. (And he wasn't all that nice sober these days either.) But that didn't make him *abusive*.

Bess frowned and put her arm around Mare. "Don't you worry. I'm going to take care of this," Bess said.

And in that moment, it didn't occur to Mare to ask Bess what she meant. But later she would wonder if she had, if everything might've turned out differently.

Amelia

MAX COOPER WAS not my father.

I said that to Gloria, the moment after the confusing words escaped her lips. But still, she proceeded to argue with me. "Annie." It felt like something inside my chest collapsed when she said my real name in a tone that almost resembled kindness, and I held on to the side of the couch. "Max *was* your father."

I shook my head.

"You have his blue eyes," she insisted. "His nose. When you turn your head just so, I see him in your profile."

I had Gaitlin's blue eyes, and from the family photo albums I'd seen over the years, my dead maternal grandmother's nose. Besides, my mother had been with Gaitlin the year before I was born. Both he and my mother had told me that my entire life. I relayed all this to Gloria now, but she shook her head.

"I know it might be a shock," she said. "But it's true. And it answers your question. It's why I brought you here."

She spoke with such a certainty, she seemed to truly believe it herself. For the first time since I'd met her, I had the sense that Gloria wasn't trying to lie to me.

"When I learned you were an actress," Gloria continued, "I thought to myself, what better person to play me than Bess and Max's girl? It all felt quite karmically fitting." She said this with such an air of arrogance that I suddenly felt dirty, like I was being used this whole time in a way I didn't even quite understand.

"That doesn't make sense," I said. Nothing she was saying made sense. I wasn't *Max's daughter*. I wasn't my mother's karmic stand-in. What did that even mean? The room rushed and whirred around me, and white noise suddenly filled my ears. I put my head in my hands and tried to breathe slow, deep breaths.

Gloria stood, and at the sound of her cane thumping toward the doorway, I looked back up. "Where are you going?" I asked. "You can't just say something like this and then leave without any more explanation."

Gloria turned back to look at me. "Remember, we had a deal," she said coldly.

"How am I supposed to show up to work tomorrow after you just dropped this in my lap?" This felt like the opposite of preparing for the role, like Gloria and I had slid backward. That I personally had fallen into a deep, dark confusing hole that I wasn't sure how to climb out of.

Gloria pulled her stole tighter across her chest. "So don't show up. You always have a choice in life, Amelia."

And then as suddenly as she came, she was gone.

After the door shut behind her, I sat there on the couch for a little while, unable to move or fully process what was happening. Max Cooper couldn't be my father. *Gaitlin was my father.* We had never been especially close, Gaitlin and I, but I'd never once questioned whether or not he loved me, whether or not I was truly his daughter.

I got up and grabbed my laptop and did a search for Max

Cooper. Now that I knew he died in 1986, I was able to narrow the results down, and I found his obituary pretty quickly. But all I learned from it was that he'd died *suddenly* in October of that year at the age of twenty-six and didn't seem to have left behind any family. The sparse obituary mentioned his co-workers at a Seattle-based law firm, and I supposed they were the ones to have written this very banal swan song for him too. I shut my laptop, suddenly overwhelmingly sad.

Max died in October of 1986. I was born in December of that year, so if he was my father, my mother would've been with him some time in the year leading up to his death.

Gaitlin, who was clueless about so much when it came to my mother, would have to know at least this much. He would have to know where he and my mother were in the months before my birth, wouldn't he? I picked up my phone to call him, but I saw the time and realized it was too late. Eight forty-five here, which made it close to midnight on the East Coast.

And then there was another knock at the door. I jumped up, hoping it was Gloria feeling remorse for dropping such a strange bombshell and then leaving. Perhaps she'd come back with some more to say, an explanation at least. *Something* that made sense. But I opened the door, and this time it actually was Will.

He smiled when he saw me. "You really like that sweatshirt, don't you?"

I'd forgotten I was still wearing it, and I tugged on the sleeves to start taking it off. "Sorry, you can have it back," I murmured, struggling to get my arms out of the too-big sleeves, suddenly feeling trapped inside of it. Everything Gloria had said was running through my head. How could I face Will right now?

He put his hands on my arms to stop me from moving. "No, keep it. It looks better on you, anyway." I nodded, but he didn't let go of my arms. He kept holding on to me as he walked into my suite and kicked the door shut behind him with his foot. Then he wrapped me in a hug and held me tight against his chest.

"Will." I inhaled the evergreen scent of him and said his name softly, suddenly fighting the urge to cry. "I…" A protest sat on the tip of my tongue, and not because of any *deal* I had made with Gloria either but because what she had said about Max Cooper and my mother, what I had remembered about knowing Will when we were younger, was swirling in my head. I wanted to talk to Will about all of it. But I suspected if I tried, he'd get upset. And I didn't have it in me to argue with him right now either.

"Remember. Just you and me," he said softly.

His latest *ground rule*. But was that truly possible? Could I stop thinking about all the rest of it and only think about him, about the fact that I liked him and he was here? Could I continue to be with him in a bubble?

He leaned down and kissed me gently on the lips. I wanted so much to forget about everything else. At least for now, for tonight.

Just stop thinking, Amelia.

I kissed him back, pushing all my thoughts and worries away. And then his hands were running up the length of my torso, pulling his sweatshirt off, over my head. And we couldn't stop touching each other long enough to walk toward the bedroom. So we stumbled there, our hands on each other, our mouths on each other.

It wasn't until later, when Will was already asleep, when I was lying with him, our naked limbs entwined, when I remembered what Gloria said about Will exactly: *You already hurt him once.*

And then it was there before me as I drifted off to sleep, a dream, or a memory. I wasn't sure which one.

Annie

1991

SHE WAS THE one who suggested hiding in the pantry.

It was late, nighttime, and the sound of the adults yelling had woken her up. Will came to find her in their guest room, and he'd suggested they go play out back on the swing set. But even though it was almost summer now, she still felt cold at night. And besides, she didn't like the swings. She didn't like the weightless feeling of the up and down, the oak trees spinning around her as she swung her feet, pushing higher and higher. And it felt too late to go outside now. At home there was always a rule she had to be *inside* the house before dark.

The pantry was in a long hallway in between the laundry room and the garage. It was large, quiet, warm. Away from the adults, and it felt like a fort. Besides that, it was filled with snacks. All the Goldfish crackers and warm Capri-Suns they could want. (And even though she struggled with the straw, Will was good at it. He helped her.)

They tiptoed down the stairs together, and got past the adults who were too busy yelling at each other in the kitchen to notice. She opened the pantry door, crawled inside and sat far in the back, underneath a shelf of dry pasta, tucking her knees to her chest. Will shut the door and then squeezed in next to her, two Capri-Suns already in hand.

He put the straw in for her and handed it over. She took a sip. Fruit punch. Her favorite flavor. "Why do you think they're yelling at each other?" she whispered.

He took a sip of his own juice pouch and shrugged. "Adults are stupid."

She nodded. That one simple sentence explained a lot about her life right now. Everything, really. The divorce. Why she had to live in Chicago. She wondered if whatever yelling was happening in the other room meant that she and her mom would be going back to Pasadena. But instead of that thought settling happily inside of her, now she glanced at Will and wondered if after they left, she'd ever see him again. "If they can't find us, they can't make me leave," she said to him.

Will laughed. "I wonder how long we could stay in here?"

There was food and there were Capri-Suns and it was nice and warm with plenty of room to spread out. It would get boring, sure, but Will was good at inventing fun games in times like this.

Let's count all the foods that start with the letter P *in the pantry.*

Let's think of a number between one and twenty and see if the other person can guess...

Then, suddenly, there was the sound of shattering glass. And all the yelling stopped.

It was very quiet. Too quiet. A pit of dread expanded in her stomach. And she clung to Will's arm.

"I'll go see what's going on." Will moved to stand up but

she refused to let go of his arm and pulled him back to sitting with her.

"Don't go," she whispered. "Let's just both sleep in here tonight." The adults would calm down by morning. The glass would be swept up, and she was not ready for her mom to pull her away right at this very moment and to never see Will again.

In the darkness, Will turned to look at her, and she blinked her eyes to try and see the expression on his face. But it was too dark. She couldn't tell if he was scared or sad or hurt.

"Let's play another game," she whispered. "Let's see how long we can stay here without the adults finding us." It would serve them right for waking her and Will up with so much yelling.

Was she old enough to understand that her mom would be worried if she went up to the guest room to kiss her good-night and found the bed empty? She was. But maybe she wasn't old enough to care. She giggled softly in the darkness. It would be funny to fool them all. To make them worry and search. And all along, they would be right here, right inside the house, underneath their noses inside the pantry.

"Okay," Will said. "I'm putting on my stopwatch. I bet we can go twelve hours without them finding us. No one knows I hide in here." He hit a button on his watch and it glowed green for a few seconds before she heard a small beep. Time ticking away.

"Twelve hours?" It felt like forever, and maybe this was a stupid game. But she wouldn't say that to Will now that he was actually interested in a game she had come up with. Usually it was the other way around.

"If we fall asleep, the hours will go by fast," Will said.

She finished off her Capri-Sun and threw the empty pouch in the corner, and then she leaned her head against Will's shoulder and closed her eyes. She really was tired, and it was warm and comfortable in here, leaning up against him. Will was right. All she had to do to win the game was fall asleep.

★ ★ ★

"Annie? Annie!"

She opened her eyes again when she heard her mother calling for her.

Her mother's voice sounded like it was coming from very far away, like she was shouting through the entire ocean, underwater.

She tried to sit up, but her head hurt and her tongue felt thick, and there was a horrible smell.

Will was lying on the ground next to her, and she nudged him with her foot. "Will," she whispered. "Will, wake up." She nudged him harder. But he didn't wake up and he didn't even move.

Then she started to cry softly, and she wanted to call out for her mother, but she picked up Will's wrist and hit the button on his watch to make it glow green. Only two hours had passed and Will had wanted to make it twelve. If she yelled now, they would lose the game.

And, anyway, she was so, so sleepy. It was so much easier just to lay her head down and go back to sleep.

Amelia

I OPENED MY EYES, with a jolt from the half memory, half dream. The horrible rotten-egg smell still permeated my nose, making my head throb. *Was there a gas leak?* I took a few deep breaths, and then all I could smell was the vanilla scent of my hotel room. No. My head throbbed because I'd hit it earlier.

But there had been a gas leak, in my dream. That's what I had been smelling. And George had died because of a gas leak. Was it possible that I had been there that night, that I had put Will in danger by convincing him to stay hidden in a pantry?

The movie—and the memoir—skimmed over the night of George's death. All I knew was the barest minimum. That the gas stove had been faulty, causing a leak that eventually caused the house to explode. Only George had been inside at the time. But the book didn't mention where anyone else had been, Gloria, or Will. And it certainly didn't mention that my mother and I had been staying there at the time. *Had we?* Was that real?

You already hurt Will once, Gloria had said earlier. Is that what she meant? Had I made him hide in the pantry with me and almost gotten him killed from carbon monoxide by not calling for help? But even if that was true, I was only a little kid. I hadn't been trying to hurt him. And why was I even there in the first place? Was it because Max truly was my father? Did that have something to do with it?

I rolled over and watched Will sleeping peacefully now. I reached my hand up and touched his cheek softly with my thumb. With his eyes closed and his glasses on the nightstand, he looked younger. I could almost see something in his face that slightly resembled the little boy in my dream. But more, I could see this beautiful man, who, in spite of whatever might have happened to him, to both of us, in the past, he was now fiercely protective of a mother who clearly desperately needed him. And that's when it hit me. Maybe Gloria was right about one thing: Will and I couldn't be together. If I stayed with him, against Gloria's wishes, we couldn't keep this a secret forever. I *was* going to end up hurting him, for real.

His eyes suddenly popped open. He looked at me looking at him, and he smiled. "You should be asleep," he murmured. He reached up and stroked my hair, tucking it gently behind my ear. His thumb traced my cheekbone, and my heart pounded against the walls of my chest.

I closed my eyes and took a deep breath to try and center myself. And then I reached up and gently moved his hand away from my face. "Will," I said his name softly, but firmly. And it took every bit of acting I had left in me to say what I did next believably: "I want you to leave."

"Leave?" The way he repeated the word like he couldn't comprehend it, hit with a steady ache in my chest.

My heart clenched, but I nodded.

He offered a gentle Will-smile of understanding. "You want to be alone to go to sleep tonight?"

I kept my expression neutral as I continued talking and spoke calmly, with no hesitation. "You said if I ever wanted you to leave, I should tell you."

Understanding seemed to hit him, and he rolled over and groped around the nightstand for his glasses. Then he put them on his face, sat up and stared at me hard for a moment. "You really want me to leave?" he repeated softly like he couldn't quite believe I'd actually said it.

I nodded. "We knew this was just a quick crazy thing," I said coldly. My heart hurt as I spoke, as I watched his face turn in surprise, disbelief and then sadness. "I want you to leave," I repeated. I kept my voice flat, emotionless. "And we should forget any of this ever happened."

ONE DEAD AFTER GAS LEAK, EXPLOSION IN GLEN COVES

June 2, 1991

A thirty-two-year-old man is dead after an explosion Saturday night in the suburban enclave of Glen Coves.

The fire department was called to the scene at 4:11 a.m. after an unidentified woman made a 911 call saying she smelled gas near the property. By the time GlenCo Fire arrived at 4:21, the house had already exploded. All occupants got out safely, aside from the owner of the house, George Forrester, who was pronounced dead at the scene.

Mr. Forrester and his family had lived in the two-story house in the Glen Coves subdivision for approximately three years before the incident. Described as "a quiet family who

kept to themselves," the Forresters had recently renovated the 1972-built property. The
close-knit suburban enclave was rocked by the
sudden tragedy, with many wondering how safe
their own homes were. However, fire personnel
were able to prevent damage to any neighbor-
ing properties.

The cause of the gas leak is still under
investigation. Though, initial evidence seems
to point to a faulty gas stove recently in-
stalled during a kitchen remodel.

GlenCo Gas Company has offered free gas line
inspections for anyone interested. Investigators say if you ever smell gas, leave the
house immediately and call 911 from a safe
distance away.

Amelia

I FELL ASLEEP on the plane, but I woke up as the wheels touched down on the runway with a thud. I felt strangely disoriented, struggling to remember exactly where I was, how I had gotten here. Then it slowly came back to me and settled like a rock in my stomach.

I'd been awake in Belles Woods in the middle of the night, searching on my laptop for any information at all about the night of George's death. But I'd turned up nothing more concrete than a short newspaper article. Gloria's words tumbled restlessly through my head: *You always have a choice, Amelia.*

If she was right about Max, then everything I ever knew about myself felt completely wrong. And I realized the information I truly needed was never going to be found searching my laptop in the middle of the night. I needed to see Gaitlin, face-to-face. I needed to understand who I really was, where I really came from, before I could even think about becoming someone else again. And more than that, in the middle of the night it suddenly hit me: playing Gloria wasn't ever going to help me heal in the wake of my mother's death. It was only making the tightness in the center of my chest feel that much worse.

If I were making a choice, then maybe it was that, for once, I was choosing myself over my career.

I'd checked out of the hotel, I was at the ticket counter at SeaTac by 5 a.m., and now I was entirely across the country, in Newark, only an hour from Gaitlin's house near Princeton. All I had to do was get off the plane and get on the train, the way I had every summer as a teenager when I'd come to visit him for two weeks. All I had to do was go talk to him about everything Gloria had told me, and certainly he would know and tell me the truth. At least, I hoped he would.

I'd texted Liza right before putting my phone in airplane mode in Seattle to let her know I was quitting the movie. And as the plane taxied to the gate in Newark now, I reluctantly took my phone out of airplane mode, feeling the tiniest pit of regret in my stomach. *Sixty-three missed texts.* Sixty of them were from Liza, and I sighed and opened those first. At 6 a.m. she was angry, but by noon Seattle time it seemed she'd already gone through all the stages of grief, up through and including acceptance. At which point she asked about when I wanted to discuss our next move. *We need a plan!* I did want a plan, but not yet, not today. So I texted her back that I had some personal things to take care of in New Jersey and that we could set up a time to talk when I was back in LA next week.

Then I looked at my other texts. Two from Jase, whom I hadn't heard from in months. He wanted to know if I was okay, and he sent a TMZ article that said I'd quit the movie after an injury on set. Well, I guessed that was how Liza had spun it. It was none of his business if I was okay. So I ignored that.

And finally, a passive-aggressive text from Cam, who was

worried he came off bad in the TMZ article but also still thanked me for the time we spent together. I ignored that too.

There was nothing from the person I wanted to hear from most: *Will*. I'd half expected him to text-yell at me for breaking a *ground rule* when he learned that I'd left this morning. I'd gone and quit the film after breaking things off with him. Hadn't I promised him I wouldn't do that? But maybe the fact that I'd told him to *leave* superseded everything else, and now he was just doing what I asked. So why was I so sad about all of it? And why did it feel like maybe Will's silence meant he'd never actually cared for me at all?

I hadn't been to Gaitlin's house outside Princeton in years, but somehow it still looked exactly the same as I remembered it. He lived in a cute Craftsman, with a wide white porch and red shutters framing the windows. The Uber dropped me off out front, and my half sister, Melody, was sitting out on the front porch steps with a golden retriever I assumed was theirs (but whom I'd never met). The last time I'd been here, Melody was maybe ten. But now she sat before me looking like a full-grown woman at almost eighteen.

She stood when I got out of the car, and I was shocked by how tall she was. At least half a foot taller than my five foot five. The golden retriever sat up too, but stared at me patiently, unlike Gloria's yippy little rat. *Stop thinking about Gloria.*

I waved, and then Melody squinted, recognition spreading slowly across her face. "Oh my god, what are you doing here?" she squealed, like she was *thrilled* to see me.

Melody and I had never been close, so her reaction caught me off guard. Then I remembered that I hadn't been back here since the success of *Addy*. Melody had probably watched me on TV.

"Hey, Mel," I said, breezing up to the porch, like we were real sisters. Friends even. "Is Gaitlin home?"

She shook her head. "He's still at work." I glanced at my

watch. It was after six. Gaitlin shouldn't work so hard. He was older than my mom by two years, which, in the months after her sudden death, felt a lot older to me than it used to.

My stepmom, Courtney, suddenly opened the screen door and stepped out. "Amelia, is that you? What a surprise!" I'd always disliked Courtney, simply for the sheer fact she wasn't my mom. But to her credit, she had never been anything but kind to me. She'd tried so hard it was almost sad, and now I wished I actually liked her more. "Is everything okay?" she asked me kindly.

"I saw on TMZ she got hurt yesterday," Melody said more to her mom than to me. "And she cheated on Jase a few months ago. Remember when I told you he broke up with her?"

"You can't believe everything you read," I said to Melody, struggling to present a happy exterior. She kept staring at me, so I felt I had to continue. "Jase cheated on me. I broke up with him. And yeah, I got a little bump on the head yesterday, but I'm fine. That's not why I'm here. I just really needed to talk to Gaitlin."

Courtney frowned, like she was altogether confused why my urge to talk to Gaitlin meant a visit, not a phone call. And maybe I should've called. But I wanted to be face-to-face when I asked him about Max, about my mother, about whether there was any truth to anything Gloria had said. And I didn't know how to explain any of that to Courtney.

Courtney chewed on her bottom lip and then pulled her long blond hair back with her hands, looking flustered. "We were just about to have dinner, Amelia. Why don't you come in and join us? I'll go call Gait and tell him you're here and to hurry home."

The last thing I wanted going on twenty-four hours of jagged sleep, a head injury, the most confusing memories and the strange emptiness I was feeling without Will, was a forced dinner with Melody and Courtney. But I'd shown up here out of the blue. What else could I do but smile and make small talk with them over Courtney's overcooked pasta?

"Melody really looks up to you," Gaitlin said a few hours later. He was finally home from work, and we were out on the porch, in the dark, just the two of us. He nursed a whiskey and had offered me a drink. But I was exhausted, my head still hurt, and I was struggling to think clearly as it was, so I'd declined.

"Melody seems like a sweet kid," I said to Gaitlin now. The truth of it was, I knew next to nothing about Melody, other than her love for TMZ and affection for Jase, and I was still kind of annoyed she had believed *I'd* cheated on *him*.

"It's pretty cool to have a famous sister," Gaitlin said, taking a sip of his whiskey.

"Half sister," I corrected, though now I wondered if even that much was true.

"Half sister," Gaitlin repeated quietly, into the darkness, like saying the word itself disappointed him. "So what are you really doing here, honey? You quit the biopic? I don't understand. When we talked last week, you were so excited."

I bit my bottom lip. I wasn't sure how much to tell Gaitlin. But right now, what I knew more than anything was that I needed answers from him. All week I'd been trying to figure out who the real Gloria Diamond was. But maybe what I'd needed to know all along was who the real Annie Gaitlin was. "I have something to ask you," I finally said. "And I need you to tell me the absolute truth. Don't sugarcoat it. Don't worry about upsetting me. Just the truth. Okay?"

He nodded and took a bigger sip of his whiskey. "The whole truth and nothing but the truth. So help me god." He let out a small nervous laugh.

I took a deep breath and then I blurted it out: "Are you really my father?"

He sputtered on the whiskey and started to cough. I slapped

him gently on the back, and it took him a moment to catch his breath. "Why would you ask me that?" He sounded hurt. "I know we don't see each other much but I hope you know how much I love you. How proud I am of you."

I nodded. I truly did know those things. But that didn't answer my question. "But are you really my father, by blood?"

"Of course I am," he said quickly. Then he put his glass of whiskey down on the steps, like he realized he needed to sober up for this conversation. "What's going on, honey?"

It all came out of me in a tangled rush. Finding out that Mom was connected to Gloria in the past. Remembering that we might have been there once, when I was very young, and finally what Gloria told me, what she had insisted, that Max was my real father. That I had his blue eyes—

"You have *my* blue eyes." Gaitlin cut me off.

I smiled a little, thinking about how we had both responded the exact same way. But I also knew that didn't mean all that much. Then I asked him if he knew who Max Cooper was.

He surprised me by nodding. "Your mom dated him before we met." He paused and then he added, "Before she moved back to Pasadena. And then some time later there was an accident, and he died pretty young."

"She dated him?" I repeated, fixated on the one piece of his response I hadn't yet known. Was Gloria right? Max really was my father? Maybe my mother had done something Gaitlin hadn't ever even known. I sighed.

Gaitlin patted me softly on the head. "I can practically hear the wheels turning in there. But Max was *not* your father."

"You don't know that for sure," I said softly.

"I do," he said. "I was there. I was with your mom when she realized she was pregnant. I was with her when you were born. And I know it right here." He thumped his chest with his fist.

I shook my head, unconvinced any of that proved anything.

Gaitlin snapped his fingers. "Courtney's Christmas present."

"Christmas?" It was a total non sequitur and I didn't understand what he was talking about. "It's... June, Gaitlin."

"She got us all those, what are they called? Thirty-three and something DNA tests but we never got around to doing them."

"23andMe," I corrected him.

"Right! Let's you and I go do it right now."

It felt like such an easy answer, but I bit my lip. Gaitlin was so convinced. What if the DNA test proved him wrong? He would be devastated. And it hit me, so would I. "I don't know," I said. And for some reason I thought about Will telling me he didn't want to know any more about the past after learning that he grew up in Max Cooper's house. Maybe sometimes not knowing was better. Maybe I should've just ignored Gloria, stayed in Belles Woods, stayed with Will, blocked out everything about my past and stuck to our *ground rules*. "What if we learn something we don't want to?" I said softly.

Gaitlin shook his head. "First of all, I already know everything I need to know. This is for you." He paused, picked up his whiskey and downed the little bit that was left in the glass. "And second of all, isn't it always better to know the truth for sure? Facts are better than conjecture."

But were they, really?

Before I could protest anymore, Gaitlin was already standing, already walking into the house calling out for Courtney to ask her where the tests were.

Mare

1991

LATER, SHE WOULD know exactly three things for sure about that night:

One, that afterward, George was dead. Two, that Will had almost died with him. And three, that Bess was to blame for everything.

That night felt calm, at first. George was working late and, anyway, once he had sobered up last week, he'd forgotten all about his threats. For a few days, he and Bess continued on, cordial to one another. No one said another word about Max. And Bess made no plans to leave.

But that night, it was after nine, the kids were already asleep, and George was still not home from work. It had been a warm and muggy day, but the night breeze had cooled it down enough for Mare to sit out on the back patio with a glass of Chardonnay, her notebook and a flashlight. She scribbled down ideas as she heard the teakettle whistle inside the house, and she knew Bess must be heating water for tea. That, as she had done many nights before this one, she would carry her tea and her Jackie Collins out back and sit down on the patio couch next to Mare, snuggling in close as she sipped from her mug and read.

But then, caught up in the sound of the whistling kettle came the sound of a howl.

Mare thought it was an animal at first. A rare coyote or perhaps an injured owl. But then she heard it again. And she realized it was coming from inside the house. That the sound was coming from Bess.

She stood up quickly, accidentally knocking over her wine, forgetting about her cane, but not taking the time to stop and pick up either one. She hobbled inside the kitchen as fast as she could, and there George was, standing over Bess, holding on to her arm, a drunken scowl on his face.

That was why he was home so late from work tonight, he'd been drinking. Again.

"Jesus, George, what are you doing?" she cried out and went to him, grabbing his arm to pull him off Bess. But George suddenly swung back, and the force of it sent her flying across the room, where she landed on her backside with a thud. Bess let out another scream, a high-pitched cawing like a bird.

Bess pushed him out of the way and ran to Mare. She knelt down and gave her a hand to help her up. George stared at them both, still scowling, breathing hard.

"George, you're drunk." Mare spoke slowly, trying, and failing, to keep her voice from trembling as she leaned onto Bess and rose to her feet. She suddenly thought about what Bess had said, that George was *abusive*.

"I told you she had to go," he said. "I warned you. And you didn't listen to me."

"If she goes, I go with her." Mare spoke defiantly, though even as she said it, she wasn't sure she would actually do it. Where would they go? How would they live? If ever there were a moment where she wished she had finished college, that she had never met George or that she had protested in his apartment that cold icy night, it was this one.

George shook his head and pulled something from his suit pocket. *A photograph?* He held it up and then she could see what it was: the picture she kept on the desk upstairs in the guest room of her, Max and Bess from college. They were standing outside her and Bess's dorm, smiling from ear to ear. It had been taken for them by their RA, on their way to the dorm picnic, a full month before Bess had even introduced her to George, when she was still a third wheel. (And why had she thought that was so bad, anyway?)

"What are you doing with that?" Mare snapped. It was one of the last pictures she had left of Max. The only one she thought suitable to display on her desk. The other one that she'd gotten developed right after she'd left the hospital—the one of her and Max at the pizza restaurant, their heads close together—she kept hidden inside a book on her nightstand. But sometimes she would get up in the middle of the night when George was asleep, take that photo into the bathroom, lock the door and lie on the cold tiled floor and cry while she looked at it.

George held this photo close to the stove, and that's when she realized the burner was still on. Bess had removed the whistling teakettle but must not have turned off the stove before George had grabbed her. He held the edge to the tiny flame and it rippled, lighting the corner of the photograph blue, then orange.

"George, stop it!" she yelled at him.

"You loved him. And you love her. But what about me?" George said, suddenly sounding like a child.

She lunged forward and grabbed his arm, but by then half the photograph was already burned. Max had disintegrated into ashes on the stove. Half of Bess's face had disappeared.

"I made him go away," George said softly, so softly Mare wasn't sure Bess could hear from where she stood across the room.

Mare felt her throat constrict, and she leaned against the kitchen counter, struggling to breathe. Was he talking about the photograph he'd just burned? Or something much, much worse? "What are you saying, George? What did you do?"

"You were going to leave me for him. You were going to take everything away from me. I told you I wouldn't let that happen." George spoke coldly, his words sounding calculated and strangely sober.

She remembered what he had said so many years earlier. That if she tried to take Will away, he would *kill her.* And she felt a sudden chill course through her.

"She's next." He pointed at Bess in the photograph, but with her face half burned away she was unrecognizable. Mare turned around, but the actual Bess was no longer standing across the room. George suddenly seemed to notice her absence too, and he dropped the photograph on the floor, strode out of the kitchen, into the dining room and then the living room, calling for her.

Mare hobbled out after him, wishing she hadn't left her cane on the patio. "George," she called after him. "Wait!" Her heart thudded against the walls of her chest, and she wasn't sure what she would say to him even if she caught up to him. What could she say to make him listen? *He killed Max.* The truth of it suddenly hit her so hard that she stopped walking for a moment and bent over to breathe, trying not to vomit. "George!" she cried out desperately.

But before she could catch up to him, she heard the sound of glass shattering. And then she heard a giant thud from the living room.

Amelia

IT TOOK EXACTLY four weeks to get our DNA results, and by then I'd been back in Pasadena for three and half of them. I'd left Gaitlin's after a few days when the Realtor called with a decent offer on my mother's house, which I'd promptly accepted. She'd offered to help me hire someone to come in and pack everything away into storage until I was finished filming, but I'd told her that wouldn't be necessary. That I would come back to Pasadena and go through my mother's things myself.

A few weeks later, I had just finished going through my mother's closet when I saw the 23andMe email hit my inbox and decided I would ignore it for a little while.

But then it was promptly followed up by a text from Gaitlin that simply said: told ya. A weird sense of relief flooded my body, and I sat down on the master bathroom floor and opened up the email and started to cry. Gaitlin was definitely my father. He was right. Everything I'd ever known wasn't a lie. Gloria was wrong.

I felt a smug sort of satisfaction that maybe my quitting the film, quitting Will and fleeing Washington had all been justified. But then here I was, literally knee-deep in thirty years of my mother's junk, and maybe winning would've looked something more like staying on the film, telling Gloria to fuck off and taking the Realtor up on her offer to hire someone to put all this into storage?

Liza had told me that Gloria's part was quickly recast after I left—Celeste Templeton of all people. And why not? Gloria loved *Seattle Med*. Celeste was a real up-and-comer. I knew they were on a break from filming for the summer so Celeste had the time. And I knew I wasn't really allowed to care since I was the one who'd walked away from the role to begin with. But somewhere in the back of my mind, I kept thinking about finding her in my bed with Jase. About her more than likely meeting Will on set. It felt like Gloria had orchestrated it all on purpose to get back at me for some sin I still didn't even understand. And that thought alone made me want to scream.

But what was done was done. I had quit. I was here. And most importantly, now I knew for sure that Gloria was out of her mind. That I had made the right decision to play no part in her film.

"No regrets," I said to my mother's elderly orange tabby, Sebastian, who walked across the bathroom floor, rubbing against my legs. "Right, kitty?"

Sebastian already looked pissed that I had his entire home in upheaval, that I had taken away all his piles, the clothes in my mother's closet and most of his furniture. He had the kind of look on his face now that made me think he was not-so-secretly plotting my murder while I slept at night. But I stroked his chin, and then he rubbed against my hand with his head.

"Don't worry," I told him. "You're coming with me to Santa Monica." I had a cute little house under contract, not too far from the beach, that I would close on in a few weeks. Sebastian had spent his whole life with my mother—she'd adopted him as a replacement for me after I'd left for college—and even though I wasn't really a cat person I couldn't bear the thought of sending him to a shelter. "We're moving somewhere very nice," I assured him.

But Sebastian had already given up on me and left to jump up on the high empty shelf of my mother's closet. If I stopped to think about it, I might've been sad that I'd downgraded my closest living breathing companion to my mother's elderly cat. But I didn't stop to think. I grabbed another box and walked toward my mother's office.

I had saved this room for last. And not because it contained years' worth of documents (like tax returns) that I knew I would have to spend an enormous amount of time shredding. But because the walls in here were lined with bookshelves, and the shelves contained rows and rows of Gloria Diamond books. I hadn't been able to bring myself to look at them yet, much less take them off the shelves and decide whether to bring them to Santa Monica with me, donate them or throw them in the trash. That last option felt particularly harsh and, yet, also somewhat deserved for how Gloria had treated me.

But now I'd finished most of the rest of the house, and armed with real proof that Gloria was wrong about my father, I walked into my mother's office, straight toward the shelves. I stopped there for a moment and stared at all the pink and purple spines. How had my mother read all these, collected all these, and never once mentioned her friendship with Gloria? I supposed it had something to do with whatever happened many years ago to tear them apart, or maybe whatever happened that led Gloria to believe that Max was my father. Gloria loved Max. My mother once dated Max, according to Gaitlin. It felt both cliché and disappointing that they had probably ended their friendship over a man.

I sighed and started taking the books off the shelves. I picked up my favorite first, *Love at the End of the World*. I had always loved books almost as much as I'd loved movies, and I could remember with perfect accuracy where I had been, how I had been feeling when I first read, or watched, something I particularly loved. This book had gone with me on a long flight from LAX to Newark, a summer trip to Gaitlin's. I was fourteen or fifteen at the time, the summer before Melody was born. I still remembered holding this book in my hand as I stepped off the plane and was confronted with Courtney's enormous belly. Knowing she was pregnant and seeing her actually pregnant had been two entirely different things, and I'd clutched the book, this beautiful postapocalyptic love story, to my chest as I'd wandered through the terminal, staring at Courtney's giant belly and feeling a little like my own world was about to be upended.

I flipped through the book again, remembering how much I loved the very first line: *Sometimes the end of everything sneaks up on you when you least expect it.* For some reason, now, though, I thought about Will. I thought about my strange memory of being trapped inside a pantry with him, and of him helping me in the snow. I thought about the way his face looked when I told him I wanted him to *leave.* A month later, Will probably wasn't dwelling on what had happened between us. In fact, he had probably already forgotten all about me.

I sighed and put the copy of the book down on my mother's desk. Maybe this one I would keep and take with me to Santa Monica, but the rest I decided I would throw in a box and stick them in the pile for Goodwill with the majority of my mother's clothes. I swept them off one of the shelves with one abrupt motion of my hand and felt the smallest sense of satisfaction at the sound of them cascading roughly onto the tile floor.

But then I noticed something stuck in the back of the completely empty shelf. A red envelope. It was hard and square— containing a card of some sort. I pulled it out of the shelf—it was sealed shut. And when I turned it over, there was one word written on the front: *Mare.*

November 10, 1991

My dearest M,

There are so many things I've been wanting to say to
you. I've been trying to write this letter since the night
I last left you, after we fought. And every time I try
and write it, I rip it up or burn it. Then I start over,
but I can never seem to get my words right. You're
the writer. Not me.

So now I'm just going to try and tell you the truth
in a few, spare words. Maybe I'll never mail this letter
anyway. (I don't even know where you live anymore?)
So I'm taking a deep breath as I write this. Here goes.

For one thing, our fight. I promise you, I turned
off the stove. I don't know why the gas was leak-

ing, but I remember going back into the kitchen and turning off the burner after I hit George over the head with the lamp.

For another thing, George was still breathing after I hit him. I didn't even hit him that hard. I only stunned him, and then he was passed out drunk when you walked into the room and saw him lying on the floor.

And this is the most important—it was Annie who saved Will. They were hiding in the pantry, and I was tearing through the house and couldn't find them. I finally found her dragging him out on her back when he wouldn't wake up. I want you to know at least this much about my girl: My Annie, her heart shines like a star, just like I always told you. Just like the song. Annie saved Will's life.

I know you blame me, you think everything was all my fault. And maybe I deserve the blame, in that me being there, being around you, made George crazy, made him drink too much that night. I could've left before things went that far. Maybe I should've left. But I was too happy being with you. I was selfish.

And yes, I did introduce you to him, back in college. You were right—that much was my fault. I didn't know then what I know now, of course. I thought he was a nice guy, if a little boring. And if I'm really telling you the whole truth, that's why I introduced you to begin with. Because—and this is the hardest part to explain—you were always a diamond, M. And George was just the plainest of rocks. I thought we could all have a little fun, go on a few double dates before you'd grow tired of him. But I never truly wanted you to be with George. I wanted you to be with me.

I tried to tell you how I felt so many times, M. And I know you didn't or (didn't want to?) or couldn't understand what I was trying to say. Or maybe I never said it the right way. Maybe I was never clear enough. It's easier to write it down, like this, knowing you'll likely never read this. But here is the whole entire truth, I swear to you on Annie's life: I never loved Max. I never loved Gaitlin. I love you, M. It was always you.

I told this to Max once, the last night I spent with him in Seattle, and then swore him to secrecy. He got upset, feeling like I'd lied to him, and he was right, I did. Maybe he had a right to be upset. He and I never spoke again after that night. And part of me thinks he told you what I said despite the promise he made to me. Maybe you've known this all along. But part of me thinks he didn't. Because I know he loved you too. And as messed up as it sounds, the fact that I knew he loved you so much is why I stayed with him so long to begin with. Being with Max felt weirdly like the next best thing to being with you.

I realize as I get to the end of this, that I probably will never send you this letter. But even if we never speak again, I truly hope you're happy wherever you are. I will always hold you in my heart.

With all my love,
B

Amelia

THERE WAS A big bay window in the front living room of my new house in Santa Monica, and once Sebastian discovered that, he forgave me for moving him out of his house in Pasadena. Likewise, I forgave him for being a cat, as I spent afternoons in the window seat with him lying on my lap purring while I read the new script options Liza sent over.

Just about two months after I moved in, I had read enough to settle on my next project, a Netflix series adaptation of a novel I'd read the summer before my mother died and had absolutely loved. It was a supporting role, so maybe it wouldn't have quite the same impact on my career as the leading role in a big-budget biopic might have. But it was a great role—my favorite character since Addy. I would be playing a live-in housekeeper for an extremely wealthy and handsome man, and I was going to start shadowing an actual live-in housekeeper in Malibu next week. We'd spoken over the phone once. She'd sounded almost more excited than I was, and I felt it again in my chest, the elation I always get from acting, from learning, from becoming.

Then, one afternoon in mid-September, Sebastian and I were sitting in the window seat, as I read through the script again, preparing for the table read. And I suddenly looked up and saw Gloria walking up the front pathway to my door.

I closed my eyes, certain I must be imagining her. But she was still there when I opened them again. And then, my doorbell chimed.

In a few months' time, I'd put Gloria and my strange week in Washington behind me. So what if I still thought about Will? So what if I had a recurring dream now of being trapped in a pantry with him? I would never see him again, and ultimately, it didn't mean more than my subconscious not cooperating with what I was doing in my waking hours.

I had forwarded my 23andMe results to Tate in an email back in July and asked her to share them with Gloria. I also let her know I was mailing Gloria something to her house, and then I sent the card I'd found on my mother's bookshelf. I had debated throwing it out, or keeping it, or shredding it along with the tax returns, but then I decided if my mother had written the word *Mare* on the front, it meant that she had wanted to share it with her. I wasn't sure why she never had. Maybe she'd lost it or forgotten about it. But in any case, I hoped it would bring some closure for Gloria.

The doorbell rang again, and then I moved an annoyed Sebastian off my lap. Gloria had never responded to any of what I'd sent her, and Tate hadn't even acknowledged my email. I could not imagine what would have driven Gloria to show up here now, out of the blue, months later.

I opened the door and stared at her for a moment before I said anything. She was dressed up today: a light gray sequin top, a black fur stole around her shoulders and black leather pants.

Her big blond wig was piled up on top of her head, and a long strand of diamonds hung from each ear.

"Amelia," she said my name softly, as she looked me over too. I was dressed in leggings and my *Saving Addy* tee. My hair was in a messy bun, and I couldn't remember the last time I'd put on makeup.

"What are you doing here?" I finally asked her, tucking stray hairs behind my ears.

"May I come in?" she asked.

It felt too rude to say no, so even though I wasn't sure I really wanted her to, I opened the door wider and gestured for her to walk inside. Sebastian stared at her from his perch in the window.

"Beautiful cat," Gloria said.

"He was my mother's." At the mention of my mother, Gloria's face suddenly fell. "Please, have a seat." I felt guilt rising in my chest, though I wasn't sure exactly why. I had done nothing wrong. I gestured toward my new sectional. "Can I get you anything, Gloria? Water? Coffee? Hot toddy?" I added, though I wasn't even certain I had the ingredients for that on hand.

She shook her head, and she sat down, resting her cane and her bag at her feet. "I actually came here to give you something." She pulled what looked like a typed manuscript out of her bag and handed it to me.

On the front there was one line, a title: *The Real Gloria Diamond.* "I don't understand," I said.

"I read everything you sent me, and I think I got a lot of things wrong over the years," she said softly. "You had so many questions for me, and I didn't know how to tell you the truth about anything. Seeing you brought up so much old emotional turmoil for me. I know I treated you terribly when we met over the summer. And it wasn't fair to you." She paused and ran a finger down the long spiral of diamonds hanging from her earlobe. "The only way I know how to do things is to write them down. So there you have it."

The pages felt heavy in my hands. *The Real Gloria Diamond?* "So this is the truth about your life? About my mother?" I asked.

She nodded. "My version of the truth, anyway. We all tell stories to ourselves, but some of them are truer than others." Before I could reason out what that meant, she cleared her throat and continued talking. "And do with this what you will. It's not meant for anyone's eyes but yours. But sell it to the tabloids if you wish. I'd probably deserve it."

"I would never sell it to the tabloids," I said. No matter what had happened last summer, I wasn't going to do anything to make Gloria's life more difficult.

She smiled a little, maybe the first genuine smile I'd ever seen from her. "You have your mother's kindness," she said. "And her passion," she added. Then she gestured to the manuscript. "Read it now. I'll wait."

"Right now?" My heart pounded furiously in my chest, and I wondered if I really wanted to know everything she had written in these pages. I thought about what Gaitlin said, that truth is always better than conjecture. But what was Gloria's version of the truth, anyway? And what could she know about my mother that I never had?

Gloria nodded. "Go ahead," she said gently. "And then if you have any questions, I'll answer them for you. I mean it this time."

Mare

IN THE YEARS that followed George's death, she would become a new person, the kind of woman who, ironically, wrote the love stories Bess had always wanted her to, stories that only had happy endings. But in real life nothing ended happily for Mare. Max died. George died. She and Bess got into a huge fight and never spoke again after the Glen Coves house exploded.

After that night, she and Will fled to Seattle, the only place she could think of to go where they could have a roof over their heads for free—the (now) dilapidated house in the middle of the woods that Max had left her. Max's clothes were still there in the closet when they first arrived, moth-eaten and dusty, and still, she wrapped herself in the red holey sweatshirt he'd been wearing that night she ran into him in that bar in Seattle, and then she set to work finishing her first novel. The novel she hadn't quite been able to verbalize months earlier became a dark literary mystery, about a woman whose husband had murdered her lover in a hit and run, never to be caught.

She sent it off to try and sell it, and an agent in New York called and told her it was much too dark for her to ever sell from a woman writer. *They want women to write romance, happy endings with a little sparkle. Give them diamonds!* Mare told her she was a new widow, and then the agent said she should write a love story based on her own. That, she said, would sell like hotcakes.

Mare listened, sort of. She wrote *Love in the Library*. An ode, not to George, but to Max. She was desperate to sell a book, to have a writing career, to earn some money writing, and so at first, it felt like she was just playing a game writing romance. Anything the agent wanted, to sell a novel.

But then, in spite of herself, even before that first book took off, sold a million copies, she understood that maybe Bess had been right all along. Writing love stories suited her. So what if she wanted nothing to do with love in her real life? In her romance novels, love could be perfect, beautiful, anything she wanted it to be. Writing love stories that actually worked out on the page made her feel suddenly and wonderfully the most alive she'd ever felt.

And that was when she transformed herself into Gloria Diamond, this woman sparkly and fearless enough to write romance novels. The more love stories she wrote, the more lies she told, the more diamonds she bought, the more it felt like Mare had never even existed at all. That truly, deep down, she had been Gloria Diamond all along.

But she supposed the real story of her life wasn't even about her career at all. It wasn't about how many books she eventually sold, how many happy endings she wrote, how many diamonds she owned in the end.

Maybe it was about the fight she had with Bess, about what

really happened that night George died. And this was the part she had been trying to write in one way or another for thirty years. In her head. On paper. Loosely disguised in a novel with a happy romantic ending she never got herself.

And yet, she could never quite work it out. She could never quite remember the details in any order that made sense.

Sometimes the end of everything sneaks up on you when you least expect it. Sometimes it seeps into your bones like a slow-growing cancer, over years and decades, until all at once, thirty years later, you're in terrible aching pain.

There was the thud when George hit the living room floor that night.

Mare hobbled in and saw Bess standing over him, clutching a broken Tiffany lamp. Rage violently flooded Mare's veins. "What have you done? You killed him? You killed my husband!" Mare screamed. But even she understood in the moment that she wasn't really yelling this at Bess. That any rage she felt was about what George might have done years earlier, to Max.

Bess burst into tears, dropped the lamp, ran out. Mare let her go, and lowered herself to the floor, closer to George.

Bess had most definitely not killed him. He was still breathing. She put two fingers on the inside of his wrist and his pulse beat on just steady and fine. He moaned a little as she touched his wrist. "Mare, I didn't mean it." His words were still slurred. She noticed he had a small red welt on his head, but he seemed more drunk than injured. "I love you," he murmured. "Everything I did was for..." His voice trailed off, midsentence.

She sighed, knowing George would likely sleep it off here for a while, and leaned back against the couch. *He loved her?* Her heart ached thinking about Max, and maybe she still didn't know much about love herself, but she understood that it definitely wasn't what George thought it was.

After a few minutes she got herself up again, grabbed the

bottle of Chardonnay and her cane from the patio, and then went to her bedroom. She slowly drank from the bottle in bed, trying to get the alcohol to soothe her. To dull the memory of what George had said in the kitchen about Max. *I made him go away.* What he had said on the floor in the living room, that *he loved her.*

She had to think; she knew she had to figure out what to do next. But every thought now started and ended with Max's blue, blue eyes. Thinking hurt too much, and instead, she finished off the bottle of Chardonnay until she was woozy and numb. Until she had no choice but to fall asleep.

When she woke up, maybe hours had passed. Or maybe it was days. There was the horrible stench of rotting eggs, and the sound of Bess's voice cutting through darkness. "Mare, you need to get up!" Bess was shouting. Then she was in the bedroom, shaking Mare's shoulders. "Wake up!"

Bess grabbed her arm, dragged her to the edge of the bed. Mare finally opened her eyes, and even in the darkness she could see the panic stretched across Bess's petite face. "Come on," Bess said. "Hurry. The house might explode."

Explode? She heard what Bess said but it didn't quite resonate as something that concerned her. *Explode.* Like George had. Like her life had?

But Bess held on to her arm, pulled her through the upstairs hallway, down the staircase, out to the front lawn. And then as Mare's bare feet hit the wet dewy grass, she suddenly understood what Bess had been trying to say. The smell of the gas. The house really was going to explode. And she remembered the last piece of Max she had left, the photograph of the two of them she'd hidden in the book on her nightstand. She pushed Bess away and hobbled back toward the house to get it.

"Wait!" Bess cried out after her. "You can't go back in there."

Going back into the gas-filled house, she hovered in a moment between life and death, between an instinct to survive and the feeling building up inside of her that it might be easier just to sit down on the couch and wait for death. But she pushed forward instead, up the stairs, found the picture and then hobbled back down, back outside, clutching Max to her chest. She exhaled with relief and gulped in the fresh night air. "I'm okay," she said to a stunned Bess. "I'm going to be okay."

And that's when she suddenly noticed Will and Annie, standing across the street from the house on the sidewalk, holding on to one another. The last thought she had before the house exploded was that she hadn't even remembered about the children at all.

Will hardly spoke for almost a year after the house exploded.

Mare took him to a doctor in Seattle who felt sure his voice would come back when the trauma of that night subsided. He was right, and when Will eventually started speaking again, after many silent days wiled away in the backyard tree house, he told Mare he remembered nothing at all about that night. Barely anything about his father or Chicago either. She supposed that was a blessing.

By the time Gloria Diamond's first romance novel was published a year and half after the explosion, Will was acting somewhat like a normal child again. He was quiet, too thoughtful, but that had practically been the way he'd acted since he'd made it through his terrible twos. He went to school, and he got good grades. He never got into any trouble. And they never ever talked again about that night.

But he was the reason why she told the greatest lie of all. Why she kept lying about George in all the books and the years that would follow. Maybe she hadn't been the one to think to save Will from the explosion that night, but she could save him in the aftermath. He deserved to have a father who was a wonderful man. He deserved to have parents who'd had an incredible love story. George was dead. Max was dead. Who was left to ever know that Gloria Diamond's entire career was based on a lie?

Only Bess. And maybe that was part of the reason Mare never spoke to her again. Mare was a coward. Gloria was, in fact, a bigger coward. And she didn't want to have to explain herself. Or ever tell Bess about what had happened between her and Max. It seemed easier to forget about Bess, to never talk to her again, than to have to beg her for forgiveness.

That night, just after the explosion, Mare screamed at Bess out on the front lawn. "You did this!" She yelled into the warm, smoky night. Her ears were ringing from the burst of noise, and it was hard to hear. "You never turned off the burner."

Bess shook her head and held Annie tight against her in a hug. "Mare, I did turn it off. I swear." Bess, who barely ever raised her voice, was yelling too. Or maybe it was that neither one of them could hear over the residual ringing of the blast in their ears.

"You wanted him to die. You killed him." Even as Mare screamed at Bess, she didn't quite believe the words she was saying. She was wrapped inside of grief that poured out of her with the hot lava of rage. What Mare yelled at Bess was what she should've been yelling at George. Except, George hadn't gotten out of the house. George was drunk, passed out on the floor. And now George was almost certainly dead.

"I never wanted anyone to die!" Bess yelled back. "How could you even think that about me? I didn't do this!"

"You brought me George in college, and now you took him away too!" she screamed, the irrational words burning up, bursting out of her in another yell. "You're just as bad as him, trying to control me. You just blew up my life. Literally."

"The kids were hiding in the pantry. Annie said they were playing a game. What kind of a mother do you think I am that

I would intentionally have done this knowing my kid was inside that house?" Bess's voice broke with hurt.

"A pretty shitty one," Mare screamed at her. The words were almost nonsensical. She knew it, and yet she couldn't stop them. "And you almost killed Will too."

"Mare, calm down." Bess's voice was softer now, and Mare's ears were ringing enough that Bess's words felt slushy, jumbled. Maybe Bess didn't tell her to calm down? Maybe Bess told her to *go to hell*.

But did it even matter what Bess said if Mare wasn't listening? Mare was so hurt, so angry. George was *gone*, her house had just exploded and her anger needed an outlet. She needed to blame someone. "This is all your fault," Mare screamed at Bess. "I don't ever want to see you again. Ever."

Bess stared at Mare's face, and even in the darkness, Mare could see Bess was crying. "But, Mare, I love you," she said softly.

Maybe Bess didn't say that that night. Maybe Bess said nothing. Or, like she wrote in the letter, she did say it and Mare couldn't (or wouldn't) hear her. Maybe she said it a lot those few months they lived together. Maybe she never said it at all.

Months later, right after her literary agent had sold her first romance novel to a publisher, Mare would learn from investigators the cause of the gas escaping into the house was not the burner after all. The line behind the stove was disconnected and the gas was leaking from there. Tiny little Bess never could've moved the stove out to disconnect the line even if she'd wanted to. There was only one person in the house big enough, strong enough to do that. The man who'd killed Max. The man who'd once threatened to kill all of them. The man who'd thought everything he'd done, he'd done for love.

Bess had done nothing but tried to save her. She knew that then, and yet she also knew that she was on the brink of becoming this new woman. Someone entirely different than the struggling girl, wife, mother. Someone glamorous, happy and sparkly who had based a beautiful love story upon a romantic and tragic fictionalized life. *Gloria Diamond* was about to publicize her new novel by spouting so many lies about Mare's life with George. And then it felt like calling Bess and telling her she knew the truth about the explosion would mess all that up.

And, in a way, she almost felt like she was saving Bess by staying away from her. By never telling her the truth about Max. It would destroy Bess to know what had really happened to Max, how she, and George, had played a part in his death.

Bess was better off without her.

And Mare needed to become the Gloria Diamond the world wanted, more than she needed Bess. Or at least, she thought she did, at the time.

And maybe you might say that Mare got a happy ending, after all. In real life, maybe a happy ending isn't always being with a person you love, but instead, becoming the person you always wanted to be yourself. That girl who lay in the field in Ohio, staring at the blue, blue sky, dreaming of all the stories she would tell would spend thirty years of her life doing just that. If that wasn't a happy ending, what was?

Though Mare never spoke to Bess again, she would still try and keep tabs on Bess from time to time by looking her up on the internet. She convinced herself that Bess had a happy ending too. The internet would reveal that Bess continued to make art, and she seemed to sell enough to get by living in Pasadena. But then one terrible spring day, the internet offered up Bess's obituary. She had died, suddenly, much too young. And her Annie had grown up to become an acclaimed actress named Amelia Grant.

It was then that she decided she needed to bring Annie to her. If Bess was dead, then there was no one left who knew the truth. And suddenly she needed to see what had happened to Max and Bess's daughter. She thought it was only right, oddly poetic, even, that Max's daughter star in the story that was truly and secretly always about her love of Max. *Diamond in the Rough* was fiction. Sort of. A recounting of her life with George, if George had actually been Max. It was the greatest lie she ever wrote.

But she was wrong about so many things.

And Annie showed her that, the way Bess might've too thirty years ago. Annie loved and lived and reasoned like her mother, so much so, that it was almost breathtakingly painful to be around her. The truth was, she had never missed Bess more in the last thirty years than she had talking to Annie, having Annie stay in her house.

But Annie was right, that she couldn't, no, she shouldn't, play the movie version of Gloria in *Diamond in the Rough*.

She deserved more than that, after all. She deserved better. She deserved to know the real Gloria Diamond.

Amelia

SHE DESERVED TO *know the real Gloria Diamond.*

I read the last sentence and then turned the page, but that appeared to be the end.

So this was her story, her *real* story? Her life as Mare, from being roommates with my mother in college to meeting George, to marrying him, to her affair with Max and then all the horrible things that happened after. She ended with the content of my mother's letter and then her explanation of how she transformed from Mare into Gloria Diamond after George's death.

I stared at the blank back page and tried to process it all. So, my mother had loved her once. Or maybe she had loved her always? I had never really considered my mother as a person who might have been in love with anyone. But now it made me sad that she had never gotten the chance to tell Gloria how she felt while she'd been alive.

But I couldn't be mad at Gloria for that either, because now

I understood her. She was a far cry from the too-happy Gloria I'd been trying to play in that first day on set, a far cry from the Gloria dripping in diamonds in her Oprah interview and even a far cry from the ice-cold Gloria who had made me feel completely unwelcome in her home. Her real story wasn't a love story at all. But a tragedy. Or was it ultimately the story of a woman who had survived—and thrived—even after every terrible thing life had thrown at her?

I finally looked up, and she was staring at me. Waiting for me to say something, or to react, but for another moment, I still didn't know what to say. I was sad for my mother that she had never been able to tell Gloria how she really felt. Sad for Gloria that she had been through all of this and then only found success by lying about it. Sad for Max, who wasn't my father, but had clearly been someone my mother and Gloria had both cared deeply for once. And then I thought about Will. Will had been through so much, that as a young boy he'd lost his voice. And as I thought about his sweet, argumentative voice now, that part made my heart ache. "Thank you for sharing all this with me," I finally said.

She nodded slowly. "You know, I kept so many secrets for so long. But when I read the letter you sent, that Bess wrote me all those years ago. I just...broke. And this all flooded out of me." She paused for a moment. "I wish Bess had mailed me that letter herself back in 1991."

I tried to imagine how my own life might've been different if Gloria had known how my mother felt about her, but it was impossible to comprehend now. "Would it have changed anything, do you think?" I asked her.

Gloria shrugged. "I wish I'd at least have had a chance to apologize to her before she died hating me."

"She didn't die hating you," I said.

"Oh no. I'm sure she did."

I shook my head. "She definitely did not. Can I show you something?"

I stood and waited for Gloria to get her cane and stand up, and then I walked toward the extra bedroom I was using as my office.

In the end, I didn't have the heart to donate any of my mother's copies of Gloria's books. They had always been my mother's prized possessions, and maybe now it made sense why. I had moved them all here to my new house, displayed them across several rows of the beautiful built-in bookcases. I pointed to them now to show Gloria.

"You bought all my novels?" Gloria raised her eyebrows, not making the connection.

"No. These were my mother's. I moved them all from her house. She loved your books so much—she always purchased them on the day they came out and kept them all prominently displayed on her shelves. I couldn't bear to give them away when I sold her house."

Gloria bit her lip and walked toward the bookcase, running her fingers slowly across the pink and purple spines. "She didn't hate me?" Gloria said softly.

"She didn't hate you," I repeated.

And then I couldn't find it in myself to hate Gloria either. Instead, I felt deeply sad for her. And even sadder for Will. "Can I ask you one more thing?" I said.

She nodded, still running her finger slowly across the spines.

"Why did you say I had hurt Will once? I'd assumed it was because I trapped him in the pantry that night. But then my mother's letter said I dragged him out. I saved him." As I spoke, the words ran through me like a chill. Had I really saved Will's life, thirty years ago? I felt impossibly disconnected from that being something that had happened to me once. But I'd been so young, too young to truly remember it for real.

Gloria looked down, stared at her feet, at her diamond-studded pumps, before answering. "That year after George died, when Will didn't talk, he actually would say one word. I'd hear him at night. He would cry out in his sleep, *Annie, Annie, Annie.* He was so distraught. And all he could manage to say was your name."

I wondered if I'd ever woken up in the middle of the night calling for Will too. I could barely remember anything before the house I lived in with my mother in Pasadena, that we moved into when I was six. In fact, now I had no idea where we went directly after that night when Gloria's house exploded or what happened in the two years between that and moving into our Pasadena house. I felt a wash of grief for the loss of my mother all over again. It was the weirdest and most horrible feeling, realizing I had a question only she could answer and then understanding there was no possible way for me to ever ask her.

Will might have complicated feelings about his mother. But he was lucky. She was still here. Still trying to protect him. I now realized that this was why she had asked me to leave him alone when we were in Belles Woods. She'd been scared what memories I might bring up for Will again. He had a great and successful life. All his trauma was behind him. "I think I understand why you wanted me to stay away from Will," I said. "Just so you know, I want him to be happy too. And I'll never bother him again."

She stared at me, and she frowned that Gloria frown I'd gotten used to seeing in Seattle. "Amelia," she said sternly. "What part of *I was wrong about everything* did you not understand?"

"I…" I didn't know what to say.

"Will is waiting in the car," she said abruptly, slapping the hardwood floor with the bottom of her cane for emphasis.

Of course, Gloria didn't drive. Gloria didn't do anything alone. I had assumed that Tate had brought her out here. (Or whoever *the new Tate* was at this moment in time.) *Will?* Had come all the way here, with her? He was sitting out in front of my house right now?

I folded my arms in front of my chest. "I don't understand what you're trying to say."

"He read my story too. I thought it was long past time he

understood the truth about me. About everything." She paused and gave me a withering look. "He's been absolutely miserable since you left Seattle, so I'm saying, go out there. Talk to him. Love each other if you both want to."

Love each other? I twisted my hands together, trying to reason what game she was playing now. "But you wrote that a happy ending isn't being with a person. It's becoming the person you want to be."

"So go be the person you want to be *with* him," she said. Then she added, "If there's one thing I know, it's that love doesn't wait for you. When it comes, it's fleeting. And if you don't grab on to it, it disappears forever."

I wasn't sure whether she was referring to Max, or my mother, or to the plotline of one of her novels. But I nodded.

"Amelia," she said my name curtly. Then waved me away toward my own front door, as if she owned this place, not me. "I brought you a gift. Go."

There was a white BMW parked in my driveway, and as I walked down the path toward it, I could see a man sitting in the driver's seat. It was only when I got closer that I could make out the shape of his beautiful bespectacled face, that I believed Will was truly here.

I stood there for a moment, unsure exactly what I was going to say. Gloria had said he'd been miserable, but maybe he was also upset by how I left things. He'd traveled with her here, sure. But he'd taken her up to set too, and even babysat Jasper when she'd asked. His being here in my driveway didn't necessarily mean he'd be happy to see me, did it?

The windows were almost all the way rolled up and he appeared to be focusing on something. Probably listening to NPR or reading the *New York Times* on his phone. And the thought of Will still being so *Will* made something swell in my chest. If Gloria was right, if love really was fleeting, then I at least had to try to tell him how I truly felt. I took a deep breath and knocked softly on the window.

Will jumped, removed his AirPods and turned to look at me. He stared at me through the window, putting his hand up to the glass as if wondering if he was imagining me here. I took a step back, and then he opened the door and got out of the car.

We stood a few feet apart, staring at each other for a few silent minutes.

"This is private property, you know," I finally said, unable to suppress my smile at the sight of him again. "You're trespassing."

He just kept staring at me, and I wasn't sure whether he was going to yell at me or hug me. "I think that's my line," he finally said and smiled a little.

I suddenly felt weightless, giddy. "Will," I breathed his name. "You're really here."

He held up his hands. "But I'm not trespassing," he said firmly. "I can explain."

"Can you?" I laughed.

"The thing is, I actually do know the woman who lives here. And I have something to say to her."

"You do?" I put my hands on my hips, but I couldn't stop the smile from spreading across my face now.

"I do. I think I'm in love with her, and even though she told me she wanted me to leave, I'd like to present a closing argument to the contrary, if she's willing to listen. First of all—"

In love with me? "Will," I cut him off, and took another step closer. I stood on my toes and put my hands on his forearms. "I didn't really want you to leave," I said. "I thought I was protecting you. And protecting myself. I had so many unanswered questions that were confusing me then. But none of them were about how I felt about you." I paused for a moment and then I added, "How I *feel* about you. I want to try this and see where it goes. For real."

He moved his hand to my cheek and stroked it softly with his thumb. "That is a much more concise argument than what

I would've said." He leaned down and kissed me gently on the lips, and then he pulled back and whispered, "And I concur."

I smiled, and he wrapped me in a hug that felt like home. I held on to him for a few minutes, not even caring what my new neighbors must be thinking about me. "I'm so glad you're here," I whispered into his chest, still not letting go. "Thank you for not listening to me, and for showing up here."

Will pulled back a little and gave me a half smile. "Actually, my mother didn't tell me where she was taking me. I didn't know until you knocked on the car window that she came to see you." He chuckled. "She's a piece of work, isn't she?" But he said it as a term of endearment, and I nodded to agree.

Maybe it was strange the way Gloria had brought me to Will, then forced us apart, then brought us back together again. As if we were a love story she was writing too, the ending still unknown. But right then all I could feel was grateful that she had brought him here, and that she had told me the truth about everything.

Will reached for my hand. "So…you live here?" he asked, pointing to my new little house behind us. I nodded. "It's cute."

"Now that we've established that you're not a trespasser, do you want to come in?" I asked him.

He squeezed my hand. "Of course."

"Oh, and I have a cat now too. You can meet him. He's awful. Almost as bad as Jasper. But you'll love him."

Will grimaced. "Well… I'm really not a cat person. But I'm suddenly hoping your cat likes me. What do you think that says about me? And also, how in the world do you even get a cat to like you?"

I stood up on my toes and kissed him softly, slowly, leaning into him long enough that we both had to pull back a little for air after a few minutes. Then I whispered, "Don't worry. I'm not a cat person either. But it's amazing what a can of tuna can do."

EPILOGUE

Amelia

SOMETIMES THE BEGINNING of everything sneaks up on you when you least expect it.

I read this once in a Gloria Diamond novel, the final novel she would ever publish before her death. It was a much-anticipated prequel to her biggest bestselling novel of all time, *Love at the End of the World*. *Love in the Beginning of Time* was the love story of the two mothers of the original protagonists from *Love at the End of the World*. Thirty-five years before the asteroid hit, they met on the beach in Santa Monica and started a torrid summer affair that would secretly span decades, right up until the asteroid killed them both.

It would be the first—and only—Gloria Diamond novel that did not have a happy ending. And critics would be mixed over whether the Queen of Romance could truly be the *queen* if the romance didn't end happily. But the book sold three million copies worldwide, and the movie (on which I was an executive producer) became a blockbuster success.

Truth be told, it wasn't the ending that made me tear up. I didn't make it past the dedication before I started sobbing, as it simply read, *For the one and only B.*

Sometimes, even years later, I would marvel at my life, at my thriving career, at my twins, at my adorably nerdy and sexy husband, and I would think that this was the truest line that Gloria had ever written: The beginning of everything really did sneak up on you when you least expected it.

The supporting role that I would go on to take after I quit *Diamond in the Rough* would end up winning me a Golden Globe, which then spiraled into a leading role in a feature film that would make me a household name. I would sell my house in Santa Monica before I turned forty and move outside of Seattle with Will where daily life was quieter. And then when the twins were born, two weeks after my forty-first birthday, I would take a year off from acting before Liza would find me a role in a long-running series that shot in Vancouver, not too far from home, and that would eventually win me an Emmy. (Liza would later quip that she could've made me an EGOT winner if only I'd ever learned how to sing. Sadly, I had not inherited Gaitlin's perfect pitch.)

Sometimes I thought about how my life would've turned out differently, if all the secrets of the past hadn't cast so many long shadows on all of our lives. Mare, Max, my mother. But then everything I knew about them now made me wonder if maybe endings were really just new beginnings in disguise.

I ran this thought by Gloria once, in her later years, after the cancer made her mostly bedridden, and she insisted Will or I bring the twins over at least once a week to cheer her up. They were tweens by then, though, and bringing them over meant that after a quick hello, they sat on their phones eating snacks in her kitchen, while I sat and talked with Gloria at her bedside by myself.

"Beginnings and endings are drastically different," she snapped back at me, when I posed the question. "Maybe you should leave the writing to me?"

She was no longer writing by then of course, but I smiled at her and nodded. Over her later years, she loved telling the story in every interview she did of how the best thing to come out of the massive flop that was her biopic was her future daughter-in-law. (*Diamond in the Rough* might've tanked at the box office, but at least she got grandkids out of it!)

"Beginnings," she clarified, "are the easy part. Endings are the hardest to get right." She paused and motioned for me to hand her her diamond-studded water cup from the nightstand. I carefully passed it over to her, and she took a slow sip through the metal straw before handing it back to me. "It's all about what you do in the middle that counts," she added. "You have to earn the happy ending, Amelia. You need to work really hard to get all those small moments in the middle exactly right." She grabbed on tightly to my hand and squeezed for emphasis.

And that's what I would remember, even years later, after Gloria was gone. That would stay with me, more than any line in any of her books. More than anything that had happened in her real (or pretend) story.

I would remember the way she reached for my hand as she spoke that afternoon, the way she held on to me, the way she smiled just a little when she talked about the *small moments in the middle*. As if somehow me knowing her, talking to her just like that, made me a part of her eventual happy ending. And maybe it made her a part of mine too.

★ ★ ★ ★ ★

ACKNOWLEDGMENTS

Thank you to my amazing agent, Jessica Regel, at Helm Literary, who is not only a literary agent extraordinaire, but also was totally with me on the front lines from the first seed of this idea to the final product. I truly could not do any of this without you. Not to mention, I'm not sure any of my books would have titles if it weren't for you!

I was lucky that I got to work with three fabulous editors on this book. Thank you to Laura Brown for your early excitement about this idea and for your extremely wise and insightful edits on the first draft. Working with you is always a dream! Thank you to Erika Imranyi for your line edits, which really helped me make this book shine. And thank you to Gaby Mongelli for seeing this book through to publication with such incredible enthusiasm and care.

Thank you to the entire marketing, publicity and sales teams at Park Row for helping this book reach the hands of readers. And thank you to Heidi Gall and Jenny Meyer at the Jenny

Meyer Literary Agency for bringing my work to readers around the world.

My family and friends near and far are always an enormous support and I'm so grateful to have them. Thank you to Gregg for always being my person (and my first reader). Thank you to B and O for always bringing me music and laughter—you inspired me to give Gloria a pretty amazing son. Maureen Kilmer and Tammy Greenwood, thank you for always being my virtual office mates and cheerleaders. My friends on the home front who share puzzles, coffee and daily text check-ins—I'm so lucky to have you in the real world when I leave my fictional world for the day. And thank you to my parents, who still get excited to read my books and attend my book events and even drive me to the airport!

Finally, thank you to the booksellers, librarians and readers who have been supporting and reading my books for the last fifteen years now. I am so grateful to be able to write books for a living and to continue to belong to such an incredible community of readers.

THE
GREATEST
LIE OF ALL

JILLIAN CANTOR

Reader's Guide

PARK
ROW
BOOKS

1. The prologue and epilogue both begin with contrasting lines from Gloria Diamond novels. Sometimes the end—and beginning—sneaks up on you when you least expect it. What is the significance of these lines to the story? How does the meaning of these lines change over the course of the novel? How do the two Gloria Diamond novels these lines come from connect to themes of *The Greatest Lie of All*?

2. Discuss the meaning of the title. What is "the greatest lie of all"? Who tells this lie? Could it have more than one meaning to the novel?

3. Though they butt heads throughout the novel, Gloria and Amelia are actually alike in many ways. Compare and contrast Gloria's character to Amelia's. Who is the

main character of this novel—Gloria or Amelia? Who can you relate to more and why?

4. There are several love stories woven into this novel, which is largely about a romance writer. But is *The Greatest Lie of All* a romance novel? Why or why not? What genre do you think it would fit into?

5. Bess tells Mare that you "always have a choice" when she decides to marry George, and Gloria repeats this phrase to Amelia near the end of the novel when she's conflicted about her role in the film. Why is this idea important to the overall theme of the novel? How does it echo through both the past and present storylines?

6. There's one chapter in this novel from Bess's point of view. What is the role of this chapter? What is the significance of Bess to the overall story, in both the past and the present?

7. Though the novel largely focuses on Amelia and Gloria, the male characters also play a significant role. Compare and contrast the characters of George and Max. George and Will. Jase and Cam. What is Gaitlin's role in the novel? Is there a villain in this story? A hero? If so, who would it be and why?

8. Amelia thinks "Writing itself struck me as somewhat close to acting. Pretending to be someone you never would truly be in real life." Do you agree or disagree that Gloria and Amelia have very similar careers? What role does method acting play in the novel? And how might this also apply to Gloria's career?

9. What is the significance of the dedication of Gloria's first novel: *For the one I love, always*? Who do you think

she dedicated the novel to and why? Why do you think Amelia's mom circled this in her copy?

10. What role do the 1980/90s chapters play? Who is "the real Gloria Diamond," as Gloria tries to show Amelia with her manuscript at the end of the novel?

11. Discuss the role of the settings in the novel: Pasadena, Chicago, Seattle and the fictional hotel in Belles Woods. How do the atmosphere, weather and landscape add to the overall themes?